*Parallel Lives*

Also by John Tagholm and
available from Quartet

*No Identifiable Remains*
*Bad Marriage*

# PARALLEL LIVES

*John Tagholm*

*Quartet Books*

First published in 2010 by
Quartet Books Limited
A member of the Namara Group
27 Goodge Street, London W1T 2LD

A catalogue record for this book
is available from the British Library

ISBN    978 0 7043 7196 5

Typeset by Antony Gray
Printed and bound in Great Britain by
T J International Ltd, Padstow, Cornwall

*To*
*Thomas, Hugo and Theodore*

Under the look of fatigue, the attack of migraine
and  the sigh
There is always another story, there is more than
meets the eye.

W. H. Auden

# Chapter 1

The room, tucked into the eaves at the top of the tall, rambling house, looked out over the whole of central London. After rain, when the air was clear, it was possible to see the broad sweep of the city, the full spread of its component parts, laid out like a planner's model. On the far horizon directly ahead, the twin metal television towers signalled the southernmost boundary. To the east rose the brash new blocks of Canary Wharf and the dark swell of Blackheath, like a pubic bone, behind. Travelling westwards, with occasional flashes from the sparkling Thames, were the shapes of St Paul's and the Palace of Westminster and the twinkling light reflecting from the London Eye. And then, impossibly slow, the succession of aeroplanes, invisibly joined like a line of camels, dropping imperceptibly to a distant Heathrow. Closer still, the smooth green of the Heath and at the foot of the garden, the dark line of the railway ruling a border under it all and a fox sitting still, oblivious.

But today the rain had blurred the scene into an amorphous grey and although Marjorie Nielson sat at her desk in the window, she could not see the view. Not even the sun would have helped her. The rain had pebbled the windows and occasionally they bled one into the other and ran quickly down the glass like tears.

The room was unnaturally still. Above the fireplace hung a portrait of the therapist, the whirls and squiggles of colour capturing exactly the essence of the woman who now lay dead under her own stare. In the corner, a tiny abstract, layers of paint on paint, colour on colour, lit up the corner of the jade green room. Beneath it, in an ornate silver frame, was a black and white photograph of a young woman. The room was full of clues to the life of Marjorie Nielson which had so recently departed.

The wooden surface of the desk on which her pale hand now rested with absolute stillness was mottled and stained with splashes of ink which over the years had been polished into random permanence. An old doll with plaits of dirty yellow and a smock of pale blue dots was propped against the base of a brass lamp as oblivious as the fox in the garden. The doll's up turned feet rested beside a closed folder marked Major Peter Harrington, the edges of the papers spilling out along one side.

Behind the motionless figure, in the corner, stood an innocuous wooden filing cabinet, again so polished that the yellow of the grain stood out against the dark brown of the old wood. In here, panned through hours of listening, were the distilled lives of Marjorie Nielson's clients. Although they had never met, the intimate secrets of these men and women lay side by side, almost touching. The details of their sexual indiscretions, the accounts of their traumas and their fears, the abuser and the abused resting cheek by jowl just millimetres apart, parallel lives, unknown to one another. Their anonymity was deliberate. They were destined never to meet and but for the events of this grey day, early in spring, their lives would have remained separate forever.

The radiator on the wall to her left began to crackle into life, sounds that would normally have led Marjorie Nielson to stand and then rest against it, to feel the warmth slowly seeping through her clothes.

A voice was calling from downstairs, happy and familiar. 'Good morning, Dr Nielson, good morning.' And then the feet on the stairs, faint at first, but louder and slower as they came higher. The knock on the door was light, so as not too disturb too much. And then it was more insistent.

'Dr Nielson? It's only me.'

Slowly and quietly the cleaner opened the door, pushing it ajar to see her employer sitting in her familiar position in the window. Calling her name again, she approached tentatively from behind and reached out a hand to touch the motionless figure.

The scream that followed caused the pigeons to clatter noisily from the lone conifer at the foot of the garden and disappear into the grey skies and the fox to turn and lope silently into the young willowherb and buddleia.

# Chapter 2

'This was an extremely stupid idea,' Toby Browning muttered under his breath as the first drops of rain chased them off the eighteenth green. Although he had played golf several times as a student in Glasgow, this was his first game in the south and there were many years between the two experiences. He simply wasn't built for sport.

'What was that?' his companion asked, the wind carrying his words up towards the tall lime trees under which they had to pass on the way to the club house which glimmered like a small cruise liner in amongst the laurel and the rhododendrons. Golf in these parts was a statement of rank rather than a democratic right.

'It was stupid of me not to bring something rain proof,' Toby lied as he felt the dampness settle on his shoulders. What was he doing on a Surrey golf course on a wet Friday in April with a man he barely knew? Well, he could answer part of the question easily enough, practised as he was at coming up with positive reasons for finding himself in situations he found uncomfortable. He would talk about this later with Marjorie and see if he could make more sense of it then.

'C'mon,' the voice cajoled from behind. 'I'll buy you a drink.' It wasn't so much an offer, more an order and once again Toby felt trapped between instinct and duty. He knew he had to be in the West End in two hours and yet he was with a man who had the potential to be one of his best customers.

'Sure,' he offered lamely, knowing it would make him late.

The rain was now falling relentlessly, somehow making the newly emerging leaves even greener, an almost unnatural chlorophyll brightness in the darkening day.

Toby had chosen to play golf against his better judgement

but he had been bullied into making the journey into the rich commuter suburbs by a man to whom it was difficult to say 'no'. So was it weakness that found him drinking a ridiculously expensive glass of Meursault and listening to a lecture on Fauvism which, however well informed it was, did not add to the sum of his own knowledge? He glanced at his watch, a movement which did not escape the attention of his companion.

'Got to go?'

'Got to go. Will you come to the gallery this week?'

There was a pause and Toby knew that every day the man sitting opposite him was offered the opportunity to part with some of the fortune that he had acquired over the years. That he remained rich was down to moments like this, when he had to measure the risk he was about to take. The eyes that assessed him were a cool grey-blue and Toby wondered which side of the balance sheet he would fall.

'I'll get my PA to fix a time.' And that was us all put into our positions, concluded Toby, wincing under the pressure of the farewell handshake.

The empty carriage of the train seemed unduly noisy as it rattled through the deserted stations back to the capital. Toby could not imagine any scene more forlorn than a suburban railway station in the late afternoon of a rainy day. The graffiti proclaimed 'hate, hate, hate' and rubbish was blown along the deserted platform to lodge against lurid pink metal benches whose modernistic design clashed miserably with the late nine-teenth century building to which they had been attached. The noisy cocoon of the carriage allowed him time to think but an extended stop just after Clapham Junction caused him to fret and guaranteed that he would be even later.

No matter how many times he prepared what he was going to say to Marjorie, it usually came out differently. At first this used to frighten him, as though his inability to collect and order his thoughts was a sign he was losing control. Now he realised it was part of the process, although it continued to surprise him what he ended up talking about. Marjorie had told him that he was being encouraged to speak in such a way that he might not necessarily understand exactly what he said. Is this a license to say the first thing that comes into my head, he had asked? Precisely, she had told him. Now he knew that that there was a mysterious space between what he thought and what he said and in this strange territory the unexpected often happened.

But, at this rate, he wouldn't be saying anything at all.

He called her office and left a message on the voice-mail, slightly surprised that Marise, the elderly and yet supremely efficient secretary, didn't take the call.

Eventually, twenty minutes late, he scuttled along the rain swept road bounded each side by mansion blocks behind whose discreet facades a thousand secrets were being offered in rooms of careful neutrality. He was sweating when he came to the familiar black door and its collection of shiny brass plates. Even after all this time, his eye still registered hers: Dr Marjorie Nielson, the letters almost rubbed to oblivion by their daily polishing. This was the first time he had ever been late for her and, although he didn't know it at that precise moment, it would be his last.

So concerned was he about his lateness, he almost bumped into the woman standing by the broad steps that led to the front door. She was wearing a lightweight trench coat, pale chinos that stopped above her ankles and trainers. That he chose to take in what she was wearing was the result of first seeing her large sun glasses which, on such a gloomy afternoon, he thought unnecessary. She appeared to be listening to an iPod and as he passed her she didn't move, which immediately irritated him. Why is it, he thought, that people with music in their ears or mobile phones in their hands, seem to lose all sense of geography. As he rang the buzzer, he looked back at her, his face conveying his displeasure. She was standing very still and something about her caused him to step back and ask if she needed any help. She turned to him and gave a slight nod of her head.

'No,' she said, 'I don't need help any more. Thank you.'

At that moment, the door clicked open and he entered the big hallway with its familiar smells. Marise was standing on the black and white marble floor and he was about to apologise for his late arrival when he noticed the look on her face.

'She's not here?'

'She's not here,' she said, slowly shaking her head.

Toby frowned. 'Is she ill?' Despite himself, he felt just the slightest annoyance that she wasn't here, that she had let him down personally, more particularly after dashing halfway across London to be with her. He was immediately to regret his reaction.

'No, it is more serious.' Marise walked slowly across to a leather chair, one of a pair which flanked a table beneath a mirror. She was looking at the floor when she spoke.

'I have to tell you that she is dead.'

Now it was Toby's turn to go over and sit on the companion leather chair, for it was as if someone had aimed a careful blow behind his knees and taken all the strength out of his legs. There was silence between them, Toby unable to form a single thought and Marise unsure about how to continue. In the gloomy light of the reception the two figures sat very still, like ornaments on a mantelshelf under the large mirror.

'This is awful,' he said, more to himself than to Marise. And he knew at once what he meant. That it was awful for him and the selfishness of his response made him look over to Marise to see if she had noticed. She appeared to be in a world of her own, the half-light of the room pressing on her shoulders.

'What happened?'

'I can't believe it,' she said. And he waited.

She looked up at him now. 'They say she committed suicide.' She sat very still as if unable to know what to do next.

It was taking Toby some time to reverse his thinking, to take on board the totality of what he had just been told.

'How did it happen?' It was the obvious question and it was aimed as much at him as it was at her.

'The cleaner found her this morning. In her study. She doesn't know, but she thinks it was an overdose.' Marise's voice was small, as if she felt that by saying the words quietly they might turn out to be less true.

'But, why would she want to do that?' Toby might just as well have added 'to me', for he could not release himself from the feeling that he had been profoundly let down.

'Poor woman.'

It was only as Marise said these words that Toby faintly glimpsed that there was a world beyond his reaction to what had happened, as if a curtain on a stage had been partly lifted to reveal a scene totally different from the one he was expecting. And what he was shown was a small corner of the life of Marjorie Nielson and it appalled him that this first appreciation of Marjorie Nielson as a real person should come after her death. He knew no more about her now than he did before.

He stood up and walked over to Marise where he knelt down and took her hands.

'I'm sorry,' he said. 'This must be terrible for you. Having to tell all the clients.'

'I have found it very difficult to,' she replied. 'Some of them have been coming to see her for years. They are like family. I'm almost frightened to talk to them. I know I will break down.'

'But you are family, as well, Marise.'

The pain of that statement made her turn away, her profile reflected in mirror.

'I thought I knew her so well,' she said simply. 'But how little we know. How little we know.' She paused and looked down at her hands which were still being held by Toby.

'She asked me never to talk about her to her clients, the people who came to see her. I never questioned why, but I knew it was important. And now it seems such a waste.'

Toby thought that, paradoxically, Marjorie Nielson had died knowing pretty well all there was to know about him and just as he was beginning to talk to her in a way that he never talked to anyone in his life, she was gone taking with her the clues and the solutions to his life. Now it was Toby's turn to drop his head and stare at the hands in front of him.

'Can I do anything, Marise?' Again, the statement was ambiguous, an offer of help or a request for advice, an admission that he was lost.

'Thank you, Mr Browning. If I said I don't know, I hope you'll understand.'

He did, only too well. He was left with a discomforting sense of unfinished business, of being in an unreal world where normal rules did not apply. He could not properly grieve a woman he knew nothing about and yet in one way their relationship had been more intimate than any in his life. And he could not rid himself of this feeling of anger, the frustration of being left in mid air half way through a journey. He was about to give Marise one of his cards until he remembered that she had all his contact details.

So often in the past, leaving through the big black door had been like stepping into a different world from the one he'd left only an hour before. In the beginning, it had been more threatening and he had felt vulnerable, as if he had been released naked. Slowly, however, he began to experience the opposite, as though he had been given the set of clothes he always knew he should have been wearing.

He took a cab back to the gallery and it was only as it pulled up in Wapping that he realised he might never make that journey again. It was a feeling he didn't like and the image of Marjorie, calm, steady, secure, came to him as he walked into his apartment.

At this stage it didn't occur to him to ask why such a model of competence should have taken her own life. He slumped down on to the leather sofa and wondered if he had been able to cry, whether it would have been appropriate. The rain splattered against the windows and he heard a bus rumble over the cobbles of the High Street.

Sometimes, when he needed to think through a problem, or when he was sad, like now, Toby rode his bicycle around the living room. It was no ordinary bike and this was no ordinary living room. The large open space, once a spice warehouse, was dominated by four large iron framed windows through which the light from the river twenty metres below was often reflected on to the brick ceiling in dancing fragments of intense white. The bike was a racer, the sort used in the Tour de France and the frame, so delicate he could pick it up with the middle finger of his right hand. But what he liked most of all was the silence. When he freewheeled over the polished concrete floors, between the grey cast iron pillars and the outsized furniture, all he could hear was the occasional squeak of the rubber tyres on the smooth surface beneath him as he glided around the great space.

And this is what he did now, weaving noiselessly around his home, turning over in his mind not just the events of the last twelve hours but the whole intricate latticework of his life that had led to this point. A passenger on a pleasure cruiser making its way against the incoming tide towards Greenwich would have seen the strange sight of the upper half of a man gliding from window to window, a graceful and surreal image on the banks of the Thames.

# Chapter 3

**Notes on Tobias Browning. Aged 39. Referred by his GP Sarah Buckman. Insomnia and panic attacks.**

He is in more trouble than he shows. Not unusual at this stage, but I just wonder. His charming manner is well practised and he is amusing to listen to. An only child, he was born and brought up in Norfolk, which he described as being on the road to nowhere. He begins to talk about his parents unprompted. Perfectly normal upbringing, he says, especially for an only child. He catches my slight reaction and explains his statement by saying that his parents only wanted the best for him. He gives a small cough at this stage and adds, you know, violin lessons and extra coaching for maths and that sort of thing. He was packed off to Germany – his phrase – to learn German with a family in Bonn when he was eight. And, using the same phrase again, he said he was packed off to boarding school fairly early as well. He says he had a happy time there and he made friends that are still with him now. He pauses here and looks around as if wondering how to continue.

He was lucky, he goes on, that the music teacher was such a wonderful man. Mr Gregory thought he had real talent, which it appears he did, passing his exams and eventually playing for the National Youth Orchestra. Here he nods at me, as if expecting approval but moves on quite quickly to talk about a friend of his in the school orchestra with whom he was good friends – John Lockyer – a brilliant player of the trumpet. Again a pause. He looks out of the window and I wait. He gave it all up, he says. It was the girls. He had better things to do than practice all day and night.

But you didn't do that? I ask.

He shakes his head. I was a good boy. Is that what it's about? he asks. Is that why I am here?

Why do you think you are here? I ask.

He cannot sit still and he laughs and tells me it is nothing. He can't sleep and occasionally he breaks out into a sweat and has to leave wherever he is. Pause again.

Tell me what happens, I say.

Again, the look to the window.

I expect everyone has it from time to time he says. Tell me about it, I say.

Doesn't everyone get like this from time to time? he repeats. It's just his body telling him to slow down and surely that's quite common. And then he starts.

Anyway, the last time it happened I was on the way to see a friend in Holland Park. I had taken the Jubilee Line from London Bridge to Green Park where I caught a bus, and went upstairs. As we came along Kensington Gore, with the park on the right, I began to feel queasy and I thought I was going to be sick. It's how it always starts. He puts his hand to his collar at this stage. And then comes the sweat. No ordinary sweat, but rather like suddenly being drenched all over. It's completely ghastly and I feel awful. I get up from my seat and I don't know whether I will be able to get off the bus quickly enough before I am sick. The bus stops and I'm not really sure how I get off but I do, and I stumble on to the pavement and sit on a wall or a step with my head between my legs. Gradually the nausea passes and I feel the discomfort of my wet shirt. Even my socks are damp. The first thing I see is the Albert Memorial, glinting in the sun. It's almost blinding. Everything seems very bright.

Again the look to the window, as if he was comparing the brightness then with the brightness now. He pauses. I was exhausted, he says and then stops, perhaps exhausted again. He has told this story before, given this self same account, I am sure.

After a moment or two I ask him how he felt when it happened.

I felt like a fool. Frightened and foolish, he confirms. And I want to pretend it never happened, that it was just one of those things.

And is that what you still feel?

I suppose so, yes. It is beyond my control. It just takes me over and

I just have to learn to live with it. He looks at me in a final, challenging way.

You're certain that this is beyond your control? I ask him and he nods.

Where else has this occurred? He pauses and thinks.

I was in a car going to a funeral. Somebody I had played in the orchestra with. Nice chap. A pretty good player, but he was killed in an accident. A waste. Here he stops and stares at the wall and I wait.

I had to open the window. I was being driven by his father. There were four of us in the car and I just felt shocking. This was their son and I was about to yell stop the car I want to be sick. I just hung on, the sweat pouring off me, clenching my teeth to stay in control. How I got through it, I don't know. I remember I couldn't talk. I kept my eyes on the open window, hoping that no one would talk to me because it would have been impossible to reply. I was ashamed, yes, ashamed.

I put his statement back to him. And this is what you just have to learn to live with? He is uncertain how to reply and he frowns at me.

Can you remember when you first had an attack like this? I ask him. He rubs the palms of his hands on the arms of the chair. I can't remember having them at University in Glasgow, he tells me. Sometime in my twenties, it must have been.

I wait.

My late twenties were a bit of a mess, he tells me. I think I lost my way a bit.

And then he sits and stares at the window until it is time.

**End of session**

# Chapter 4

She could smell the dust and feel its fine particles against her teeth. And with the dust came the noise, all around her, filling the air, the clank of chains from the tall cranes, the insistent bleeps of reversing trucks and the calls of men high in the scaffolding. This was a landscape in transition and she was at the centre of a cacophony of sound. She had once known these streets well in the days when the old red brick bridges covered the crossroads by the two gasometers. Back then, the prostitutes worked this section and they would occasionally shout to her as she made her way to the rehearsal room, thinking that she might be one of them. Most of what she had become familiar with had gone, swept away by the great concrete supports that brought the new cross Channel rail link into its London terminal. The working girls had now been pushed up towards what was once the Caledonian cattle market, but she knew the canal remained and she was aware of the fresher smells of water and trees and she could hear the coots clucking madly in park to her right. She felt the shudder of a big diesel engine as it pulled laboriously out of the station to begin its journey northwards.

But other sounds were with her now. As Perdita Landberg made her way through the new landscape of St Pancras, her mind was playing with the thought of the Archbishop of Narbonne, the Primate of Languedoc, lying in the churchyard up ahead of her. She imagined a colourful figure from a warmer climate, driven from his native France by the Revolution, ending up in this run down and impoverished corner of London. The graves in the ancient parish church, home to many of his countrymen, were sometimes piled at least five high, coffin on coffin. The jumble of bones, she had discovered, had been moved twice, each time to accommodate the building of the railways. Perhaps, originally, they had been buried according to family ties, or religious affiliation, but more likely, she thought, they had been randomly laid in the ground, strangers cheek by jowl, unknown to one another except on their journey to eternity. She heard a theme develop, a series of repetitive notes which seemed to work and which she memorised. She knew she was at the beginning of something and it excited her.

She walked up the old stone steps and through the elaborate metal gateway into the churchyard. She had been told that the Coroners Court was housed in a charming if somewhat gloomy Gothic building tucked in one corner of the cemetery, between the graves and the main railway line. The idea that this was a place that people passed through on their way to somewhere else added further to the themes evolving in her mind and she stood for a moment, resting against the flaking trunk of an old plane tree. It was as if the quietness of the cemetery was kept in place by a circle of sound at its perimeter. And now another life was about to pass through this strange corner of London and the thought that Marjorie Nielson was at one and the same time both known and unknown to her, further intensified Perdita's mood. Perhaps, she wondered, it was this that had brought her here today, nothing more than a selfish accumulation of facts for her work. Or was she driven to discover more of the life of Marjorie Nielson, a woman who had been an intimate part of her life for over a year but nevertheless remained a complete stranger?

The last few metres to the court were more difficult and she paused at a junction in the paths where, unseen by her, a sign indicated that the buildings to her left were home to Pest Control and Dog Warden and the Mortuary.

'Have you come for one of the inquests?' The voice broke into her thoughts and she turned to face her questioner.

'Yes,' she replied. 'The case of Marjorie Nielson.'

'That will begin in about ten minutes. Will you come with me?' She was shown into the court by one of the coroner's officers and sat on a long wooden bench, one of a row of six which were lined up a few feet lower than the coroner's bench directly ahead of her. At right angles to her left were the benches for the jury, although these would not be used today. Above her, the wooden ceiling painted corporation scarlet and hanging from it, on long chains, were a series a brass chandeliers. An elaborate and rather fine coat of arms in wood or plaster filled the wall behind the coroner's chair.

Toby Browning had noted all these details as he waited for the inquest to begin. He had arrived so early that he had sat through a previous case, the death of a ninety-seven year old man through smoke inhalation. What a strange way to go, thought Toby, after such a long life. There had been a modicum of doubt as to whether the man had started the fire himself but a rather portly and obsequious fire investigator had assured the coroner that 'in his opinion, sir, it was extremely unlikely that the fire in the range in the room of the deceased had been spread deliberately. There was no evidence of accelerants being involved.' The coroner duly recorded a case of accidental death and another life was accounted for.

Now he watched as the woman was led into the courtroom. There was something familiar about her but he could not immediately decide where he had seen her before until he saw the iPod which she took off as she sat on the bench. She sat very still in the same row as him and then, as if sensing he was there, she turned and looked towards him. Her eyes were hidden by dark glasses and he recalled now the same querying look when he had seen her outside Marjorie Nielson's consulting rooms in Harley Street. She continued to regard him for a moment and then slowly turned away. He examined the blistered varnish on the bench in front of him and wondered what had brought her to this Victorian anomaly amongst the railway lines. Three other people now arrived, another one of whom he recognised. Marise was wearing a black skirt and jacket, her small frame slightly stooped. She was clearly nervous and barely looked around her as she sat in the row in front. Sitting next to her was a woman only a few years younger who was even more agitated, squeezing her hands together and quite clearly distracted. Towering above them both, uncertain where to sit, was a tall dignified man with close cropped hair and a tanned, lined face. He stood very straight and held his chin high, a rolled newspaper under his left arm.

They were all startled by three sharp knocks from behind the door to the left of the coroner's chair and a court official ordered that they all stand. The coroner, a small wiry man with the air of a preoccupied prep school headmaster, entered the courtroom and as he sat so did everyone else. For a moment he shuffled the papers in front of him, reading sections here and there, seemingly unaware of the people around him. Then, looking over his glasses, he quietly addressed the court.

'We now come to the case of Marjorie Nielson. My condolences to the family and friends of the deceased.' And then quickly, as if not wishing the emotions to get in the way of procedure, onto the business at hand. 'I have here reports from A and E, autopsy and toxicology results, which I shall come to later. But first, I wonder if we might call Vera Stanovic, please.' He looked up and around until he saw the women sitting next to Marise rise tentatively and make her way towards the witness stand where she took the oath. The coroner confirmed her name and details in a kind reassuring voice, emphasising to the woman that this court was not here to lay blame but to discover more about the deceased and the manner of her death.

'I believe you were Dr Nielson's cleaner?'

'Yes, I had looked after Dr Nielson for almost ten years. She was a lovely woman.' She dropped her head and began to weep softly into a crushed handkerchief.

'We quite understand, Mrs Stanovic. It must have been an awful shock for you.'

'It was. It was.' The woman gathered herself before continuing. 'I looked after her three times a week, Monday, Wednesday and Fridays. She was very organised and my routines were nearly always the same. That Friday morning I arrived at the normal time and called up to her as I always do. She didn't respond, as she sometimes didn't, so I went upstairs to see if there was anything special she wanted me to do. And that's when I found her.'

'Yes, indeed, Mrs Stanovic.' The coroner raised his eyebrows in expectation.

'She was just sitting there. And when I touched her, she was so cold.' She wiped her eyes and held on to the rail in front of her, her white freckled hands bunched in anxiety.

'Tell me, Mrs Stanovic, what sort of woman was Dr Nielson?'

'The kindest, the kindest.' Vera Stanovic looked towards the court as if to affirm her comments. 'I had nothing when I came here from Yugoslavia. She helped give my life back to me.' She turned to face the coroner. 'She can't have killed herself. She was too, too . . . I don't know quite the right word, but maybe too . . . responsible.'

'Of course, Mrs Stanovic. That is the purpose of this inquest. Perhaps you could tell us how she was when you last saw her alive?'

'It was on the Wednesday and she was downstairs in the kitchen when I arrived. I remember she was bright. She was always bright in the morning. She didn't really have to tell me what to do because we had such a routine. She joked about my hair because, well, I had just been to the hairdressers and it was different.'

'So you didn't notice any difference in her? She seemed her normal self?'

'Oh yes', Vera said firmly. 'You must understand, that although I did not know anything about what she did, I think I would have known if she had been unhappy.'

'And what did you do on the Friday after you had the misfortune to find Dr Nielson's body in her study?'

'It was such a shock, such a shock. I phoned Marise – you know, her secretary, first – and it was she who called the ambulance. It arrived very quickly and the men tried to revive Dr Nielson. It was horrible.' She put her handkerchief to her mouth at the memory.

'Very distressing, Mrs Stanovic. When you were in Dr Nielson's study, did you notice anything unusual? I am thinking particularly of any note she might have left anyone? Or any medications?'

'No, no. Well, I didn't really look. I couldn't think like that. You must understand that I was very upset and I cannot say that this was the first thing on my mind.'

Toby Browning felt like he was watching the proceedings through layers of plate glass, a stranger deliberately removed from the events taking place. He was angry at this exclusion, an anger directed at the dead woman and, although he could barely perceive it now, himself. He now suddenly realised his very closeness to Marjorie Nielson was an illusion, and this knowledge made him feel somehow abandoned. For a moment he wondered why he was there at all, unable as he was to identify the real reason in amongst the swirl of indignation and frustration that was enveloping him. Whatever worm of curiosity or unconscious impulse that had brought him to this hearing, he now regretted.

'Did Dr Nielson appear to be in good health to you, Mrs Stanovic?'

'Dr Nielson always seemed to me like a rock,' the woman said clearly. 'I never in ten years saw her ill. It makes this so much more difficult.'

'You didn't know, then, that Dr Nielson was a diabetic?' It was clear to Toby that this news came as a surprise to the cleaner.

'No, but I don't really know what that means. And, anyway,' she added somewhat defensively, 'there was probably lots I didn't know about Dr Nielson.'

'Thank you, Mrs Stanovic. That is all for now. You may return to your seat. You are still under oath, so if you have anything else to say or want to respond to what other witnesses say, you may do so from the floor of the court.'

Along the row from Toby Browning, Perdita Landberg gently nodded her head. And this is the limit of what I know of Marjorie Nielson, she thought. A strong woman and kind, someone who coped with problems. I wasn't allowed to discover more but then neither did I really ask, for our boundaries were well drawn and we kept to them. So why am I here, she wondered, what has compelled me to cross London to sit amongst strangers and listen to accounts of the last days of Marjorie Nielson? And, as she asked the question, she knew instantly the answer, for at the very moment Marjorie Nielson had given something to her she had died, leaving inside Perdita a profound sense of unfinished business.

The next witness was already in the process of taking the oath. 'You are Dr Emma Ridley, Dr Nielson's GP, am I correct?'

'That is correct, at least theoretically so. I barely saw Dr Nielson at all, and certainly can't claim to know – to have known her – like some of my other patients. She came to me about four years ago exhibiting early signs of diabetes and she began injecting insulin about a year later. The last time I saw her – apart from after her death – was three months ago when she came for a regular check-up and repeat prescription. She was, apart from, or in spite of her diabetes, a very fit woman.' Emma Ridley was small, grey haired and matter of fact and she delivered her sentences in the somewhat brusque bedside manner she used with all her patients. She did not have to be prompted by the coroner to continue.

'I was called by Marise Dubarry, Dr Nielson's secretary, on the morning of April 2 and I arrived just as the ambulance men were trying to revive her. There had been no signs of life when they found her and their attempts at resuscitation were futile. I estimated that she had been dead for at least two hours. There was a syringe and insulin on her desk. She normally injected herself in the stomach and there were signs that she had done this some hours earlier. I examined the body for further puncture marks but could find none. I surmised that the probable cause of death was a stroke.'

'You are aware, are you not Dr Ridley, that the autopsy report shows that Dr Nielson died of hypoglycaemia? The estimated time of death has been put at around four in the morning and she must have gone into a coma some time before that. Had you any reason to believe that Dr Nielson might have taken more than her required dose of insulin?'

'As I said', Dr Ridley responded with just a hint of impatience, 'I checked for further puncture marks and could see none. She could have injected herself in the same place twice, but it seems unlikely.'

'The toxicology reports', the coroner continued, 'cannot confirm this but it is possible, as you say, that she may have, perhaps, injected herself more than once'.

'It is of course quite possible that the coma that led to her death was entirely natural,' the doctor added abruptly, implying that the coroner could have reached this conclusion himself. 'I have no idea if Dr Nielson was a user of alcohol – I imagine the autopsy showed this – but, if so, it may have been a contributory factor in bringing on a coma. Certainly there was a tumbler on her desk which smelled of spirits.' The doctor spoke in a manner that probably disappeared in England around 1958.

'Quite, quite, Dr Ridley. The PM showed the presence of alcohol but not in excessive quantities.'

Dr Ridley continued, barely allowing him time to finish his sentence. 'We are still finding out about hypoglycaemia and in my opinion what happened to Dr Nielson was most likely entirely natural.' She adopted a tone she might have used to discuss with a bored husband what colour to paint her living room.

'Thank you Dr Ridley,' said the coroner, adjusting his glasses perhaps as protection against this formidable witness. 'On the infrequent occasions you saw Dr Nielson,' he ventured, picking his words with care, 'were you able to form an opinion of the character of your patient? Did she seem the type of woman who might have taken her own life?'

'Certainly not,' Dr Ridley fired back, although which part of the question she was responding to with such certainty was not clear and the coroner did not seek to find out.

The windows of the court rattled in response to another large diesel train tugging up the slope out of St Pancras. Toby felt it reverberate through the wooden bench and he looked along the row to see whether the woman in the dark glasses was reacting, but her attention seemed entirely focused on the doctor giving evidence. The idea crossed his mind that she might also have been a client of Dr Nielson and once again he experienced a faint wave of disapproval.

One of the paramedics who had tried to revive Dr Nielson gave evidence next, his modern green uniform out of place in the Victorian interior. The young man, Toby estimated he could not have been more than twenty five, described the several methods he and his colleague had used to try to restart her heart. 'She was declared dead by Dr Ridley', he said, nodding towards her on the benches.

The very matter of fact way he and Dr Ridley accounted for the last moments of Marjorie Nielson's life, prompted an unexpected response in Toby Browning, a sudden feeling of remorse that rose in him without warning. Once again, he looked over to the large Gothic window and hoped that his attention would be taken by someone or something outside amongst the gravestones.

'Marise Dubarry, you were secretary to Dr Nielson . . . '

' . . . *friend* and secretary,' interrupted the witness.

'Quite so, Ms Dubarry. Perhaps you would be good enough to tell us something of your friend, how long you had known her and what she was like.'

'I met Marjorie in London in the late 50s,' said the small woman in a voice much more certain than the look on her face. 'A few years later, when she started her practice, I began to work with her. She was a remarkable woman and it is impossible for me to believe that she is not here.' Marise Dubarry's words filled the room and Toby Browning concentrated hard on the heavily accented words spoken by the French woman.

'We were both children of refugees and we both washed up in London. We both never saw our parents again and so, I suppose, we had a special bond. She trained as a doctor and I did all sorts of things before joining her.'

'Am I right in thinking, Ms Dubarry, that Dr Nielson has no family?'

'Correct. She was an only child and, as far as I know, there is no other family. She told me her parents were killed in the war.'

'May I bring us up to date now? When was the last time you saw Marjorie Nielson alive?'

'It was the day before, the Thursday. She saw her patients as usual. She had five, the usual Thursday five. She saw three in the morning and then two in the afternoon. She always finished her days writing up notes on her patients. I know we shouldn't call them patients these days, but I can't help it. Clients . . . I don't know.'

'Describe them as you will, Ms Dubarry.'

'They all came and went as normal. As was sometimes our custom, Marjorie – Dr Nielson – and I had lunch in the park. It was clear and bright, I recall, although a little cold and we ate in the café by the Broadwalk.'

'And how did she appear, Ms Dubarry?'

'She seemed happy and content. Serene, I would say. These lunches we had together were always very important to her. She used to call them her 'buffer zone', time to draw breath and to think of nothing except what was in front of her, the trees, the birds and the sky. She was no different that Thursday.'

'You were aware that Dr Nielson was a diabetic?'

'Certainly. She rarely spoke of it for she rarely complained about anything. She saw it as a mild irritant to her life and ignored it as much as she could.'

'And, I'm sorry to ask you this Ms Dubarry, can you think if any reason why Dr Nielson might have taken her own life?'

'Absolutely not,' Marise said clearly, pronouncing each syllable separately to emphasis her response, placing the palms of her hands together in a silent clap.

'She finished with her last patient at four o'clock and then stayed in her rooms until six, as she always did,' Marise continued. 'She came down the stairs. Occasionally we would go to a pub in Marylebone High Street but that evening she said she wanted to get home and so we said goodbye. She appeared happy, no different from most evenings, in fact.'

What do we know, thought Perdita, listening carefully to the reasons why Marjorie Nielson could not possibly have committed suicide? Suicide takes everyone by surprise. If it didn't, there would be fewer suicides. The calm and assured woman she had sat opposite once a week for almost a year had been sympathetic and inspiring, but what did this mean? Who was listening to Dr Marjorie Nielson? She felt a momentary spasm of guilt, a sudden regret. She had the image of ships passing in the night, with her own radar blank but Marjorie Nielson's registering every movement of the vessel close to her, ready to take action if necessary.

'Major Peter Harrington?' The coroner called the next witness and Perdita was surprised to hear the low Yorkshire tones of the man taking his oath.

'You were, Major Harrington, the last patient, client, that Dr Nielson saw on that Thursday, is that correct?'

'I would prefer it if you called me Mr or Peter Harrington. I am retired now and I do not use my military rank. But to answer your question, yes, I saw Dr Nielson as I have been doing every Thursday for about a year now.'

'And how did you find her during that last session?'

It might not have been too difficult to guess that Peter Harrington had been in the army but Toby thought that he looked too young to be retired. His face was fit and lean, his blond hair running to grey was short and he stood upright as if by habit. He would put him at no more than late forties.

Peter Harrington paused before he spoke, drawing himself up as if deliberately thinking about his answer. When it came it was slow and measured.

'You must understand', he said, 'that the relationship between a therapist and a client is an unusual one. The act of perception, if you like, is only one way. So when you ask me how did I find her, I can only reply, the same. She was sympathetic and attentive, as ever. She was a formidable woman and nothing in this world would make me think that she had taken her own life.'

The authority with which he said these words seemed to bring a quietness to the courtroom and Perdita felt the atmosphere change. Some voices command attention and Peter Harrington's slow northern diction seemed to have silenced even the thunderous diesel engines outside.

'But I can give only one side of the story and that's from a strange angle. But you must believe me, this woman did not take her own life.'

Peter Harrington's certainty provoked the coroner to return to his papers which he shuffled through with a degree of perplexity before realising that his witness was still standing in the box.

'Thank you Mr Harrington, that will be all. You have been most useful as, indeed, have all the witnesses.' The coroner continued to study his papers as the witness made his way back to the benches. Perdita felt him settle in front of her, the creak of the wooden bench responding to his tall body. She had no idea of what would happen next.

'This has been an inquest into the death of Dr Marjorie Nielson, aged seventy-eight, of 28 Parliament Way, London NW3. Dr Nielson's body was found on the morning of 2 April 2006 and she was declared dead at 9.22 a.m. Toxicology and post mortem reports show that she died following a coma induced by hypoglycaemia. This may be have been caused by a number of factors. The PM shows that she had not eaten in the previous four to six hours but that she had drunk some alcohol. Higher than normal levels of insulin were found in her bloodstream but there appears to be no evidence to support that she administered these herself. I cannot therefore say that this is a case of self-harm. There is simply insufficient evidence to support the taking of her own life. Perhaps she took insulin by accident or perhaps, as her doctor has said, this death was entirely natural. In view of this, I am able to pass a verdict of death by natural causes. The body may be released for burial.'

Peter Harrington looked down and appeared to be trying to remove a liver spot from the back of his hand. Toby Browning was frowning as though the inconclusiveness of the proceedings had displeased him. Perdita Landberg, further along the row to his left, was thinking of the body of Marjorie Nielson joining all the other dead souls in the field outside, another life to add to the thousands that lay around the old courthouse. In reality she realised this was not possible, but in her mind it had a poetic neatness. As she thought about it the music began to play in her head, the repeated theme she had created earlier, louder now and more elaborate, it filled the room up beyond the chandeliers and into the very apex of the roof so that she didn't hear the shuffle of feet on the wooden floor and the slow emptying of the Coroners Court of St Pancras.

Then she was back in the present, a transition so sudden that it might have been brought about by a clash of cymbals and rumble of timpani. Marjorie Nielson with whom she had confided for over a year but who was almost entirely unknown to her was dead, a life reduced to a series of statements in an old fashioned coroner's court.

Peter Harrington watched her stand there, lost in her thoughts and looking upwards at the spread of the plane trees and he involuntarily glanced towards the trees himself but he could see nothing to hold his attention. Instead, he turned and walked down through the graveyard, past the small parish church and onwards to St Pancras station. His stride was purposeful, his bearing strong and upright and the clip of his shoes could be heard even above the traffic on the road. But although he held his head firm and his eyes were fixed on a point directly ahead of him, this was all a front for those eyes were glistening with tears which, much to his annoyance, now rolled down his cheek so that he had to raise the leather gloves, which he held in his right hand, and dab them away.

# Chapter 5

**Notes on Peter Harrington. Age 48. Referred by Dr William Jones at the Royal Scots Regiment. Problem unspecified.**

Major Peter Harrington is a commanding presence. It is difficult for me to be here, he begins. We, by that I mean the army, doesn't believe in this sort of thing. Well, at least it didn't until recently with all the health and safety business. It's hard to square health and safety with the army, don't you think? He talks slowly and carefully and his speech, like his movements, are surprisingly precise for such a big man. He tells me he has left the army, took early retirement and now lives in the south of France. He runs a business looking after people's swimming pools and gardens. I fell in love with the area during a joint exercise with the French army just north of Draguignan, he explains. It's wilder than you think he adds, not like the coast which I suppose is wilder in a different sort of way. He smiles and waits, quite at ease with himself, it seems to me.

As I say, it is difficult for me to be here, he repeats and I'm not sure what it is all about. I feel, though, that there is something stopping me living my life. Does that seem a bit vague he asks me?

It seems very precise, I tell him.

Well, perhaps you can tell me why? he responds.

I think I need some help from you before I, we, can achieve that. He looks directly at me as if trying to take in what I have said.

It's not easy to explain he says but I feel uneasy a lot of the time. I ask him to describe what he means. Sometimes it is so vague I'm not sure I can, he says, it's like having a car with a governor, if you know what I mean. He sees that I need an explanation. Well, he continues, quite a few army vehicles have governors, limiters, to stop them going beyond a certain speed. I feel that I have been fitted with one of those.

And what effect does it have on your life? I ask.

I just don't seem to be able to relax, he says. I thought when I left the army it would change, but it's got worse. It's like I'm followed by a cloud that's always just behind me. He stops as if imagining the cloud.

When did this start? I ask him. He shakes his head. I'm dashed if I know, he says, it just was there.

Can you remember having this cloud as a child? I ask him.

He takes some time to answer. Well, now you mention it, he says as though it is a surprise to him to be asked to think so far back, I don't think I did. I come from a large family in a poor background but I can't remember feeling bad. I had bad days, of course, but, no, I don't think I had the cloud then. He pauses again, looking beyond me as if trying to unpick his childhood for clues. This is a long silence before he turns back to me. The silence continues.

So what made you come here now?

It was Taffy Jones, he says. He was one of the Regiment's doctors, he explains, and a friend of mine. He came to stay with me in France and he was telling me about what happened to lots of men like me who retire early from the army and go to pieces. They come out of a very disciplined world where to some extent everything is done for them, into a world where there are no rules. Lots of them fall apart and a disturbingly large percentage commit suicide.

Pause.

That hasn't happened to me, I told Taffy, although I do feel a little odd from time to time. Taffy wondered what I meant, so I told him what I've just told you. Odd really, because I had the feeling really badly the day Taffy came down.

Pause.

Why do you think it was particularly bad that day?

I'm not really sure, he says.

OK, I say, can you describe the feeling on that day? Long pause.

It's difficult for me to say this, he says, but I suppose I felt tearful. He looks at me as if wanting to challenge any reaction I might have to his statement.

37

Why? I ask him.

I don't know, do I, he says and he appears irritated. If I bloody knew that I wouldn't be here would I? He doesn't say this aggressively, more in exasperation.

So you told Taffy a bit about the way you were feeling. And did he suggest that you might see someone about it?

He thought I might be depressed, yes. I hate that word and it's not a word I associate with myself. I don't believe in it. It's seems to me a form of self-indulgence.

Pause.

But Taffy must have thought that the way you were feeling was beginning to spoil the quality of your life?

I was in the army for over twenty years and you learn not to show any side of yourself that might, shall we say, be open to exploitation. You don't let on, for example, that you read poetry, or that you paint. And so you would never let on that you were 'depressed'. Here he deepens his northern accent to emphasise the contempt felt for the word and the condition. Perhaps it was because I had left the army that Taffy could broach the subject with me and, by the same token, it was why I was able to talk to him.

I want you to think further about why, on the day that Taffy came to stay, that you felt bad, I ask him. Tell me what happened.

There wasn't anything, he said, but I'll try. I had to pick Taffy up from Nice airport and I left with plenty of time because there can often be problems on the autoroute. I remember I was working early that morning at a big house on the hill to the east of Draguignan. I arrived there shortly after six and began the routine maintenance on the pool. Although it was the end of the season it was hot, even at that time in the morning and my dog lay in the shade by the side of the pool. It was odd, for that day the owner came out to see me. She is a Parisienne, very smart with lots of money. I wasn't aware of her at first and then I saw her standing there, her arms folded. She was wearing a brown robe, almost like an Arab. Not sure if it was a dressing gown, or not. She made me coffee and told me she was going back to Paris the next day and had sometimes heard me in the morning and wanted to meet before she left. Anyway, she delayed me so I was slightly late on the autoroute and then there had been a crash on the opposite carriageway. A large lorry had caught fire and the fire engines could only get to the scene from the eastbound side, the one I was travelling along. So I crawled by the scene and lost at least another half an hour. Fortunately the plane was delayed and it didn't matter. It was very good to see Taffy again and we drove back and I made him lunch. The rest I told you.

Long pause.

**End of session.**

# Chapter 6

The further east he drove, the bigger the clouds became, great white billowing cumuli filling the sky above the flat horizon, muscular and threatening, gathered off shore and held there by the wind coming from the land. Toby stopped the car just after Burnham Market, on a rise of land topped by the ancient church and its round tower. The wind was behind him, pushing his hair forward as he looked over the familiar scene. He had come here to prepare himself for the undoubted confrontation that lay ahead of him, down in the village, where Norton Hall stood, its flint and brick façade and neat lawns butting into the salt marshes which lay between it and the sea. Although this was familiar land to Toby, it held uneasy memories for him and he found it hard to simply accept the beauty of the panorama in front of him for it always came tinged with unease, the very width of the horizon indicating an uncertain future and an unclear past.

His father had called him the day after the coroner's hearing. 'Couldn't get you yesterday,' he had announced unceremoniously, not really interested in discovering why his son had been unavailable. ' 'Spect you were busy with one of your artist chappies. Well, anyway, I want to see you and thought you might be able to drop by the Hall at the weekend.'

Charles Browning's concept of time and space was entirely predicated on his own life and needs. His selfishness, about which he had been told many times, not least by his own son, he always denied, failing to see it just as he failed to see the needs of those closest to him. And, as is the curious case with people like Charles Browning, he nearly always did get his own way, which is why Toby was just completing the three hour drive to Norton Hall and why he was now preparing himself, on the low wind-swept hill overlooking his family home, for another dose of his irrepressible father.

'Shame, shame,' were his father's first words as he greeted his son at the door. 'You just missed Roy Ponting. There's a man who knows a bit about art.' There were several implications contained in this series of abrupt sentences. Firstly, that Toby was late. Secondly, that he didn't know as much about art as Roy Ponting. And, thirdly, that if he had really knuckled down to things, he, too, might have become Director of the National Portrait Gallery.

Toby followed his father through the long hallway to the large living room at the back of the house where tall windows looked onto the garden and beyond that to the creeks and ditches lining the marshes. Although his mother had been dead for several years now, Toby always felt the house had the softening touches of a woman's hand. On the table was a tall vase of white lilies and the cushions on the sofas were plumped up and neat. The smell of wax polish lingered in the air.

'Drink?' His father was already pouring himself a decent sized whisky.

'Go on, then. But I'll have a glass of white wine, if you don't mind.' This was a little dance the pair of them did regularly, his father knowing full well that he preferred to drink wine to spirits.

'Roy has just been putting on that old poofter, y'know, whatsis-name?' This statement was interrupted, after the word 'poofter', with the pop of the cork being withdrawn from the bottle of wine. The coincidence was not accidental.

'Would you mean Hockney, by any chance, father?'

'That's the one. Chap that painted bare bottoms in Californian swimming pools.' Charles Browning spoke in short, clipped sentences as though he was discussing horses with a few chums at his club, in a tone of voice unchanged since he used to order first year boys to do his bidding when he was a prefect at school.

All this was an act to see whether he could make his son rise to the bait, but Toby had been round this course a few times before.

'Huge success, I gather,' Toby replied genially. 'I once sold a Hockney, did I tell you?'

It was as if his father had not heard, so busy was he adding ice to his drink and swirling it noisily with a glass stick.

Charles Browning was a Luddite to human relationships, deliberately upsetting the machinery of family and social life as often as he could. For years Toby thought his father had done this unwittingly, but now he saw it much more cynically, as the way his father always got what he wanted. The man sitting opposite him now may have been his father, but in some many ways he remained a stranger to Toby. Clubbable and amusing he could be, with a seemingly endless circle of friends, but this was the man whose desire to make life easier for himself began when he sent Toby away at the age of six thereby putting a distance between the two of them that Toby could not, or would not, bridge.

'Spring tides brought up a whole load of rubbish again this year,' his father said, out of the blue. 'We used to have sea weed at the high water mark and now we've got miles of plastic. If you fancy it, we could clear some of it from in front of the garden.'

'Sure,' replied Toby, knowing that whatever it was that his father wanted to say to him this weekend, would be more easily conveyed if the two of them were doing something. Toby had barely taken a sip of wine before his father was heading for the outhouse where he kept the boots.

The wind had turned colder now and the bank of clouds still lay out to sea waiting for the sun to disappear before they moved in over the land. The flint and brick wall which ran the length of the garden served as both a boundary and a defence. Occasionally, like the week before, the tide would lap against its base. Charles Browning was forever being told that global warming would soon have the sea coming over the top, but he dismissed all this talk as 'modern poppycock', as he did now whilst dragging a large tarpaulin through the side gate and onto the path which ran at the foot of the wall. The departing sea had deposited a tide mark of detritus, plastic containers, broken and discoloured packing foam, condoms, which lay on the sea grass like an artist's installation. Toby said as much to his father.

'What are you talking about, boy?' was his abrupt and fairly typical response. Charles Browning could not relinquish his role as senior partner in this relationship and never tired of emphasising the fact. The two men worked for the next two hours, feeling the wind die down and watching the clouds approach and add to the gloom of the darkening day. They wrapped the tarpaulin over the heap of dirty plastic as they caught the first hint of rain in the air.

'George will come along with the tractor in the morning,' Charles told his son. George was the local farmer, as unable to rebuff the demands of his neighbour as was Toby.

'C'mon,' he ordered, 'let's have another drink.

'Perhaps I could finish the one you poured me earlier,' said Toby to his father's back, but the remark was lost in the scrunch of their feet on the gravel path. Either that or his father chose to ignore it. So far he was running true to form in a pattern that Toby had grown only too familiar with over the years, increasingly so after his mother's death. He had once mentioned it to Amy, when he had convinced himself that their relationship was becoming permanent, and she had rather disappointed him by siding with his father, describing him as charming and amusing and not to be taken too seriously. Toby remembered how his father flirted outrageously with Amy, telling her risqué stories about his past and scattering them with the names of the great and the good. Toby had only just begun to understand that Amy's inability to see his father in perspective was an early warning that their relationship was destined to founder, as indeed it did when she abruptly left him for a hedge fund manager, stranding him, now he came to think if it, above the high water mark like a useless piece of flotsam.

There had been a Norton Hall on this spot for almost six hundred years and the present building was the third that fronted up to the winds which blew relentlessly across the salty marshes to buffet the windows and strip the paintwork. This house had replaced its half-timbered Elizabethan predecessor in the middle of the eighteenth-century and during its building the foundations of an even earlier house had been discovered. Everyone who visited the present house fell instantly in love with a building so easy on the eye that it was impossible to imagine it ever being designed; it was merely part of nature, at one with the surrounding landscape. And, as Amy had once declared, the eccentric and larger than life Charles Browning was the perfect owner, filling the rooms and corridors with his exuberant life.

'Now,' his father said, handing him a glass of whisky, 'there are a couple of things we need to talk about.' Toby put the whisky back on the silver tray and retrieved his half finished glass of wine from the book shelf where he had left it earlier. In a small gesture, he raised the glass to his father, only partly as a rebuke, but his father seemed distracted by something on the other side of the room.

'As I was saying,' he said, turning to face his son and pointing with his drink towards a wing chair by the fire, 'there are a couple of things I wanted to discuss,' by which Toby understood his father to mean 'tell'. This used to happen a lot in the old days, when Toby would be called to this very room where his father pretended to debate important issues relating to his son's life when in fact all he wanted to do was issue a series of commands. But even the advantage of experience had not prepared Toby for what came next. Toby watched as his father paced to and fro in front of the big window, passing his drink from one hand to the other in time with his steps. The choreography was familiar to Toby and he knew it was the prelude to some fairly important information as it had been, for example, when his father had expressed his extreme disappointment at his son's wish to study art history at Glasgow and not law at Cambridge by withdrawing his not inconsiderable monthly allowance. But this was nothing compared with the cold contempt Charles Browning had expressed when Toby had declared that he was no longer interested in playing the violin. Even now Toby could feel the discomfort of those days but his father's peremptory cough brought him sharply back to the present.

'I am getting married.' The statement made it sound as though this was about to happen for the very first time thus condemning the twenty years he had spent with Toby's mother to oblivion. 'I am getting married,' he continued, 'which means there are going to be some changes.' If Toby felt surprise at this he certainly wasn't going to show it and he waited for his father to continue on his imperious way.

'Penny lives in Wiltshire and I have known her sometime.' Charles took a sip from his glass, his back to his son as he looked down the garden towards the sea, omitting to explain that 'sometime' included eighteen months before Toby's mother left him. 'She's a Trottman and her old father popped his clogs a few months ago and she's inherited. You know, the Clayburn Estate.'

Toby did, indeed, know the Clayburn Estate and he could see his future stepmother now welcoming him into her father's vast Georgian living room with its double aspect over the Capability Brown landscape. Clayburn House, a stuccoed Palladian mansion, stood four square in the middle of two thousand acres of the best countryside in England. Toby was there to discuss the sale of an early Francis Bacon which old man Trottman didn't think suited the house. He was wrong, but Toby was not going to inform him or his daughter who had been deputed to look after the sale. He recalled that she could not have been more than five years older than him and he looked over towards his father and shook his head at his broad back.

Toby knew that whatever he said next would either be ignored or misunderstood so he remained quiet.

'And so,' his father went on as though he had never expected a response from his son, 'I shall be moving in there after the wedding. Which leaves me the question of what to do with Norton Hall.' Now he did turn to face Toby who wondered, having gained a stepmother almost his own age and been told that there was a question mark over the future of his family home, what could possibly come next.

'Now I've thought a lot about this', Charles Browning explained, to which Toby silently replied 'but not with me', 'and I have decided that I can't be doing with tenants and that it would be a folly to sell now. So I've decided it should be yours. You're going to get it in the end, anyway, so, for all sorts of financial reasons, it might be best if you have it now.' It was a statement and it was final. Norton Hall was to be Toby Browning's, not because he coveted it, nor because his father felt that emotionally he should have it, but because it made financial sense to him, Charles Browning. No discussion, no debate. *Fait accompli.*

Charles helped himself to another drink and just stopped himself offering the whisky bottle to his son. 'Don't worry,' said Toby, 'I'll get the wine from the fridge.' The few seconds it took him to walk to the kitchen allowed him time to assemble his thoughts and they came to him wrapped in suspicion and doubt. On a table in one of the alcoves in the kitchen, a photograph of his mother was framed in silver. Toby raised his glass to it so that the pale yellow liquid blurred the outlines of her face. What do you see now? he wondered. What can you tell me? He was unable to accept his father's offer straightforwardly, for he knew instinctively that there was a labyrinth of reasons behind every decision his father made. Even the picture was there for a purpose, a reminder that it was his mother that had left the family home, a reproach in black and white.

'Well, for a man of considerable property, you appear particularly glum,' his father said as Toby walked back into the room and again it was said as an accusation rather than a statement of concern.

'Do not misinterpret "thoughtful" for "glum",' Toby said quietly, knowing full well that his statement would fall to the ground between them, unheard.

'A prime piece of Norfolk real estate, much sought after by

most of North London,' his father rolled on, making a sweeping gesture with his drinking hand so that a splash of whisky splayed over the polished top of the mahogany table beside him. 'Thought you'd be absolutely delighted. But, then, you've always been a strange one.'

It's a monologue really, thought Toby. He doesn't need me here because he has already pre-decided the answers. Now all I have to do is find out what they are.

'It's a lot to take in,' Toby said. His father looked at him with wide-eyed puzzlement. 'I wonder if you would allow me a moment or two to gather my thoughts? I won't be long.'

The tide had now come in and changed the view from the embankment walk, the advancing water soaking into the marshes until the last of the light from the sky was reflected uniformally by the sea. Far away in the distance came the lonely cry of a curlew but the sight that Toby had come out for was in the sky in front of him, a great swirling mass of grey, shifting one way and then swerving another as if guided by some giant magnet. The closer he came to the exhilarating display, so he could hear the babble of noise coming from the swooping cloud as thousands upon thousands of geese enjoyed the final moments of daylight before descending, almost as one, to the fields around for the night. It was a sight that even on this rain-specked evening, where the birds were merely a grey mobile mass against an even greyer backdrop, that never failed to halt him in his tracks and hold him for the few minutes of its enthralling performance. And, as suddenly as it started, it was over and the chatter of the birds subsided as darkness closed over the scene.

Toby walked back along the sea defence, marking each step of the familiar path with deliberately slow strides, delaying the moment of return. It was not difficult to know what concerned him but what eluded him was how to avoid it. To accept the gift of Norton Hall was to hold out his arms and receive the hand-cuffs which would shackle him to his father for life. There would be a penance for such bounty, a permanent debt of gratitude payable in ways that Toby could only too well imagine. He could see the house ahead of him now, defined by the lights in the downstairs rooms. The big copper beeches in front were just beginning to bud and although he could not see them clearly he heard the wind blow through their branches. The sweep of the long boundary wall defined this oasis of tamed nature from the land around but it was an artificial strength and at a whim the sea could breach it, just as his father could breach his defences whenever he liked. Toby would have liked to be impervious to his father but he had not yet devised the strategies and so for the second time on that grey night in early spring, he told his father that he needed more time to think about the offer, a statement which merely caused his father to toss back his head and declare 'fool boy'.

It wasn't until he was some way beyond Fakenham that Toby realised that he was running away, a discomforting sensation and one that caused him to pull into a lay-by. He was in a stretch of forest not far from Thetford and the wind shook the dark trees to his right and he looked into the darkness trying to make out their shapes. All he could see was the reflection of his own face, a middle-aged man, who had just been offered the chance to become a millionaire and doubted that he should take it. As he sat there, the lights of the occasional vehicle approaching and blinding him before suddenly disappearing, he felt the loss of Marjorie Nielson in a way he had been unable to do at the inquest. Her absence now seemed enormous and the future as black as the forest outside. Another car swished by and he flinched at the light and caught a brief glimpse of his white face in the rear-view mirror. His own eyes regarded him without emotion and as he returned his own stare, he recalled a similar look from the woman in the dark glasses in the coroner's court. He tried to put more detail into his memory, but all he could recall was her white blond hair and the stone coloured mackintosh which she had belted tightly around her waist. He felt a glimmer of relief at the memory, this lifeline to Marjorie Nielson but not for an instant did he wonder why the image should have come to mind. He had yet to understand the nature of such accidents.

## Chapter 7

Perdita Landberg lived in a mansion flat just off Marylebone High Street with a minimal amount of clutter, save for the grand piano which dominated the small living room. It was here that Perdita now sat rocking slowly backwards and forwards. To her left, on a small table almost hidden by the piano, was a laptop computer, its blue light reflected along the shiny curve of the instrument. For the moment Perdita Landberg was in a cocoon. Double glazed she liked to call it, wrapped in her own room and then again by the concentration of writing and recording music. Every so often she would tap a key on the computer and then play a phrase or two on the piano, pausing and replaying until she was satisfied with the theme. She repeated this process many times until she estimated that she had accumulated enough to approach the next stage of the special alchemy that was her work. Although all the phrases she had collected during the morning were played on the piano, she was able to change them in the computer to any instrument she chose. At first, she found this abundance of possibilities too much to cope with so now she decided beforehand what instruments to choose. Piano and violin would dominate the piece she was now writing, a process which began on the walk through Kings Cross to the coroner's court. Although, now she thought about it, it had really begun when, in researching more about the court, she had discovered the story of St Pancras Parish Church and the strange history of those that have been buried around it in the thousand years of its existence. And it was Marjorie Nielson who had prompted and focused these ideas, both before and after her death.

Strangely, the piece emerging in front of her, or around her, contained more joy than pain and she wondered, as she always did at this stage, of the curious process of creativity. She had been trying to capture, on that walk to the court, a feeling of movement through time. She had not attributed a mood to it, merely a dynamic, but from it had developed a theme which would be at the heart of the composition, recurring at different points and in different tempos, and this would define it. And this theme, which she saw as both wistful and questioning, was also positive and spoke of future opportunities.

She went into the kitchen and made herself a camomile tea which she did at regular intervals when she was working like this. She was excited and took the tea back into the living room. She sat on the piano stool and pressed 'play' on the computer and for the next twenty minutes listened to the various digital tracks become something altogether more ethereal, extracted from the logical world of commands and programmes, into something indefinable and entirely magical. When the piece had finished, she felt simultaneously elated and exhausted. As she listened her head had dropped slowly to her chest, so that at the end her chin was resting on the top of her sternum. She could not move and her stillness was reflected by the silence of the room. She hardly wanted to break the spell and she stayed liked this for several minutes, the echo of her own music in her head. She had rarely experienced the feeling of knowing that one of her compositions had emerged in such an exciting and complete form. It wasn't for her to judge it as a success, but she knew absolutely that she did not want to alter any part of what she had just heard. Curiously, she also knew that she had completed only the first movement of the composition and with this realisation came two thoughts, tumbling one after the other to take her by surprise. The first was the certainty that she could finish the piece and that the other movements would match the first. This was not arrogance or false bravado for she knew that the inspiration for the first would carry her through to the end. But it was the second thought which caused her to raise her head; she knew that she couldn't continue unless she discovered more about the woman who had been the inspiration so far.

It was not difficult, perhaps, to see why Marjorie Nielson should have been the inspiration for Perdita Landberg's composition. She had been an integral part in her life for more than a year and her death had produced a powerful emotional response. It had also brought a responsibility which Perdita was only just beginning to comprehend. All of a sudden it seemed unjust that she should be able to take any more from Marjorie Nielson. Both in life and in death she had provided guidance but the process was hideously one sided. She understood that she had to redress this balance for it was as if the therapist had left the golden thread which had been her life for Perdita to follow.

She moved back to the piano stool in a gesture which was as much practical as it was superstitious. It was here she felt most comfortable and entirely within her own world. She placed her hands on the keyboard and felt the coldness of the ivory keys and with a slow sweep of her upturned right hand, ran the nail of her middle finger over the succession of notes, hearing it click over the joints. She wondered then if the next movement of the new work would be discordant, in contrast to the first. She surmised that it might, for ignorance produces fear and Perdita realised that the process of discovering more of the life of Marjorie Nielson might reveal facts that would disturb the perfect but unrealistic picture she had of her dead therapist. She set in motion the old parquetry metronome that sat on a polished shelf which slid out from above the keyboard and she measured the slow tick of its beat against her thoughts.

She was back in a recording studio almost two years earlier, about to record a series of short pieces she had written for a television series, each conveying a different mood and tempo to match different scenes in the drama. She had enjoyed creating the music which she found relatively easy for, unlike the music she wrote for herself, which she regarded privately as 'art', it only taxed part of her brain and the mood was already dictated by the pictures. The producer of the series was there and he stood behind the glass screen, more an observer than a participant.

Perdita was playing the piano with a quartet with whom she had collaborated before. She enjoyed the pleasure of listening to her own music come to life and was both elated and grateful that the other players took her work so seriously.

It was afterwards that the mood changed. The musicians left and Perdita, as she often did, went back into the studio alone. She sat at the keyboard and listened, for she believed that in the very silence of the room she could hear not only the echoes of her own music but remnants of all the other compositions that had been played within those soundproofed walls, ricocheting invisibly in the corners. It was as she sat listening, head slightly cocked, that she sensed someone behind her and felt hands placed lightly on her shoulders.

'I thought that was brilliant today.' The producer's voice was calm and rich and he pulled up a chair that one of the violinists had used and sat beside her.

'Thank you,' she said. 'I am blessed with very good players.' She had detected in his tone an interest beyond the musical and she was immediately on guard. She had heard the others talk about this man, of his charm and good looks but she did not feel at ease.

He handed her a CD of the music she had just recorded. 'Can we celebrate', he said, tapping the Perspex case against her knee, 'with me buying you a drink? There is a champagne bar in the hotel round the corner.' His voice carried an assumption of compliance, as if his question had been rhetorical, and this further set her against him.

'Would you mind if I didn't?' Her reply was perhaps a shade colder than she would have wished but his next comment made her not regret it.

'You're a funny one, aren't you? I'm only asking if you'd like a drink, not if you'd like to get into bed with me. Or maybe that's what you're frightened of.' He laughed. 'Lighten up, girl.' And with this, he put his hand on her thigh in a gesture that might have been affectionate had it not been accompanied by the words and a slight squeeze of his fingers upwards towards her groin.

'Don't.' She spoke the word as a command.

He looked coldly at her. 'And what are you going to do about it?' he said slowly, all warmth now departed. 'Precious bitch.' As he put his hand on her breast she flayed out with her arm and caught his face on the bridge of his nose. The chair clattered over as he stood and the CD case span across the floor.

'Who'd want to go to bed with you, anyway?' His words were cold and dismissive, spoken poisonously into her face.

She heard the heavy door of the studio sigh shut and she was alone again. Her heart was racing and her body had shrunken protectively in on itself. But a different sort of damage had already been done to her mind and she began to weep, not only at the hostility and crudeness of the assault but at the corrosive effect his words were now having on her. If his comments were unforgivable, they now resonated in her head finding strange echoes of earlier thoughts that had plagued her for years. As many cruel people are able to do, the producer had intuitively detected a fault line in Perdita's psyche.

As the insistent tick of the metronome continued, Perdita Landberg felt the tears slide down her face and drip onto the keyboard just as they had done in the studio. Two years ago those tears would propel her towards Marjorie Nielson's door. Today, they acknowledged the sadness of her passing.

Her hands formed two chords on the keyboard and she pushed her body forward as she depressed the keys. Contained in the sounds the different notes made was both discord and harmony and Perdita's ear was able to separate and identify the different layers so that when she adjusted her fingers and leaned forward again, although the sound was different, the two sets of chords were quite clearly a progression from one another. It was another beginning and the spirit of Marjorie Nielson was tangible in the room. Perdita played the four sets of chords again and recorded them into the computer. Then she lengthened them so that the reverberation of the first set bled into the second. This was the opening into the next movement and into it walked Marjorie Nielson. Perdita imagined her standing in the room in one of the brightly coloured shirts she said she liked to wear to match her mood, her greying hair pushed back and a pencil in one hand lightly tapping the knuckles of her other hand. She spoke to the therapist who was as real as the keys under her fingers.

'But who are you?'

She held the image of the therapist as her right hand began a series of rapid repetitions between the notes that had formed one of the themes in the first part of the work. Against this continuous background of sound, her left hand played the chords so that, taken as a whole, the effect was both melodic and discordant, clangorous and challenging. It was a perfect embodiment of the emotions that had gripped her in the studio, her enjoyment of the recording broken into by the physical and verbal assault of the producer. But now it also reflected her unease at something unknown in the life of Marjorie Nielson. Outside, in another world, she heard children calling in the street and knew that it must be four o'clock and school over for the day. Their sounds, brash and excited, were funnelled up from the main road pushed upwards with all the other noises of the city street, the diesel clatter of a taxi engine idling at the zebra crossing, the beep of a horn and the angry shout of a motorist, the call of a startled blackbird, each separated by Perdita into different layers, the modern opera she listened to every day of her life.

# Chapter 8

**Notes on Perdita Landberg. Aged 38. Referred from a previous client. Unspecified symptoms.**

When she phoned, Perdita did not tell me she was blind and so my first encounter with her catches me slightly at a disadvantage. Even walking into a strange room for the first time, she has a certainty to her movements which belies the fact that she has no idea of its geography and leads me to think that the dark glasses were merely an affectation. It was only when she stands still in front of me and speaks my name that I realise that I should move forward to shake her hand and explain where the chair is and even then she doesn't explain her blindness. Uncompromising.

Something unpleasant happened to me and I wanted to talk to someone about it, she begins and then stops.

Tell me about it, I say and she shifts her position slightly, my words clearly helping her to orientate herself with me.

A few weeks ago I was sexually assaulted whilst at work. To tell you the truth, nothing actually happened. I was groped. He put his hand on my leg and touched my breast and he was verbally unpleasant and that was about it. But in some ways that is entirely incidental, the touching I mean. No, he laid bare my doubts. He wanted to have sex with me and when I wouldn't he became aggressive and in doing that he released so many fears in me, so much so that he made me doubt the thing that I had been more sure about than anything else.

She pauses and I wait for her to continue.

I have never believed that my blindness was a disability. I was born like this and as far as I am concerned it is all I have known. It's only other people who seem to have a problem with it. I never wanted it to matter and it never really did matter. This is my life and I'm not complaining about it and never did complain about it. She pauses here. This is familiar ground for her.

I wait, again.

Well, I suppose, until now. Suddenly, I don't know why anyone should find me attractive.

She says this boldly, almost as a challenge. I tell her that the majority of women who come through these doors, even, or perhaps especially, the most beautiful, believe they aren't attractive.

But they can see themselves, she replies.

Well, usually they can't, I want to reply.

But it is not just that, she continues, more seriously, I now don't know why I should be attracted to anyone else. What are the criteria? If attraction is initially based on looks, I have to trust someone who finds *me* attractive. And what do I base *my* reaction on?

What happened with the man who molested you?

I had heard about him. He had a reputation. I knew he had been married and that he had been out with one of my players.

Here she tells me that she is a composer and had been recording one of her pieces in a studio.

He asked me for a drink and I said no.

Why?

Why, she repeats. Why?

What did you think of him before he asked you for a drink?

I just didn't like him. He barely said a word during the recording. I suppose it was instinct, really.

And what was wrong with that?

Nothing. But I suppose later he made me realise that I couldn't see myself. Really couldn't *see* myself. OK, I have an idea of what I am as a person, but not as a physical entity. And when he said 'why would anyone want to go to bed with you, anyway' I began to doubt myself and couldn't imagine what anyone would actually *see* in me. What was attracting them in the first place?

But men must have been attracted to you before?

Yes and I have been out with a few. But it appears I pose them a problem.

Pause.

My blindness. It is a massive obstacle for them.

But surely they know about your blindness before they ask you out?

Yes, they do.

So, they must have been attracted to something in the first place?

Yes, but I can't *see* what they have been attracted to.

And why is that important?

I think it is because my inability to see myself – or my sudden awareness that I can't see myself – has made me doubt the fact that I can't see the man who is asking me out. That somehow the whole infrastructure of a possible relationship is built on sand.

Are looks that important then?

What do you think?

There is certainly a challenging quality about Perdita. Her directness is a mix of self-belief, of which she appears to have a lot, and defensiveness which may or may not be the result of her blindness. She is undoubtedly a striking looking woman.

But I imagine you have not been short of suitors in the past?

I have been made aware that I am not unattractive.

And how do you gauge attractiveness in a man?

Voice. Hands. Humour. Politeness. But you cannot know about these in advance. I am excluded from that initial point of connection and until now, I didn't think it was that important. Presumably it is for the man who finds me attractive? Isn't that the way it works?

She is very matter of fact, as though this was a philosophy class on the chemistry of attraction.

So tell me how you felt when the man, the producer, spoke to you?

I felt that he knew something about me that I didn't want him to know, that he was taunting me with his knowledge. It was as if I was naked and he was staring at me.

Tell me about that.

For the first time she looks less than sure of herself. It is disconcerting not to see her eyes but she is notably less comfortable and appears unsure how to continue.

I'm finding it very difficult to talk about.

Pause.

Given that he had just molested you, this is perhaps not surprising.

Who would want to sleep with me? he said. And I don't know who would.

She raises her hand to her glasses and runs her fingers along the upper rim as if confirming that they are there. She shakes her head.

I cannot talk about it.

**End of session.**

# Chapter 9

Toby Browning walked across the gallery floor and straightened a large canvas by just a fraction before returning to his original position and regarding the imposing work by a leading colourist, greens, greys and deep oranges contrasting with the duck egg blue of the walls. There is a moment before every opening when the hectic preparation, the endless cajoling, the tedious detail of marketing is complete and a strange and unnerving calmness descends. From where he stood, Toby could see the majority of the pictures hung in the two large studios which made up the ground floor of his gallery in Wapping. The space had been divided by several large, portable panels, painted in what Toby called dirty badger and the eclectic mix of contemporary art hung comfortably against the colours, neither announcing themselves too strongly nor shrinking into the background. As much as he could ever declare himself satisfied, Toby let out a long sigh and glanced at his watch. This peculiar moment of peace would soon dissolve when the buyers, critics and the general hangers-on who came to openings burst into this perfect symmetry.

As if to make the point, the buzzer on the front door broke into his thoughts and he turned to see who it was. He had to acknowledge that deep in his stomach he felt a dread, a familiar apprehension that he now regarded as part and parcel of his life. Standing outside he could see a small woman in a large black coat and by her side, almost as tall, a battered cello case which she held like an old friend slightly the worse for drink. Puzzled, Toby clicked open the door and cocked his head in query.

'I'm a present from your father,' she said with a bright smile, her white teeth clear against the deep red of her lipstick. 'At least, that's what he told me to say. I'm going to play at the opening.' And with that she picked up the case with practised ease and walked past Toby and into the gallery. 'Where would you like me?'

A group of thoughts had formed simultaneously in Toby's mind, so much so that like logs in a river, they jammed against one another and ground to a halt. As if responding to the silence, the young women stopped and turned.

'He said he was sorry he couldn't make it tonight, but that I might bring a little class to the occasion.'

The fact the Toby had not invited his father to the opening seemed irrelevant at this moment for this piece of theatre was classic Charles Browning, a deliberate muscling in on his son's territory, a coup de theatre aimed at showing who was top dog.

'Oh, I am Samantha Hardy. I'm with the London Phil and Mr Browning has hired me for the night.'

Well, not this Mr Browning Toby thought, but kept the response to himself. The young cellist pressed on.

'Do you have a chair and where would you like me? Or has a cat got your tongue?'

She had very dark and shiny hair and as she pulled off her coat, which she did by shaking first one shoulder and then the other as she held tightly to the cello case. Toby vaguely recognised her from pictures in the paper.

'Well,' he responded uncertainly, giving in to the idea without really knowing why, 'over there, by the Hodgkin.' He walked across the painted concrete floor to a door which led to his office and returned with a chair which he placed to one side of the picture.

She flicked open the case and lifted out the cello but before she stood it on the floor she placed a rubber thimble on the spike on its base. And then, looking up at him, she said 'Do you mind?' and before he could answer she pulled the bow across the strings and the studio was filled with the most astonishing noise out of all proportion to the small figure creating it. It was undoubtedly beautiful but Toby was not marvelling at the music but at his father's ability to invade and dominate his territory even from a distance.

Later, as the room filled up, the music faded into the background only occasionally drifting above the chatter and the banter. From time to time, he caught glimpses of her through the bodies or over the shoulder of someone talking to him. If he concentrated hard he could separate the music from the other noise, filtering it, allowing it to distract him. He was doing this when he felt a hand on his arm. He turned to find his golfing partner holding out his hand and fixing him with his grey blue eyes. Well, partner would be putting it too strongly given the feudal nature of their relationship. Servant would be closer. Toby took William Gilbert's hand and felt the grip close over more than just his fingers.

'This is a nice space,' the businessman said simply. 'I'm glad I came.' He made it sound as though he had made the journey by bus and tube but Toby knew that outside a large dark vehicle would be waiting, its engine quietly running with a grey suited driver at the wheel.

'I've decided I will have it.' Few words, no preamble, cut to the chase. Great wealth allowed a certain directness but for that moment Toby could not think of the several millions of pounds that William Gilbert was about to pay for Rain in Venice, but of the music which seemed to be louder and clearer than ever, rising and falling in the room, weaving between the bodies so that although people's lips were moving Toby could not hear the sound of speech but only the drifting beauty of the cello.

'But I want to take it now.' It was a statement of fact. Yes, and money allows you to do outrageous and unreasonable things, Toby thought, aware that to refuse such a demand would be futile. The music seemed even more dominant now, pushing in on him and he could see the white arm of the cellist jerking backwards and forwards as she fought to make the music master the room. Why couldn't he feel the pleasure of selling such a valuable and beautiful painting? A sense of panic began to rise in him and in order to deflect it, he nodded acquiescence at his buyer and threaded his way through the crowd to his office where he tripped a small switch in a cupboard by the door. William Gilbert was already on the phone and seconds later the chauffeur appeared. He was wearing grey gloves and with great care he lifted the Hodgkin off the wall, holding in his hands, Toby thought, not merely a painting but the embodiment of an emotion, a mood of sadness in Venice caught with just colour and brush strokes. And this moment now departed the room, accompanied by a small round of applause from those who realised what had happened. Toby saw the faces looking at him, pointing their applause in his direction, acknowledging his success. Meanwhile, by his side, the cellist played on, apparently oblivious of the transaction that had just taken place and of the people in the room, locked into her own world.

As he watched her, Toby began to feel faint and as he leaned back against the wall behind him he recognised only too clearly the early signs of what would happen next. He raised his arm in a weak gesture of thanks before taking small steps towards the sanctuary of his office. A nausea rose in him now and with it his body began to sweat. He unlocked the back door of the gallery and almost fell on to the cobbled road before stumbling down a narrow stairway to the river. Here he sat on the stump of an old wooden pier and thrust his head between his legs, retching. He watched his sweat drip onto the dirty stones and waited for the moment to pass. The smell of the Thames, both sweet and foul, assaulted him and he gagged again. The sheer ludicrousness of the situation appalled him, his black patent shoes poking into the debris of the river, his suit and shirt soaked with his sweat, the people behind him in the gallery wondering at his absence, his very helplessness at what had overtaken him.

A cold wind, encouraged by the river, was now chilling him, his jacket flapping in the breeze. He turned and looked up the stairs, wondering how he was to go back in, his mood as black as the night that had now closed around him. He picked up a stone and tossed it towards the river, hearing it splash in the distance.

'Well, Marjorie Nielson, what do you think of this?' he challenged the night air. 'What would you make of this? It's the same old story, isn't it? Come on, give me a clue. I know you're out there somewhere.' He was shouting now, his words carried on the wind over the river.

He walked to the stairs, trudging up the slippery steps, pausing at the top to straighten his clothes and pat his hair into place, before re-entering the party. He stood for a moment at the door of his office and remembered to turn the alarm system on again. He looked at his hand on the switch and hoped that as he pressed it down, the people in the room would magically disappear and leave him alone. One of his two assistants came over, full of smiles and put both her hands on his forearm as if to confirm his success and perhaps to hope that some of it would rub off on her. The opening had been a triumph, she told him and not even the sight of his muddy shoes could dampen her enthusiasm. She wheeled him around the pictures and the rash of red spots to show of their sale. People were beginning to leave now, some calling their thanks as they left.

Samantha Hardy had stopped playing. He watched her as she removed the rubber tip and then carefully laid the cello in its case, a mother putting her child to bed. She clicked the case shut and the looked around her, as if for the first time. He carried over a glass of champagne to thank her.

'You know, your father's one of the rudest men I have met,' she declared without hesitation. 'But for the fact he paid me a lot of money to do this gig tonight, I would have told him where to go. You see, he said I might want to entertain you with more than just music.'

Toby grimaced at the news, which didn't come as a surprise to him at all. 'I can only apologise,' he said. 'My father has a degree in not being aware of other people's feelings.'

'Are you alright?' she asked, looking up at him. 'You look pretty terrible.'

Toby Browning was like the captain of a one-man submarine, hatch firmly battened down in a quiet world beneath the surface, hoping to escape detection. He deliberately chose not to engage with those around him beyond the niceties that society and business demanded. He dealt in paintings and if they spoke to him, which often they did, they never threatened him. And they never answered him back.

And he really didn't know how to respond to what had been posed by the young cellist. This was a language alien to him, as foreign as Serbo-Croat. He had even found it difficult with Marjorie Nielson where she said he had permission to talk about how he was feeling. But out here, in the real world, it was a different matter.

'Well, cat got your tongue again, I see. Hope you're feeling better soon,' she called as she manhandled her cello towards the exit and neatly danced through the swinging glass door. He heard the pop of another bottle of champagne being opened and he received the glass with a polite smile. He sat on the chair where the cellist had played as the caterers cleared up around him. Behind him, where the Hodgkin had hung, the wall was bare.

The absence of Marjorie Nielson made his desire to talk to her even more extreme, rather like a smoker's anxiety at discovering there are no cigarettes in the house. He couldn't remember feeling as low as this, not even in the early days with Marjorie when he believed at one and the same time that there was nothing and everything wrong with him. He recalled the therapist telling him that suffering happens when there is too big a gap between who a person feels himself to be and who he wants to be and for the first time he caught a glimpse of what she meant. It was as if he was in a loop, a series of repeated actions that brought the same results each time.

He went upstairs to his flat and sat at his laptop, barely

registering that William Gilbert's bank had confirmed the transfer of money into the gallery's account. Neither these millions, nor the millions that his father had offered him, not even the pretty young woman whose eyes he had not seen, could impact on him now. He had other things on his mind now which it was clear money could do little to help.

He tapped a number into his phone and waited.

'Marise? This is Toby Browning. I wonder if you could help me?' Later, much later, he would realise that this was the most important phone call he would ever make.

# Chapter 10

He estimated that this was the last day of the Mistral, the wind having now dropped to a breeze. The sky, though, remained intensely, almost frighteningly blue as though it had been polished clean by the fierce winds of the previous days when the cypress trees had been bent almost double by the gale flooding off the hills to the north. This had been a twelve day Mistral, the longest variety and whilst it was meant to drive some people mad Peter Harrington saw it as a cathartic wind, cleansing the landscape and leaving the air and sky pin sharp and perfect. He looked across to the Massif des Maures, so clear in the early morning light that he could pick out every tree and crevasse in the looming mass.

Already it was hot and the limestone paving around the pool was warm under his feet as he made his way towards the two filters at the far end where the bougainvillea was in full bloom. He worked quietly, removing the debris from the filter buckets and replacing the salt tablets. He was wearing a faded blue T shirt and similarly bleached shorts and the parts of his body that were exposed to the sun were deep brown and weathered. He worked steadily for an hour, happy to be absorbed in a series of routines which he found comforting and which, he acknowledged to himself, reminded him of the army. He skimmed the pool of the debris blown in by the wind, leaves, black beetles and, this morning, a large iridescent blue dragonfly, before tipping the assortment on the compost heap by the olive grove. The wind had almost disappeared now and the heat was encouraging the insistent clatter of the cicadas.

He loved this time of stillness before the rest of the world woke, when he knew his mobile would not ring and where his thoughts were his own. In the distance, a hoopoe announced itself, probably from the compost heap where it would be break-fasting courtesy of Peter Harrington. The swimming pool terrace was just below the house, an ancient *mas* which had been sympathetically restored and his favourite of the twenty or so he looked after. He came here once a week, more if there was a problem but the notion of a typical working week didn't exist in his life any more. Today happened to be Saturday but the fierce structures which had bound him – happily – in the army, had loosened and he had begun to accept the freedoms that this life offered and he was increasingly able to accept the times when he didn't have a specific task in front of him.

He had chosen to come here this morning because he knew the owner was in Paris for the weekend. He enjoyed being alone in the gardens, which dropped away from the house in a series of large terraces each planted in different ways. On either side of the steps leading from the house huge domes of lavender were now in bloom and the smells from these mixed with the honey-suckle which clung thickly to the limestone walls. He walked up the stairs, worn smooth over the years, to his car, an ancient Renault 4, and returned with a black canvas holdall out of which protruded the end of a wooden easel. He extracted this and as he began to assemble it he moved along the terrace, his eyes on the distant hills, until he stopped and placed the legs as he wanted them. He fetched a metal chair with an orange striped seat cover from under the pergola outside the kitchen and then slowly unpacked his materials with the care of a surgeon about to perform an operation: a battered black tin of water colours, various clean brushes in an old pottery beaker and finally several sheets of thick cartridge paper, one of which he placed on the easel, securing it in each corner. Moving the brushes from the pot and laying them on the ledge at the bottom of the easel, he walked along to the outside tap by the pool pump house and filled the beaker with water. The routines satisfied Peter Harrington and they helped clear his mind before he began painting, which he often delayed for a surprisingly long time.

Is it possible to paint a Provencal landscape in a way that is not trite or which does not ape the great Impressionists whose paintings have been reproduced throughout the world? Peter had been through this phase of thinking which for quite some time had prevented him from painting what was obvious and what was in front of him, so now he felt at ease with the magnificent view he had chosen to capture. And, yes, the cypress trees at the foot of the garden flanked the blue-grey hills in the distance and the land in between was made up of a series of irregular shapes in varying shades of brown and green. What had been obsessing him for some time was not the familiarity of the scene, but how to capture its essence in as few brush strokes as possible. The key limitation of the watercolourist is the inability to revise what he has done. The medium demands a certainty of approach and planning and it was this that fascinated Peter Harrington.

In the army this had been very much a secret passion, strictly hidden from his colleagues. Often, when away on manoeuvres, he would sneak off and attempt to capture the local countryside in his sketchbooks so that now they formed a visual diary of his life. But to be artistic in the army was to open yourself to a degree of ridicule which Major Peter Harrington decided to avoid. Only poofters and nancy boys paint, he had heard several times and even an admission that he had been to an art exhibition appeared to some as an admission of critical weakness. So the Peter Harrington that was poet and painter was kept, quite literally, under lock and key.

It was well over an hour before he began to paint, although in the meantime he had experimented in a small sketchbook, some-times simply trying to capture colour and texture but also attempting smaller versions of the scene in front of him. As the morning drew on so the light changed but the post-Mistral clarity persisted and the mountains remained extraordinarily detailed. Like a battle plan a long time in the making, but swiftly executed, after he committed his first strokes to the larger white sheet it was not long before he was finished. When he had, he stood up from his easel and walked away, stretching his limbs. He sauntered around the garden, smelling the flowers and running his fingers through bunches of thyme. He was an animal circling his prey, waiting for the right moment to approach. Peter Harrington was a hard taskmaster and on reviewing many of his paintings he had felt disappointed and had destroyed them. He was down at the lower terrace now, where water trickled out from a spring line and gave this part of the garden its character, green and fresh and calming. It was as he cupped some of the gently flowing water and splashed it onto his face that he heard the sound of a car arriving on the gravel driveway in front of the house. Puzzled, he made his way back through the garden and when he reached the top he saw Natalie Dinan wheeling a small suitcase towards the back door.

'*Bonjour*, Peter, *ca va?* I saw your car so I assumed you were here. How is the pool?'

Peter liked the owner of the house, a small, attractive woman a few years older than him, but he was surprised and, to be honest, a little irritated to find her here now.

She saw him glance over to the easel and when she said 'Oh, Peter, I am so sorry. I have interrupted something,' he immediately forgave her. 'I am honoured that you should want to paint my garden. May I?'

He could not stop her walking towards his painting any more than the feeling of vulnerability that began to grip him. It would have been less concerning if he had been able to assess his work before her, for he would have known then whether to dismiss his efforts. But it was too late and she stood in front of the easel, hands on hips. There was a pause and the cicadas became louder in the silence.

'*Extraordinaire*,' she said quietly, and she turned to look at him before redirecting her gaze at the painting.

'I think this is absolutely beautiful, Peter. I had no idea that you painted. I had no idea that you painted,' she repeated, 'so beautifully.'

And Peter Harrington had no idea how to respond. The habit of keeping his work secret in the army had become second nature to him so receiving a compliment was a new experience. And because so few people had seen his work he had never been able to gauge if it was any good, not that this really mattered to him. At least, he thought it didn't.

'So little and yet so much,' she said. 'It looks so easy.'

Still absorbing this reaction, he approached his painting with more confidence. Standing behind her, he looked down at it and then up again at the view it represented.

'How do know where to begin?' she asked. 'Isn't it so difficult with water colour?'

He still hadn't spoken, but somehow he didn't need to. He picked up the sketchbook from the canvas bag and showed her the preliminary sketches and experiments with colour.

'Oh,' she exclaimed again, 'these are almost more beautiful than the finished painting.' She looked back at him. 'Excuse me,' she added, 'that was meant to be a compliment.' He nodded his understanding.

And then Natalia Dinan realised that her presence, even in her own home, needed some explanation. It was a sudden strike on the TGV which she should have anticipated because it seemed to happen every *jour de fête*.

'But,' she added, *'j'ai de la chance*. Without the strike I might never have discovered you were a painter.'

'And I must apologise', said Peter speaking for the first time, 'that I did not ask your permission to paint here.'

'Piff.' She dismissed his statement with a quick flick of her head. 'But now I have you, I cannot let you go. I have bought some lunch and you must stay.' And with that she trotted back up the stairs between the lavender. Peter stood alone with his painting for the first time, rubbing a hand over his cheek as he assessed his work. There was a confidence and certainty about it, a collection of brush strokes, some containing several different shades of a colour in a single sweep which had transferred one reality into what he saw as a different, more profound one, both a homage to nature and a refinement. 'Talking is different from thinking', he remembered Marjorie once telling him, 'what you think is not always what you say.' He felt the same about painting, that something happened between the eye and the paper that he did not necessarily fully understand before.

Lunch was a simple cheese omelette served with the minimum of fuss and the maximum of pleasure by Natalie, her small frame ferrying dishes and glasses from the kitchen to the terrace and chattering as she did. Peter did just wonder if her sudden re-appearance with two pre-cooked lobsters was too much of a coincidence, but he immediately dismissed the idea for normally he would have left the house much earlier. She opened a pale pink wine and they sat and talked on the shady terrace. He liked to think it wasn't the drink, more his pleasure at her unstinting praise for his painting, that led him to agree to show her some of the other sketchbooks which he usually kept in the black holdall. By now the fine detail of the Massif des Maures had begun to disappear as the shift of the sun and the heat of the mid afternoon blurred their outline and deepened their purple bulk.

The books, all with similar black covers, he picked out at random and he told her, in his slow and steady Yorkshire tones, where each of the sketches had been made and what he had been doing. There was one particular book he was keen for her to see and he offered it to her without explanation. She recognised the landscape immediately, the rough limestone plateaux and deep gorges to the north of Draguignan.

'I fell in love with this landscape ten years ago. It has a deceptive beauty. It's not what it seems. I was here on a joint training exercise with the French army. You have to respect what the landscape can do to you before you fall in love with it.'

She was enthralled by the pages of watercolour sketches, as much by the recognition of the scenery as by the facility of the artist. A different Peter Harrington was emerging before her. 'I don't understand how you do it,' she said simply.

She was eager to see more of his work and he dipped into the bag to bring out another book. When he opened the pages, he made to return the sketchbook, but she stopped him, having seen part of a very different scene. He gave up the book and she confirmed what she thought she had seen, a simple but powerful ink sketch of what she assumed was a concentration camp.

'It's Belsen,' he said. 'I was near there with my regiment and at first I was reluctant to go. The idea that it should be on the tourist trail, I suppose. But I was wrong. It has a power, a presence, that is greater than that. I was told by my sergeant to be aware of an extraordinary thing. Although the camp is in the middle of woodland there is absolutely no birdsong. And there isn't.'

She looked at him and then back at the drawing, merely a series of lines in black ink which caught precisely the isolation of the camp and seemed to suggest the awful history that lay behind the twisted wires.

She continued turning the pages of the book and the sketches became darker, more brooding. One page seemed almost black, until she could make out the faint outlines of trees, conifers at night. This work was quite unlike the others she had seen. It contained several simple line drawings of faces, placed at different angles on the same page.

'Chums,' he said simply.

He took the book from her and gently closed it, bringing the afternoon to an end. He thanked her for a delicious lunch but it was Natalie who appeared more grateful. Before he packed up his equipment, he unclipped his picture from the easel and with a small pen signed the corner. 'To Natalie with thanks. Peter.' She smiled as he gave it to her, perhaps the perfect way of ending the day, except that his mood, like the light, had now shifted and become, like the flanks of the mountains he had painted, darker and colder. As he drove home the warmth of day, in every sense, seemed to evaporate.

# Chapter 11

If the rich are different, so are the blind, but only up to a point. If she thought about it at all, which she rarely did, Perdita believed that for all its disadvantages, blindness still allowed her to see in ways that others couldn't and she was, for the most part, happy to accept her lot in life. One of the first pieces she had ever written, in fact, was based on a childhood experience of running through a pedestrian tunnel under a shopping centre near her home. She was between two friends, holding their hands, no more than seven years old and as the three of them hurtled along the white-tiled and echoing passage she remembered screaming in exhilaration and joy at hearing the mix of feet and voice bounce back off the walls and repeat itself over again, the affirmation of joy at her freedom. Since she had been born blind, she knew nothing else and as she had told Marjorie, it was only other people who made her feel different. 'I'm only blind,' she would say with withering simplicity to those whose condescension, well meaning though it may have been, ran too far. We are all born with advantages and disadvantages, Perdita concluded and it is how we exploit the former and diminish the latter which is important which is why Perdita was spending the afternoon with Henry Beadles, the first man to make her think she was beautiful.

'My dear,' he exclaimed, 'it's simply divine. Now try the mauve.' They were standing in the middle of what Henry had just described to Perdita as 'darling, the height of vulgarity, I love it. It's an enormous space, at least two stories high, beautifully lit and designed to within an inch of its life and all, my dear, for the sale of girls' frocks. I've seen churches less divine than this.' Perdita's idea of her physical self had been ushered into reality by the unswerving certainties of Henry Beadles, a pot-pourri of a man, fashion editor, interior designer, fabulous cook, collector and, sometimes, Perdita's eyes.

'Darling, I'll tell you, if I didn't bat for the other team, the game would be up.' Perdita laughed and was aware, not for the first time, that this indeed was a reason that she felt so comfortable in his company, but it was by no means the whole story. She had met St Bede, as he was generally known, at a photoshoot for the cover of a recording of contemporary music which contained one of her compositions. He was writing a piece, he told her without any sense of embarrassment, about the 'flogging of classical music. Darling, these days is no good simply having spent the whole of your childhood practising your fucking scales, you've got to be gorgeous looking as well and if you aren't, you've got to be lit as though you are. Fortunately, you are gorgeous looking, if you don't mind me saying so. Henry Beadles.' And, so saying, he took her hand and introduced himself. If men had called her beautiful before, none had done it in such an incidental way as Henry Beadles, as if the beauty and her blindness were just an ordinary conjunction and not one thing to be seen against the other. In fact, Henry had barely ever spoken of her blindness, it was just something he embraced, like discovering she didn't like milk in her tea.

She took Henry's arm and he led her to the changing room where Perdita was reflected by eight free-standing mirrors, each tilted at slightly different angles. Shutting the door, he left her for a moment and then shortly afterwards, hearing her say St Bede, he opened the door to find several images of Perdita Landberg confronting him. The dress was short, slightly longer at the back than the front, and showed off her slim legs and flat stomach but it was the paleness of her skin, emphasised by her platinum white hair, which caught his attention now and in an instant she became a still in a magazine spread. He told her to wait there and seconds later he returned with some grey footless tights and a thin pale pink-striped scarf. Perdita's trust of Henry's taste was not blind, although in the most basic sense it was, for she knew that the clothes and style he chose for her brought a positive response from others.

'Perfection, darling,' he concluded. 'We have here the black ballet pumps, the pale grey cut off tights, the mauve cotton dress with the lightest sprinkling of black dots and the silk scarf with the almost imperceptible pink stripe. And there is some heavenly underwear over there, darling . . . ' For Perdita, St Bede was more than just a release from her naturally more serious nature. He was a touchstone and behind the banter and carefree manner there lay a deeply sensible soul and it was this more than anything that struck a chord in Perdita. That, and an impeccable taste in clothes, particularly womens.

'Right, darling, lunch. It would be churlish to push our luck in Bond Street too far.'

Lunch with St Bede could be quite an unnerving experience for he had a forensic interest in food and its preparation and would often accompany its eating with a running commentary on the dish in front of him whether successful or not.

'What could he have been thinking of,' he announced in a voice that was typically not sotto, as his knife separated the small tower of ingredients in front of him. 'Let me tell you what we have here, a melange of self-defeating tastes, over complicated, over fingered and unfortunately over there in front of you now.' The restaurant, all glass and steel, he had described to Perdita as so new that chef hadn't had time to throw anyone out yet.

'Shouldn't be long, though,' Perdita said, smiling, 'if this review goes on much longer.' This prompted him to tell a story about a chef who used to do outrageous things to his dishes, particularly his soups, in order to get back at any ungrateful clientele. 'My dear, you have no idea.'

'But, wait, methinks I do detect a certain melancholy in mademoiselle P this lunchtime. Or am I mistaken?' She looked up at him and instinctively sought his hand. 'St Bede, Henry, you're not so much a magician as a witch. It's true, I'm a little out of sorts. I have been working very hard on something which is becoming more and more personal by the day. I think I have rather underestimated the impact it is having on me.'

Henry waved away an over fussy waiter with a sweep of his wrist.

'You know that my therapist died,' Perdita continued, 'and I've been inspired, well, found myself involuntarily, writing a piece that is connected to her. Is it possible to be exhilarated and miserable at the same time?'

'Well, darling, Billie Holiday managed it on a regular basis. But I don't mean to be flippant. Well, only a little. Deep breath, change of paragraph, perceptive response. Not surprising. These are deep waters easily muddied. I have to say that I have noticed a new seriousness in you, which is quite a thing since you are somewhat of a serious girl in the first place.'

She knew that it had not been Henry's intention to upset her in any way, but his observation caused a shift in her feelings for which she was barely prepared, like a sudden wind catching her skirt and blowing it into the air. She instinctively put her hands on to her thighs in response. It was an unusual experience for Perdita, someone commenting on her state of being; most people didn't dare, so completely did she give off an air of competence, or they offered platitudes to her blindness. Henry was different, of course, but his observation unsettled her probably because she knew it was the truth.

'But, perhaps, my dear, I should swap the word serious for troubled?' It wasn't really a question although the lightest of queries might have been attached to his remark. 'I'm not particularly up on the impact of losing a therapist but I imagine it may be reasonably high in the top ten of life's major bothers.'

'I can't distinguish my feelings,' Perdita said. 'I know that guilt is one of them, guilt for somehow exploiting what happened to her, her death. And, then, for knowing so little about her.'

'We're not meant to know about our therapist, darling. It doesn't work that way round. It's one of the reasons we pay money for the privilege. But, I digress, there's more, isn't there?'

'Marjorie was helping me come to terms with something that has been bothering me for some time, a repeated pattern of reaction that I don't seem to be able to break. I think she understood what it was all about and was leading me gently to the fountain, but then she died. I think my eagerness to write about her is a way of keeping that process alive, of hoping that I can come up with a solution by holding her memory in place.'

'Sounds perfectly reasonable to me,' Henry responded. 'She appears to have given you the momentum to do it. It's what she would have wanted to happen, anyway. My old mother would have said "I'll give you some of the clues, Henry my boy, but you'll have to come up with the answers yourself."'

Perdita smiled at Henry, but she was thinking of Marjorie Nielson's kindness, the tone of her voice which conveyed the message 'I'm with you now, you can go wherever you like, it's safe.' And she was thinking how much she missed this weekly lifeline, for however much she agreed with Henry she knew that the loss of Marjorie Nielson had knocked the wind out of her and she was still in the process of assimilating the change. She knew she could talk to Henry, but at the moment she was not sure of what she wanted to say.

'Look, mademoiselle,' he said as they parted, 'remember you're beautiful. Inside and out.' She felt neither.

On the way home, Perdita remembered a phrase that Marjorie had used on a couple of occasions, probably to place it in Perdita's mind to see what it might dislodge. At first it was in response to Perdita's questioning about why people go to therapists in the first place. 'There is no single reason, of course,' the therapist had replied, 'but generally speaking they come because there is something they cannot forget, or cannot stop telling themselves, about their lives and these repeated actions need to be examined and talked about.' Perhaps Perdita knew what it was she kept on telling herself, but being sure was like catching mercury in the palm of her hand.

She arrived back at her apartment exhausted. She sat for a

moment and allowed the atmosphere of the room to assert itself. When she was composing, as she had been that morning before she left to see Henry, Perdita always turned off the telephone and now she plugged it back into the wall and tapped the keys to see if there were any messages. Perhaps because Marjorie Nielson had been so much in her thoughts, she was not particularly surprised that there was a message from Marise, a woman who, to her recollection, had never called her before.

'Thank you for returning my call, Ms Landberg,' said Marise. 'There was one message I wanted to give you and a question I had to ask. I thought you would like to know that the funeral of Dr Nielson will take place next Thursday at the church of St Clement's in the City of London at 11 a.m. It will be followed by the cremation out in Manor Park. There will be a notice in *The Times* tomorrow. I saw you at the inquest and I hope you don't mind me calling.' She hurried on before Perdita could reply. 'The second point, the question, is would you mind me giving your telephone number to someone else who was at the inquest and who phoned me in order to get in touch with you?'

'Well, who is it Marise?'

'His name is Toby Browning.' Perdita could hear the hesitation in Marise's voice and understood why.

'I take it that Mr Browning is, was, another of Marjorie's clients? You don't have to answer, Marise, I understand. No, I don't mind.'

That he called so quickly was both a surprise and a relief. Even though his voice was rather tentative, she realised, instantly, that this was the second time he had spoken to her.

'I know this is rather strange,' he ventured, 'but I think I saw you at Dr Nielson's inquest and I wanted to make contact. If I'm quite truthful, I'm not sure why.'

'In these situations, I'm not sure there has to be a reason,' Perdita replied in a tone which Toby thought was a touch sharp and discouraging. In fact, Perdita had rather liked his voice and the lack of assumptions it contained. Toby pressed on.

'I was a client of Dr Nielson's and I'll be honest her death has seemed so sudden and has left, well, a bit of a vacuum.' Here he paused and Perdita waited, sensing that he wanted to continue. 'And, I don't know, I just felt so dissatisfied after the inquest that I wanted to talk about it with someone who knew her.'

'But I didn't know her, Mr Browning, any more than you did.' And, she nearly added, any more than I know you but stopped herself as she realised that his reactions were not too far removed from her own. They both wanted something more from Marjorie Nielson. And yet she waited again, hearing his breathing on the line and the faintest crackle of whatever it was that provided the ambient background to all her calls. To this was now added what sounded like the stubble on his chin being rubbed and at this point she did speak.

'Not everyone likes to admit that they are seeing a therapist. Or is it OK to do so if you know that you are talking to someone who is a fellow traveller?'

'To be perfectly honest,' Toby replied, pressing on regardless of Perdita Landberg's tone, 'that hadn't crossed my mind but now that you mention it, perhaps we are like members of the same club. Maybe I felt that when I phoned you, that somehow this wasn't really like cold calling.'

Perdita laughed. 'The Abandoned Client's Club. It has a ring to it.'

It was as if he hadn't heard. 'Will you be at the funeral on Thursday?' It seemed a ridiculous question given what they had been discussing.

'Of course,' she said. Again her tone prompted Toby to wonder whether his call was intrusive, but he pressed on. 'Perhaps we could speak then? I will recognise you.'

'More than I will you, Mr Browning. Thursday it is.' Perdita slotted the handset back into its mount and heard the little bleeps to confirm that it was correctly lodged. She knew that she had been too sharp with Toby Browning, brusque even. She turned on the computer and played again the beginning of the second movement on which she had been working that morning. It was only as she listened to the mix of harmony and discord that she understood the reason why she had been so dismissive with Toby's call. She was jealous. Marjorie Nielson was hers and the idea that she may have been equally caring and supportive of someone else was a fact that did not sit comfortably with her. She placed her fingers on the keyboard and for the next two hours added to the composition, the darker tones filling the room, condemning the sounds of the street to oblivion.

# Chapter 12

The tens of thousands of commuters who stream across London Bridge every morning are not looking for St Clement's and even if they were they would not see its tower. The church of St Clement's does not announce itself. To all intents and purposes it appears not to exist, only visible if you stand in front of it in the narrow lane between Lombard Street and King William Street. Approach from London Bridge, as the commuters do every morning, marching purposefully over the river, it is directly ahead of them but hidden, hemmed in and almost overgrown by the anonymous grey buildings of the financial quarter. It is a fixture, though, around which everything else has accumulated, a force of nature, permanent. The tower hardly juts above the tops of its secular companions and unless you seek it, you will pass it by. It is like a discreet banker and does not have to proclaim its power. A different sort of business is done in its calm, plain interior and if bankers do ever share their sins, this is where they would come.

Peter Harrington had flown into Stansted the night before and had stayed in a small hotel near Liverpool Street station, waking to the unfamiliar roar of the City, the dull light and the cloying smell of the air. The speed of travel makes comparisons much sharper so that the juncture of the thyme and lavender laden perfumes of the south of France with the diesel and petrol polluted air of central London seemed that much more abrupt. There was an intensity about cities, an incessant demand to move quickly, which did not sit comfortably with Peter. It wasn't so much the numbers of people, for he had spent most of his life in close proximity to others, more their fierce preoccupation and apparent disregard for one another. There were also no horizons, only the looming proximity of buildings and the intrusion of sirens.

It was an act of reconstruction, of uncomfortably putting back what he had been carefully shedding since he left the army, so this Thursday morning he stood in front of the narrow mirror in his bedroom barely recognising the figure who looked back at him, the dark blue jacket, the grey trousers and black shoes and the black tie against a white shirt, all the whiter for his tanned and weathered skin. He felt alone, almost a child again. This man, able to command others and be decisive in the face of danger, was now an uncertain visitor to an event he dreaded. We seek the help of others, Marjorie had gently offered one day, to break the cycle of what we tell ourselves. Curiously, whatever it was that pre-determined his worst moods, which caused him, like now, to feel that he was on a steep scree slope of emotion, unsteady underfoot and ready to slide deep down into a ravine, was created by himself, a programming that arrived unbidden at a time when his body and his mind felt he needed it most. In their later sessions, this is what Marjorie had explained as she explored the hinterland of his life and encouraged him to think, as she put it, 'without thinking', to abandon his measured and careful accounts of his experiences.

The City assailed him this June morning, a day shrouded in grey skies, a day to match his mood and the occasion. Opposite the hotel, the outline of a new skyscraper rose into the air, the lower parts clad in green window, the upper part still a raw skeleton of angular steel struts, impossibly simple and yet hard for him to comprehend. For all the ancient permanence of the old City, it could never rest. Turn your back for just a moment and a corner would change, the lines that were so familiar eradicated and somehow immediately forgotten as in its place came first an open space, so rare in the crowded centre of London that it was almost astonishing, and then a new structure, nearly always taller and more daring than the last, buildings that seemed to grow with enormous speed to what, in the end Peter Harrington thought was a dull similarity. As if to provide an antidote, he walked slowly up to Bunhill Fields, past the Artillery Ground where he had been temporarily stationed during the IRA bombings in the late seventies. The old graveyard had not changed, could not be changed and the path took him through the old tombs and stones protected now and likely to remain like this way beyond the lifetime of the brash new building he had seen earlier. He paused in the centre and the trees, now fully in leaf, held the City at bay so that only the buses roaring up the City Road spoilt the illusion of being in a country churchyard. He chose a gravestone at random, the weathered Portland stone just managing to hold on to the name of the departed it commemorated. Isabella Pike, it told him, had died in 1824 at the age of thirty-six and that she was now 'embarked upon a journey to a better place.' She probably died in childbirth, he thought, and since life expectancy then wasn't much longer than her thirty six years, she probably was indeed off 'to a better place'. His own mother had died when she was not much older. He had been eight and he always measured his self-sufficiency from this point, his ability to get by no matter what, the very characteristics which made him so suitable for the army. Since he couldn't imagine anything worse happening to him, he was prepared for whatever life would throw at him. Until he met Marjorie Nielson, he had a series of carefully preserved memories of his mother which he had clung to over the years and honed to perfection. It was only when the therapist asked him to talk about them that he found some began to evaporate and others take their place. This process of speaking his thoughts, as Marjorie called it, was both unsettling and exciting and he knew that she was deliberately disturbing the alluvium of his life in order to dislodge or reveal whatever it was that had brought him to her door. She had gone and the waters were still muddied but she had made him believe that somewhere in the complicated circuitry that made up his thinking and his memory, there was a faulty chip that continued to impede his life but which his body, for the most part, had learned to accommodate. As he left the graveyard to meander back into the City his thoughts were of Marjorie Nielson.

*   *   *

I have been looking forward to seeing you, he begins and he leans forward with his elbows on his knees. I'm glad I make the journey every two weeks. It's curious, but since we started talking about my mother I have remembered a whole heap more.

Like what?

I thought I only had good memories but I think I recall my mother being cross with me. Well, not exactly cross, maybe serious.

Pause.

Maybe I took her seriousness as her being cross with me, I'm not sure. I had been playing with my friend Colin and I can't recall now exactly what we had been doing but I can now remember her face looking very sternly at me. Now we don't do that, Peter Harrington, she said and I can see it now as plain as plain. Pause.

Can you remember any more?

For the life of me I can't.

What sort of things did you do with Colin? He looks puzzled at the question.

I suppose we did what boys do. We jumped ditches, played cowboys and Indians. Cricket, football that kind of thing.

Pause.

She didn't like it when we failed to show up at the right time.

Pause.

But I don't think it was that. Colin was always getting into scrapes. He was part of a big Irish family, I think he was number five of eight or something like that.

Pause.

I don't think my mother liked him that much, now I think of it.

Why?

I don't know and I can't remember. It's just an abiding feeling I have.

Did your mother like your other friends? He looks at me at this stage, as if to say I know I am being led.

I immediately want to say no, but I can't tell you why. That's odd, isn't it?

Why is that odd?

Because I can't back it up with any fact. It's just a feeling.

Describe the feeling. He settles himself the chair as if really engaged with this request.

It's one of unease, I suppose. Even the image of my mother looking cross, or serious, or whatever, makes me uncertain.

Pause.

As if I am being disloyal now, talking about her like this. How do I know it is true and why, all of a sudden, have my thoughts about her changed. Well, not changed, but been added to. My father said she could be a difficult woman but I never wanted to believe him. Particular, was the word he used to use about her. Very Yorkshire is that.

And what did he mean by particular.

I suppose he meant that she liked things just so. He used to say that she had a very clear idea of the world and was not keen on people disagreeing with her. Not that I remember her like that.

Pause.

I do remember telling her once that Colin had thrown a stone at a neighbour's garden shed and broken a window. I don't want to hear stories like that she said. I don't want to hear any more about that boy Colin. He'll do you no good. And, what's more, you shouldn't go telling tales.

And do you think that this was the cross, serious story you might have been remembering?

Do you know, I suppose it might be. Isn't it that odd? I don't know where it came from, that thought. It was just sort of there.

And he smiled at me as if saying I understand the process and I am prepared to let it happen.

I suppose my views, my defence if you like, of my mother was put into place by my father, who was a wonderful man but I think from what he said rather in the shadow of his wife. He never remarried and always appeared happy. He ran a builders' merchants, quite successful. As I say, he was a lovely man and he took to single parenthood pretty well. Why am I saying this? Yes, to try and define my mother. What does an eight year old know? Anyway, looking back on it, joining the army wasn't a bad thing to do.

How did your mother die? He replies immediately.

She had a stroke by all accounts. The doctor said it was quite unusual in a woman, particularly one so young. It was a problem men had, the doctor told my father, and not women. I remember it was a Tuesday. I remember it like it was yesterday, the strangeness of being told to go and see the headmaster and finding my father with him, both of them looking uneasy. Or am I just making all this up, fitting appropriate images to the scene? Later, much later, I recall my father saying that he discovered, presumably from the doctor, she'd been to see him the week before complaining of pains in her chest. I could never understand that, my father told me, going to the doctor and not telling me. Sorry, I'm rambling.

Perhaps your mother felt embarrassed? Or didn't want to upset your father?

Maybe. It's true that he adored her and it would have worried him. But he used to say – and I haven't thought about this for years – that she liked her secrets, that she believed secrets were power. But what does it matter now? My father died a couple of years ago and it's all in the past, isn't it?

His look is both one of challenge and defeat. He wants me to continue, to guide the conversation, but I wait. I suddenly think of swimming in the sea and moving from a warm current to a cold and I imagine him doing the same thing. It has gone cold for him at the moment.

Taffy believes in talking therapies. He says the army could do with a lot more of it. It all seems a bit random for the army but then again a lot of the decisions taken by the army are random and only work because people follow them because they have to. That's the nature of the beast, isn't it?

You never wanted to speak out?

Well, you don't, do you? In a sense, you can't. If you went around doubting, querying, there'd be chaos. That's the beauty of the army. In some ways, uncertainty is taken away from you entirely. Decisions are black and white.

And you liked this?

That's the way it was. That's the way it is.

**End of session.**

# Chapter 13

Sometimes, when the weather was damp and the air was filled with a fine drizzle as it was this morning, Toby Browning believed he could smell the spices that had once been stored in the warehouse that was now his home. Certainly in the early days he had been aware of a hint of cumin and the occasional drift of saffron, but since there was an Indian restaurant less than a block away he was never quite certain. Even so, he went over to one of the walls in his living room and smelled the warm bricks, coarse and dry against his skin, hoping for just the vaguest hint of the past. The tide was low and the river looked exhausted, flat and listless and a pair of cormorants, black sentinels perched on the ancient wooden moorings at the entrance to the old dock on the opposite bank looked equally defeated. He walked on to his balcony and tapped the barometer, watching the arrowed finger drop further towards the cloud which marked low pressure before placing his coffee on a small, round white marble table. In his other hand he held a letter from his father, the bold handwriting in black ink a perfect embodiment of his father's character. 'Don't believe in this e-mail malarkey. If we lose the ability to write a decent letter then we've lost something of our heritage,' the mantra went. The balcony, more of a garden terrace with wooden decking, was partly protected by a glass roof extension, a series of overlapping semi-circles of glass similar, but on a larger scale, to those that can be found over the front door of countless French provincial houses. The curve of the terrace led out over the river, like the bridge of a ship, although this morning it stood over dark wet mud which gave off the rank odour of decay.

'I'm surprised I haven't heard from you,' the letter began, without preamble, 'and for the life of me I can't think why you find my offer quite such a problem. I have briefed my solicitor and he's ready with the paper work so it's just a question of you getting your arse into gear. I also wanted to give you early warning that the wedding's going to be on November 21st over at Clayburn at the church on the estate with a bash at her mother's place afterwards. Yours ever Charles.'

He writes to me as though I am a business subordinate, Toby thought, there to facilitate his needs. I am his only son, but my father cannot be bothered to check beforehand that the date of his marriage is convenient with me. As it happened, Toby was due to be in New York for an exhibition of contemporary art on that day. Not that it mattered to his father for he would merely assume that Toby would change his plans and, Toby thought, putting the letter on the table, he was right. As for Norton Hall, Toby let his thoughts tail away, unable or unprepared to deal with the issue on this grey, drab day and a mood of resignation took hold of him, a reluctance to face what was ahead. What would he have said to Marjorie about this or, more to the point, what would she, in her way, have said to him? He wandered back into the kitchen which was at one end of the big, open living area and divided off by an L-shaped working surface into which was set a hob. He stood there recalling the last dinner party he had given, a disastrous affair in the days when his relationship with Amy was entering its end game. The other couple had been a very pretty woman who ran a gallery across the river in Southwark, which had suddenly become London's new Left Bank and her entirely irritating boyfriend who was into hedge funds, whatever that meant. He had taken so much against the man that he had been only barely aware of the chemistry that was taking place between him and Amy. From his semi-detached position behind the hob he had seen the animation in her face and had wondered from a distance what intricacies of the financial world could cause such fascination. But more fool he, for what they were saying on the outside disguised what was happening inside and by the end of the evening it was clear to all except Toby that his relationship with Amy was over. When she had called the next day it was not to compliment him on what he reckoned had been a first class turbot and aïoli but to announce that she was leaving him 'for a man I have fallen instantly in love with.' He was neither disappointed nor sad, as if this was just another problem along the road of life. It was a state of mind that Amy reflected in her parting words. 'I don't know what's happening to you Toby, but it is as if the life has gone out of you. You seem so preoccupied and although I've tried to talk to you about it you seem not to want to listen. Anyway, it's too late now and I'm sorry.' She wasn't sorry, of course, and then to some extent nor was he, at least not about her departure. Yes, his male dignity had taken a hit beneath the water line but he had never thought that his affair with Amy would develop into something stronger and more permanent. Looking back on it now, he realised that he had never been properly involved with her at all. He could glimpse, though, that she represented the malaise in his life, his inability to control what was happening to him as if he were merely a twig in a very strong current being carried along willy-nilly. He had abdicated responsibility, preferring the comfortable position of leaving the action to others and being the passive recipient of events. This is what he had ended up discussing with Marjorie or at least this is what Marjorie had manoeuvred him into realising. During his sessions with her he came to realise that the process he was involved in was not about sudden revelation, a conjuring trick with self knowledge produced from a hat with a dramatic flourish at the end. It was a more gradual process when an insight could almost pass you by or dawn on you slowly, like a subtle change in temperature.

He set off to walk to the funeral, along the cobbled lane that ran towards Tower Bridge, the new apartment blocks fronting the river where the docks had once been. The sky had come down to lend a dull grey uniformity to the scene and not even the sight of an Italian destroyer nosing its way between the raised bascules of the bridge could deflect Toby Browning from his thoughts.

*   *   *

**Notes on Tobias Browning. Aged 39. Referred by his GP Sarah Buckman. Insomnia and panic attacks. Session 8**

He looks bad, almost slumped and hardly talks for the first five minutes of the session.

You said you wanted me to talk about the things I didn't know I wanted to talk about, but I don't know how that works.

Pause.

My girlfriend left me. Right in front of my eyes. And I didn't really see it and yet I suppose it was inevitable.

Why?

I don't suppose I was doing that much to make her stay. I don't know whether I am upset or not. It doesn't seem to matter.

Pause, glance to the window.

She said that I lived in a parallel universe and I suppose she was right.

Do you think you have always been like this?

It's ridiculous, isn't it, a man of my age having to talk like this? You would have thought that by this stage I would know how to get on with things, to understand how to get by. Pause.

Tell me what you mean.

It feels such an indulgence to be here with you talking about myself.

You don't think that it is important?

Well, I do but again I feel that it is something that happened to me rather than something I instigated. It was my doctor, as you know, who suggested that I see you.

It was a suggestion. You didn't have to take it up.

Pause. My mother left my father. In the end she just upped and left. She did something about it. I admired her for that.

For what?

For making a decision. I'm amazed she stayed as long as she did. He was livid, of course, although I'm not at all sure that was genuine. I think he had been having an affair for some time. But she decided, that's that and for my own sake I need to get out.

Pause.

I don't know why I raised that.

Why do you think you did?

Because in the end my mother didn't just let events carry her along. She did something about it and made a radical decision.

And you feel you need to do something similar?

Oh, I don't know. It's as if, a long time ago, I chose to take the wrong road and now I can't get back to that point to take the right one.

When do you think that point was?

Pause.

I was talking metaphorically. I'm not sure I think there was actually a point where things went wrong. Pause.

In an earlier session you said that things went badly wrong in your late twenties.

Did I?

Pause.

Well, it was a bad time, yes. I had an important relationship which fell apart around that time. She also left me, you won't be surprised to learn. Women leaving me, it seems to be a pattern in my life. We had been living together for about three years and it all seemed to be going well when she announced she was leaving. It hit me pretty badly.

What went wrong?

Pause.

It's funny, but now I think of it she – her name was Diana – had the same criticisms as Amy. I appear to be a bit of a dead loss when it comes to women. Maybe it's to do with commitment. That's what they say, isn't it? That I couldn't go beyond a certain point and that I allowed the relationships to stagnate. But I don't suppose that's the whole story.

Is there something else?

These attacks got pretty bad around that time, you know, the sweats and things. I can't have been easy to live with.

Pause. Glance at the window and then the door.

I was frightened, I suppose. I used to anticipate when the attacks might happen. It was almost as if I induced them.

That you knew when they might take place?

Yes. When I felt isolated and exposed, which appeared to be a lot of the time.

Can you remember when you had your first attack, as you call it?

As I sit here now I feel they have been with me all my life. All my life. I can't, no. I think at first I regarded them as one-offs, that they would go away but they've got steadily worse. It's like walking around with a time-bomb strapped to your body with a timer you can't control.

And you don't think you can control it?

Well, no. Except by not doing anything, I suppose, by not putting myself at any risk at all. But that would be giving up, wouldn't it? I'm not allowed to do that, am I?

Why do you think that?

Because I can hear my father ringing in my ears.

Pause, look away.

He's always there somewhere. I hear him in my head, but he's just someone I have to deal with. He would just say that I have to pull myself together, that life wasn't meant to be easy. My father doesn't take prisoners.

What do you mean?

He has scant regard for other people's feelings and it would appear absolutely none for mine.

He says this in a jokey way, almost in embarrassment. How do you feel about this?

Oh, it's just a fact of life. I'm not going to change my father, am I? I've just got to get on with things.

Like your father wants.

Yes, if you like. You can damage yourself resisting a force of nature.

That's how you see him?

In a way, yes. If I fought him all the time it would be fruitless. Even if I won it would be a pyrrhic victory. I would lose an arm or a leg in the process.

Tell me more.

Pause. I suppose I am saying that the act of separation might do me more harm than it would do him.

Do you want it to do him some harm?

Pause. Well, no, even though I do hate him sometimes.

How did you get on with him when, say, you were a teenager?

Never saw him. Either I was away at school or he was away at work. We came together at key moments and usually not for the better. You know, discussions about money, the future, university, careers. He had my life pre-constructed for me and it seems that at every turn I let him down.

Let him down. How?

Oh, the usual stuff. Wrong university, wrong career. The only thing I seemed to get right was my girlfriends. He appeared to flirt with them all. And he used to say of my violin playing that I might make it to somewhere in the middle of the orchestra. I suppose he would say that he was only keeping me on my toes. I expect even if I had become principal violin for the Berlin Phil and Lord Chancellor he would still not have been satisfied.

And would you have been?

Pause. He drops his head and is preventing himself from crying.

I can't even bear to think of it.

He cries.

**End of session.**

# Chapter 14

She was awake just as the first light seeped its way between the turrets on the mansion block opposite. Perdita could not see this but on clear mornings she could feel the warmth of the sun on her face and it helped her tell the time and gauge the state of the day. Today, though, the sun was hidden and the sky was as grey as a nun's habit. Light was the concept that was most alien to Perdita, except in its metaphorical sense so that while she might have been told that her work helped shed light on the human condition it was an idea she could only understand intellectually. She had woken thinking of Marjorie and it seemed only natural that she should continue working on the piece before she left for the funeral of the woman who inspired it. But it was difficult this morning as if Marjorie Nielson was somehow nearer to Perdita, a shadow behind her and this proximity, like a hovering emotion, was unsettling and she found it hard to concentrate. She was relieved when the buzzer went and St Bede announced himself. The day before he had helped her buy a simple black jacket and skirt for the funeral and he was here to offer support before she left.

'Darling, you look divine. To die for, if you'll excuse the expression this sombre day.'

He had offered to escort her to the service but she had refused, telling him that she preferred to be alone. As much as this was true, it was only part of the story. She didn't want the experience of being at the funeral mediated through anyone else.

'Shame, Perds, I love a bit of high drama with a few solemn hymns. Still, let's get you looking the part. Gorgeous. Enough to bring tears to your eyes, my dear. Black, with just a touch of silver.' He clasped a simple silver necklace behind her head and put his hands on the sides of her shoulders and declared himself happy.

'Dear St Bede, I hope you'll understand about not coming.'

'Of course, darling. Even Larry Olivier's dresser knew that he couldn't actually go on stage with the master. How are you getting there?'

'I'm taking the Jubilee Line.'

'Have you got your gubbins?'

She smiled at him and he leant forward and kissed her cheeks. As she walked down St Christopher's Place towards Bond Street tube she knew that later she would cry.

*    *    *

**Notes on Perdita Landberg. Aged 38. Referred from a previous client. Unspecified symptoms. Session six**

She once again comes in with great certainty and has clearly thought about what she is going to say.

When I first became aware that I might be what they call good looking I felt immediately insecure in a way I hadn't before. I was about fifteen and my friend Sylvia told me that a couple of the boys fancied me. I knew them, they were part of the group I went around with, but I had never really thought of them in that way.

Why not?

Perhaps I didn't want that complication. Friendship is not about looks, is it? But to go to another stage and have sex then we are talking about something quite different. I didn't have the necessary bearings.

I wonder who does at that age. Did your mother give you any advice?

As I have told you before, my mother is a deeply pragmatic figure and I bless her for this. My parents always made me believe that I was in no way disabled and scorned all notions of special concessions and that sort of thing. I suppose my mother treated me like any other teenager. Do you expect emotional logic from a teenager?

So you thought you were just like any other of your teenage girlfriends, then?

Pause.

I don't know. I think I erected a shield, a mask. Some of this is retrospective thinking, mind you. I'm not sure I saw it as clearly then. I pretended to be cool and distant when in fact I was frightened.

But many young people are, surely?

Of course.

Her reply is quick and abrupt. Having raised the subject it is as if she doesn't want to go any further.

And did this continue?

What?

The fear?

Pause.

Yes, it has continued for a long time. Blindness is not the cocoon people think it is. I am not in a separate world of my own, but people assume that I am.

Pause.

Are you saying that some people may interpret your fears as the result of blindness rather than, shall we say, the fear of sex or relationships?

Pause. Perhaps. There is, as I have said, an element in my blindness which is relevant, however much I would like to try and discount it. It was only when I was a teenager that I began to doubt my criteria for judging – liking – other people.

A lot of people with sight find exactly the same problem.

Pause. It is quite clear that she doesn't know how to take this. On the one hand she doesn't want her blindness to differentiate her from anyone else and on the other she is aware that it might.

Pause. She looks at me now as if about to step across a threshold.

I have carried my uneasiness about relationships – and sex – with me for a long time now. I remember a review of one of my compositions which was released not so long ago on a CD. It said that I wrote with childish simplicity. I think it was meant as a compliment, but I wasn't sure. It seemed to me that it was observing that the music lacked some maturity.

And do you think that it did?

It is not easy for me to talk about. I don't analyse my music in that way. Pause.

Perhaps because Perdita is blind she has a stillness about her so that any movement of the hands or body are more obvious. She lifts her hands from the wrists now as if she was about to place them on a keyboard.

I met a man a few years ago with whom I became quite involved but it seemed eventually to fade away. He was a musician and travelled quite extensively which probably didn't help.

Pause.

But was this the reason it didn't flourish?

Pause. Partly. I remember the strange sensation of him kissing me. It was like putting flesh on a face. I don't like talking about these things. It makes me feel uncomfortable.

Why?

It just does. It is such a personal matter.

And do you not talk personally? You can in here.

She looks around, as if taking in her surroundings for the first time in the session.

When he touched my breasts, I felt his hand was alien, somehow disconnected from his body. He had wonderful hands, a musician's hands, strong and fine which I had held many times before. But now they appeared to have a life of their own and he must have seen how unhappy I was.

And what were your feelings?

Relief. When he stopped, relief. And, when he left, sadness. Conflict, in other words.

So it wasn't just that he travelled a lot?

She snorts a laugh.

You mean because he couldn't have sex with me he left?

Pause. What do you think?

I am not an unconfident woman, Dr Nielson. I know my own worth. But if I say to you I don't know what he saw (and here she stresses the word) in me, would you understand? I couldn't see what he saw. In one straightforward way, I cannot see myself.

99

But, perhaps, in a more important way you can see yourself. What did you see in him?

Kindness, generosity, mutual interests. Some laughter.

Pause. Considerable virtues.

I am aware of that. I am also aware that something was missing. I couldn't describe exactly what any more than I could describe him.

You have just described him.

Up to a point. But we've had this conversation before. If you deduct looks and appearances from the factors which bring couples together, then you may just as well have arranged marriages.

Some arranged marriages work very well and many marriages based on mutual physical attraction don't. This is not a simple equation.

For all my life (she is angry) I have been able to assess people reasonably well. It is in the region of sex that I lose my bearings, which is quite clearly the reason I am here. Isn't it?

Perhaps. It is often at the root of many things but not necessarily in the way that you think. However much we try to understand it, there will always be an element of mystery about it, don't you think Perdita? Again, the look.

I don't think I know. My mother never really spoke of it. She was reasonably dismissive of men, although she loved my father. I think she believed they were an occasional necessity in life and that being self-sufficient as a woman was all important. She acknowledged, though, that in some areas men were useful.

And sex was one of these?

Not that she ever mentioned it to me. She was not a woman easily embarrassed but she just never spoke of it. I learned about periods by default and I think one of the reasons that they started so late for me was that I didn't know they existed. I sort of denied them.

As do many young women.

What about you?

My periods didn't start for a long time, but this is another story.

Obviously not a happy one.

Why do you say that?

I can hear it in your voice, perhaps more than just a therapist's reluctance to talk about herself, something more.

(It is true, of course, but I did not think that I still showed myself like that).

There is a book to be written about women and their periods, I should imagine, if there haven't been many already. And how did your father regard you growing up?

From a distance, I would say. Daughters tend to be close to their fathers, don't they, but maybe he felt the bond even more closely because of my blindness. They live in Helsinki now. My mother is part Finnish.

Do you miss them?

Yes. Perhaps if they were here, I wouldn't be here seeing you.

It is a possibility but I don't think the two things are related. From what you say, you wouldn't have been able to talk like this to your parents anyway.

I think my father believed in the fairytale approach to love and marriage, that you meet someone compatible and the rest happens in slow motion with the couple wearing white clothes. It doesn't seem to work like that.

It can occasionally work like that.

Can it?

Pause. There is genuine surprise in her voice.

You're not a romantic?

I don't think I can be. Life doesn't work like that, does it?

It's quite true in this modern world that we have been misled, often deliberately into thinking that we should get reality, whatever that is, to conform to our fantasies, fantasies that have usually been fed to us from different sources, our parents included. But remember, it can work the other way round from the one you think.

How do you mean?

That your fantasy can be of pain and misery and the reality might be quite different.

Pause. I hadn't thought of it like that.

Our expectations are there to be fulfilled, it appears, rather than refuted. We know the result before we start. But if we can understand the pattern we can begin to look at it a little more carefully and from a slightly different angle.

And will I be able to see the pattern?

You will.

**End of session.**

# Chapter 15

As far as coincidences go, this one was not remarkable and might well have been deemed predictable, but Toby still thought it was significant. He had approached London Bridge along the river having walked under Tower Bridge and along the front of The Tower of London. The Thames had risen now and as if in response the sky had lightened and in parts the blanket of cloud had broken to reveal glimpses of pale blue. From these came shafts of sunlight which patterned the river and its banks with lighter patches, like alopecia. He was early, as he knew he would be and he paused to the east of the Bridge in front of the ruins of St Magnus the Martyr, one of Wren's churches which had miraculously survived the Luftwaffe intact. His eye was now caught by the light reflecting from the spiked golden ball on top of the column rising between the buildings to the north, a monument to the Great Fire, an event that had destroyed at least as much as the German bombers. But without it the church of St Clement's and so many of its beautiful sisters tucked away in the narrow streets all around would not exist. He began to look for their spires, starting in the east at the Tower and gradually back in a semi-circular sweep to the Bridge. Perhaps this is what Marjorie would have called a typical Toby displacement activity, concerning himself with matters of little importance in order to avoid thinking about the major event in front of him. If so, he was saved at the last minute as the sunlight, having picked out gold, now did the same with silver as a part of the Bridge was caught in a random spot light which lit up several figures. Toby immediately recognised one of them, the unmistakeable silver white hair and the familiar large black sunglasses. From below he watched her make her way slowly across the Bridge and his first instinct was to run to the granite stairs which led up to the Bridge itself and intercept her but for some reason he stopped himself and he just watched her, one face among many, but curiously not looking down on the river as most of the other pedestrians were doing. No doubt she was as preoccupied as he was with the event that was about to happen. It was only as she disappeared out of sight that he realised he did not know her name and that this was perhaps the reason that had stopped him running to greet her. Marise, in her caution, had not mentioned it when he first contacted her and when she phoned back a few hours later it was merely to give him a telephone number. In his gratitude, he had failed to ask Marise for a name to attach to the number and then when he called it a combination of his nervousness and Perdita's somewhat brusque manner had allowed this vital piece of information to slip through the net. Marjorie would perhaps have made more of it than that.

From the top of the narrow lane he could see Marise, small and smart in a black dress, standing in the entrance to the church and for a brief moment Toby wondered if his apprehension was a prelude to one of his attacks. He waited, his back against the solid wall of a merchant bank and looked across the street to a doorway above which a kangaroo and an ostrich were framed in a stone pediment. He smiled at this incongruity, a distraction which allowed him to conclude that his fear was once again to do with sharing Marjorie Nielson with others, a selfishness he sadly recognised, that did not sit easily with today's occasion.

'Hello, Marise.' He greeted her with a slight bow of his head before stepping into the church to the low, almost ominous notes of a hidden organ. Although the interior of the church was small it was nevertheless much larger than Toby had expected from the outside. Uncluttered without being austere, three tall plain windows faced him above the blue and gold altar, with more light coming from several higher windows to his right. Once again she was sitting on a wooden bench as she had at the coroner's court. Since there were barely half a dozen people in the church he hesitated to sit next to her and instead chose a pew a few rows behind her and to one side. She was sitting very still, frowning as if concentrating on a distant object, her head slightly bowed. He watched her remove her iPod and fold it neatly into a case and place it into her handbag which she clicked shut. Now that he was sitting, he could feel his heart racing, his body at odds with his surroundings. He glanced up at the small windows and then again behind him at the door where several other people were arriving. He shut his eyes but all he could feel was the beating of his heart.

*　　*　　*

As she crossed the Bridge she felt the patches of warm light come and go. She was aware of the river to her right and she heard the commentary from a cruise boat telling the passengers that this was the 'third major bridge across the river at this point if you discount the two wooden ones that came first. You Americans on board will know that you've got the one before this one tucked away in Arizona somewhere, although some people think you bought the wrong one. What you wanted was the one ahead of us, Tower Bridge.' His words faded as the boat headed down river leaving Perdita once again with the idea of Marjorie Nielson caught up in the layers of history. It also brought to mind something the therapist had told her during one of their sessions. In our lives, she had said, we are rather like spies. We all build many false bridges, usually to hide our faults or our fears. We carve our identity out of compromise and we put on masks to present ourselves to others. We disguise ourselves, our voices, our looks, even to those whom we love. These pretences we use to get through life but they are false bridges and don't necessarily get us anywhere. What was it she was trying to hide, Perdita asked herself, what disguise had she adopted to throw others off the scent, what false bridges had she built?

She crossed the difficult junction at the north end of the Bridge and turned up Clement Lane.

'Hello, Miss Landberg.' She heard Marise's voice and held out her hand.

'This is a sad occasion, Marise. I'm sorry for you.'

She sat in the church and breathed in the musty air of the interior, laced with a hint of polish, the smell of a thousand churches. The organ played traditionally sombre music entirely at odds with the themes continuing in Perdita's mind, a mix of what she had already written and new themes which were forcing their way to reality. The discordance was there again but more jarring now, uncomfortable and unresolved. She frowned at the pain of the clash that was happening in her imagination and she put her hand to her forehead. She was conscious of other people arriving in the church but she could sense that it was far from full. She heard someone sit behind her, perhaps on the benches across the aisle as she heard the creak of wood. It was only now that Perdita wondered why this church had been chosen for the funeral. What connection did Marjorie have with this corner of London? It was one of a multitude of questions she wanted answering.

\*　　\*　　\*

Peter Harrington approached Clement Lane from the north, finding his way through a series of alleys that ran like vital arteries through a fast changing city. They hid ancient pubs and curious shops that spoke of earlier times and a different way of life. Occasionally he would look up and see the corner of a giant new block looming above him, a vivid contrast to the ancient byway which was leading him towards the church of St Clement's. A white van loaded with plastic bottles of drinking water hooted at him as it bumped up onto the pavement and parked. The driver, with a shaved head and a tattoo of St George and the dragon on the back of his neck, slammed the door and pushed past him flicking a cigarette stub in an arc towards the gutter. A foul smell rose from the grooved metal grating worn smooth in the middle of the narrow lane. At the far end, brightly lit unlike the lane, a succession of buses and cars crossed to and from the bridge. A woman walked purposefully towards him clutching a mobile phone to her ear and talking loudly. She, too, walked past him as if he didn't exist, causing him to step into the road as if she knew he would. He looked back at her, her elbow raised as she spoke into the phone like a scimitar on a wheel of Boadicea's chariot clipping all those who got in its way. Some instinct in him wanted to call her back, give her a dressing down as he would have done a young subaltern for sloppy dress. How easy the lines of authority had been in the army, a world within a world with its own codes of conduct and rules of behaviour. But many of these did not transfer well to the world he saw around him this grey morning in London where although the sun was trying to push through, Clement Lane remained resolutely in the shade.

Despite his disaffection with London, it was Marjorie Nielson who had compelled him to make the journey once a fortnight from the quietness of his life in the south of France and as he neared the church he registered once again her importance in his life. We are after, she would say to him, the forgotten material in your life which, as a pragmatic man, he had found a puzzle. Surely, he said to her, we remember what has happened to us, don't we? We often think we choose what to remember, she had replied. Occasionally, in the later sessions, he had been unable or unwilling to speak and she had merely said that it was her job to help him understand his resistances to speaking. Only now did he understand what she had been saying and it pained him again to think that he would never see her again and look into the wise eyes that he had found so reassuring.

He greeted Marise as he entered the church aware he was leaving the noise of the City behind him. He immediately saw several of the people he recognised from the coroner's inquest but chose a row to sit in by himself. Religion had been an important part of his army life but more out of tradition than belief. It was yet another element of the separate world from which he had come and which bore less and less reality to the world in which he now found himself. As if to match his thoughts, he heard the doors to this world close behind him and a silence descend on the tiny congregation. He wasn't sure what to expect and they remained in silence for several minutes before it was interrupted by the sound of feet from one side of the altar. Four men appeared carrying a coffin which they laid on trestles waiting for it just below the steps to the pulpit. Even though the coffin was sealed it was a shock to be reminded of the physical presence of Marjorie Nielson and he saw Marise, a few rows ahead, bring a handkerchief to her eyes. And then, as if appearing from nowhere, a priest stood on the carpeted step in front of the altar, his back to the congregation and bowed to the cross. Somewhere outside, a long way away, a bus hooted and there were distant angry voices.

'Let us pray. Our Father . . . '

There were perhaps twenty people who joined in reciting the Lord's Prayer, uncertain at first and then gradually in unison but their voices were still faint in the body of the church. Afterwards, the vicar climbed the wooden stairs to his elaborate pulpit, pausing to take in his congregation before speaking.

'You all know why we are gathered here today, for the funeral of Dr Marjorie Nielson. Some of you, though, may wonder why here at the church of St Clement's in the City of London. For this we have to thank Marise, Marjorie's long time friend and colleague who approached me not long after she died. Over half a century ago, it seems, these two women lived in this parish in the days when this great window behind me lay in ruins on this floor, a victim of the War which had played such an important part in pushing the pair of them to these shores. The window was repaired although sadly, as you can see, not with the stained glass which had been shattered beyond repair or recovery, but with the clear glass that you see now. If I may continue this symbolism, it was Marjorie's task to put back together the shattered lives of those people that had been broken by one bad experience or the other. In this she believed that the church and therapy walked hand in hand. It was perhaps her own experiences that led her to this vocation. Marise has given me various parts of the jigsaw that make up the background to the doctor's life and work and I would like to convey some of these to you now, in celebration of Marjorie Nielson. Her father was a violin maker who was born in Austria but who fled to Russia three years before the Anschluss. His choice of new home was both fortunate and unfortunate. For there he met his wife, who was to give birth to Marjorie not long afterwards, but there, unfortunately, was Stalingrad. He was to die here in 1945 and a few years later so did his wife. How Marjorie came to London is a story in itself but by all accounts it was one of her father's violins that was, quite literally, instrumental in providing her passage. An English musician, wanting to replace the violin he had lost in the war, tracked down the family to find the father dead and his wife and child in dire straights. Marjorie's mother died whilst he was there and so he did then what would be impossible now and arranged for Marjorie to be brought to this country. It was 1950 and she was fifteen. She was encouraged to train as a doctor and showed astonishing talent. She went on to become a psychiatrist and to help generations of men and women to come to terms with traumatic backgrounds like her own.'

Once or twice, on night patrols in difficult situations Peter Harrington had experienced the feeling he now had as he heard Marjorie's story unfold. Out of the murky darkness he had perceived something moving, a figure, an outline, barely visible and like a hunting dog picking up a scent he had stopped, immediately alert. This is the sensation he had now, the certain knowledge that he had heard some vital piece of information even if at the moment he wasn't able to give definition to it and to decide whether it was friendly or not. He shut his eyes and absorbed what he had heard, eager to further assimilate it and give it more form. The disparate congregation sang a hymn as his mind scanned the last exchanges he had with Marjorie seeking a key word or a phrase to add substance to his instincts. Some-where, though, a door had been opened, not completely, but enough to show a gentle light and to offer him a way forward.

'As you know, ladies and gentlemen, the actual cremation of Dr Nielson will take place at Manor Park where the coffin will now be taken. Will you please stand.'

The doors were opened and the sounds of the City flowed back into the church as the four men carried the body of Marjorie Nielson to the hearse waiting outside. It was temporarily blocking the narrow lane and behind it the driver of the white van earlier encountered by Peter Harrington sat fuming in scant regard for what was happening in front of him. The dead should not hinder his progress and he was yelling at the driver of the hearse to get a move on. The vicar went over to him to offer a word of advice, Christian or otherwise.

Toby took this moment of distraction to walk over to the opposite pews.

'Hello,' he said tentatively, 'I'm Toby Browning, we spoke on the telephone.'

She turned to face him, her eyes still hidden behind the dark glasses and held out her hand which he took and felt its firm grip around his. 'I don't know how you are getting to the cemetery but I wonder if I might offer you a lift?' In the pause whilst she absorbed this question, he looked at her more carefully, the fine silver hair cropped in a boyish manner, short at the sides and pushed back off her brow, the fine line of her chin and what he took to be the faint smile on her lips. She slightly cocked her head at him.

'And where were you able to park around here?' It was said with the sort of firmness that implied she knew that it was nigh on impossible.

He found himself apologising almost immediately. 'I'm sorry,' he said, 'but before I answer that question, could I, would you mind telling me your name? I seem to have got this far without knowing it.'

Now she did smile, the white of her teeth breaking through the strong mouth.

'Perdita Landberg. Pleased to meet you. And the parking?'

'Yes, well, I live not far from here and I was going to take a taxi back and pick up the car. You're very welcome to join me.' He said the last sentence with a certain diffidence for fear at the reaction it might provoke.

'I should be delighted to. It will save me a great deal of trouble. I won't need this now.' She had been holding what Toby took to be an iPod and she put it back into her bag.

'Why would an iPod be of help in getting to the cemetery?'

If it is possible for a face to express three different emotions almost simultaneously, then Perdita Landberg's did as she absorbed Toby's question, shifting from astonishment, to puzzlement and then to pleasure.

'Look at me,' she said. 'Do people normally wear dark glasses in church?'

'Well,' Toby said uncertainly, 'you may have wanted to hide the fact that you were crying.'

'Possibly,' she replied, 'but did it not strike you as odd that I should wear an iPod as well?'

'Well, yes, I suppose it did.'

The church had emptied now and the sun slanting through the narrow south facing windows lit up the wall behind them and the marble plaque of a long forgotten hero of a colonial war.

'If I asked if I could take your arm, would this help as a means of explanation?'

She is mocking me, Toby thought, still unable to grasp what she was telling him.

'I am blind, Mr Browning.'

It was as if at first Toby did not comprehend what he was being told and even now as he looked at her he could barely believe what he had been told, perhaps to hide his embarrassment which now swept through him like a giant wave.

'But that's wonderful,' he said and immediately regretted it.

'Wonderful? How so?' she asked sharply.

'Well, what I mean is, what I am trying to say is, how wonderful you managed to get here and to the inquest well, you know, without a problem.'

At this Perdita's face changed and hardened and she looked at him coldly.

'I am blind, Mr Browning. But I am only blind. Now, if you'll excuse me.'

He stood aside, too astonished to speak and watched her fish about in her bag and bring out what he now knew could not be an iPod and place the white leads in her ears. Her hand felt the end of the pew and she turned confidently into the aisle. She paused at the double doors and held the short brass rail on her left before stepping down the shallow step into the ancient lane to disappear from his view.

# Chapter 16

No one is buried in the City of London any more. There is no room. Instead, the dead leave the City en route to the vast cemetery at Manor Park, where hundreds of thousands of Londoners end their journey caught between the dreary expanse of Wanstead Flats and the thunder of the North Circular Road. For almost one hundred and fifty years, the dead have come this way careless of their surroundings. If you have the misfortune to be buried on the eastern fringes of the cemetery, close by the Aldersbrook, the tiny river which struggles along its boundary, then the constant sound of the traffic will carry away the words of the last rites and the gentle sobbing of the mourners.

It was an unpleasant journey by car made worse by Toby's internal post-mortem on the debacle with Perdita. He had met her three times and failed to recognise that she was blind. Was he too wrapped up in himself to notice? When he had first encountered her on the pavement in Harley Street, standing alone and apparently bewildered, could he have known she was blind? And in the coroner's court hadn't she turned to look at him? Yes, he had thought it was odd that she didn't glance at the river when she crossed London Bridge but this he had put down to her preoccupation with the funeral service ahead. And hadn't she arrived at these three destinations by herself apparently unaided? The hinterland of the cemetery was no advertisement, a succession of cheap used car lots and run down shops but eventually Toby turned off the Ilford Road and quickly arrived at the boundary of the cemetery marked by metal railings topped with barbed wire. And why had she reacted so strongly to him? He ran through the exchange which seemed to start well and end disastrously, her anger fierce and dismissive. It had taken him more than an hour from the architectural simplicity of Wren's small but perfect church, to swing under the faux medieval arch which marked the entrance to the huge cemetery. Marise had told him to follow the signs for the Catacomb Columbarium and he drove slowly through the trees on a narrow road beyond which the graves stretched into the distance, a sea of different shapes and sizes apparently tumbling one on the other. A girl from Stalingrad, forced to leave her own country, should not end up here on the fringes of London amongst strangers.

Again he was early and he walked towards the strange modern building in which the cremation would take place. In here, dying was big business and Marjorie Nielson was part of a production line slotted between Ibrahim Zarawi and Barbara Symmonds, their families mingling in sombre disarray in the gardens and lawns all around. He walked up a grassy bank towards a line of older graves, some of which displayed small green triangles which had caught his attention. 'This memorial has been identified for possible reclamation', they declared somewhat mysteriously. Did it mean that the stone memorial could be taken and used elsewhere in the cemetery, or that this particular spot could be reused for a new burial? Neither option seemed appropriate to Toby. The idea that Marjorie might end up in a second hand grave seemed as ghoulish as it was ridiculous, a recycling step too far. From the grassy knoll he could look back over the graves, the older greyer stones nearer to him and the shiny black and white marble affairs with bright gold letters in the distance. Even in death there is competition, Toby thought, looking at the jumble of shapes and sizes. Mine is bigger than yours and from beyond the grave I declare I am better than you.

And now when he saw her coming towards him between the yew trees he still wouldn't have known she was blind. She was walking slowly but then everyone did in the cemetery. Perhaps, as he looked at her feet, he could sense a little hesitancy. Marise was on one side but in no way was she leading Perdita. Toby was partly hidden by a larger memorial and he watched their approach unnoticed. This was the first time he had properly regarded Perdita Landberg and he observed a slim but not thin woman, not beautiful in the traditional sense but attractive in a way he found hard to define. Her hair, of course, made her outstanding even more so in the dark surroundings of the cemetery but it was more than this. The picture was incomplete, however, for he was unable to see her eyes and the dark glasses only served to increase the mystery of what conjunction of line and shape made Perdita Landberg so compelling. He watched as they approached with some of the group he had seen at the church following close behind. As Perdita came level with where he was standing she turned and looked towards him as if she had sensed his presence, just as she had in the coroner's court. His instinct was to slip further behind the memorial so convinced that she could see him. Her look was powerful and direct and he was transfixed, immobilised like an animal caught in the powerful headlamps of an on rushing car.

The mechanics of cremation completed the contrast between the quiet and dignified ceremony at St Clement's and the business of death reflected at the cemetery was marked. He watched the coffin slip through the gap towards the flames and although Marjorie Nielson was about to be reduced to ashes she remained tangible and ever present to Toby whose hands, clenched as he watched the curtain close, reflected his emotions. And then she was gone, the woman who had patiently listened to the stories of his life, who had offered gentle advice and nudged him imperceptibility this way or that, was no more and the tears rolled slowly down his face, tears not for the therapist but for himself. Marise was also crying, her small frame shaking, a bunched handkerchief pressed against her face. He looked over to her. Would this annexed corner of Wanstead Flats be the final resting place for Marjorie Nielson or would her ashes still have another journey to make?

Afterwards, in a large paved area covered in the flowers and wreaths from the multitude of other funerals taking place, they waited, standing separately, somewhat uneasy in each other's company and not quite sure what to do next. Toby recognised the distinguished man he had seen at the coroner's court but could not remember his name. Perdita was standing by the flowers and without thinking he went over and stood just behind her shoulder. 'There are some ghastly yellow irises directly in front of you and a particularly tasteless bunch of red and white roses to their right. However, slightly to your left is a most unusual, for here at least, array of cornflowers and eucalyptus with a discreet bunch of white freesia alongside. I can't remember the name of the Indian ceremony where they float flowers on the Ganges, but that's rather what it looks like.'

She spoke without turning. 'I have most of this picture, thank you,' she responded somewhat discouragingly. And then she continued. 'I have never seen the Ganges but I once went to the flower festival in Sikkim. I remember the air was full of the scent of flowers. It was as if I could hold out my hand and catch it. I can smell the freesia and the eucalyptus.' Before she could say anything else, Marise now appeared wiping away the tears which had wet her cheeks. It was a surreal moment both sombre and ludicrous and Toby felt like an intruder. However important he believed his connection to Marjorie Nielson to be, she was a stranger to him. Marise had been a friend and companion for decades and if this ceremony was for anyone it was for her. As if in response to his thoughts but speaking to the group of them, Marise made an announcement. 'I will not leave my friend here with all these people.' She looked around her before continuing. 'Quite often Marjorie and I would walk in Regent's Park and sit and eat lunch. Usually we didn't speak. She would have been listening to people's stories all morning and now she wanted peace.' As she said this she kept her eyes on her hands. 'When I receive them, I am going to take her ashes into the Park and sprinkle them there. I know it is what she would have liked. I'm sure I'm not allowed to do this but I don't care, I don't care. It is the least I can do for her.'

A pair of magpies began to quarrel noisily in the trees behind, a nasty screeching which caused the group to turn as the birds tumbled into view in a blur of black and white, falling on to the grass before disengaging and flying away, their ugly calls fading away over the graves.

*     *     *

The cries stayed with Perdita, an echoing menace that joined other fragments from the day which she had been hoarding just as a magpie might. She had hoped that the music that had begun in her mind behind St Pancras and been brought to life in her living room, would have developed further during the course of the day but she could not get beyond the themes she had already confirmed. This was partly due to the anger she experienced in the church when Toby Browning had spoken to her and had made such a blatant assumption of her frailty. But she had been further thrown by her new knowledge of Marjorie's background which she had yet to assimilate properly. She disliked the stifling atmosphere of the cemetery and she detected in the air a smell which she found vaguely offensive. It was as if this place did not fit in to the story of Marjorie Nielson's life and was at odds with her character. She should have been buried in the City with a marble memorial in the church of St Clement's, Cheapside in the Ward of Candlewick. As she had entered the church she had felt the old font which was directly in front of the door and run her fingers over the old carved wooden dome which topped it. Inside that, the vicar had told her when she arrived, was an even older carving of a dove made out of marble and she thought the image of peace and baptism would have appealed to Marjorie. She had enjoyed the intimacy of the church, the small number of pews and the way it contained the tiny congregation but the feeling had evaporated and she had been unable to regain that equilibrium.

'May I try again?'

She heard Toby Browning's voice behind her and turned to him.

'Try what?'

'Try and offer you a lift again?'

'Because you think I might not be able to get back to London by myself?'

'Well,' Toby Browning continued, 'it is quite clear that you could. I'm not really quite sure what I said wrong before but I apologise.'

Perdita's instinct was to say 'no' in line with the overall dissatisfaction she felt, but a small voice inside her made her hesitate and that gap allowed Toby to speak again.

'I phoned you originally,' he said, his voice smaller now, less sure 'to talk about Marjorie Nielson. Perhaps we could do that in the car? I wouldn't mind getting away from here.'

As they stood there the next clutch of mourners began to spill out of the chapel, the women in long white saris and the men in dark suits. Two or three passed in between Perdita and Toby as if they didn't exist.

There was no assumption in his voice, thought Perdita. So many men gave the impression they were doing her a favour when offering to help and their questions were often rhetorical, if indeed they asked questions at all.

'Thank you,' she said as a succession of cars, large Mercedes and BMWs began to purr out of the car park towards them. As he stepped back she took his arm and copied his movement. She kept her hand loosely on his forearm as he led her to his car. At least he knew how to do that. Normally she was grasped by her upper arm and marched into position. He opened the passenger door and she slid into position. It was a relief that he did not talk about her blindness and even before they left the cemetery he had opened the conversation.

'I must confess that I felt at rather a loss when I heard that Marjorie had died. Why I should call her Marjorie now, I don't know. I never did when I saw her. Maybe death brings familiarity.'

He drove easily with no sudden stops and starts but whether

he was doing this for her or drove like this anyway, she couldn't be sure.

'Part of it I still cannot believe,' she said. 'For part of me she is still alive and I imagine always will be.'

He looked across at her and she wondered if he was going to ask her what she meant.

'Precisely,' he said. 'But I wonder if this is because we really didn't know her and on one level there wasn't a lot to lose? You know, if you lost a brother then a whole heap of shared memories go down the drain.'

Now it was her turn to look at him. 'I thought we were like ships that pass in the night and that her radar was working and mine wasn't. She knew exactly where I was but I had no clue about her. This struck me at the inquest.'

'Oh dear,' he responded. 'My emotions were much less generous. I was just jolly cross that she had abandoned me. Isn't that awful?'

She heard the click of the indicator and felt the car turn and accelerate. As if to explain the movement, he added 'we've just turned off the North Circular and we're heading back into town.'

She was certain that he wouldn't have given a commentary on directions to a passenger with sight but she resisted saying so.

'My reactions to her death were similar,' she replied after a moment. 'I thought it was a shame that I had gone so far with her and now it had come to an abrupt end. I wanted warning, if you know what I mean?'

'Like she used to do if we were going to miss a session. She used to warn me weeks in advance.'

'Yes,' replied Perdita seriously. 'I didn't really understand that at the time, but I can now.'

The cluster of towers that made up Canary Wharf was now on the horizon, the sun glinting off the top of the tallest, a lighthouse for the motorist heading southwards into London.

'I live by the river, in Wapping,' he offered, to end the silence that had suddenly developed between them. 'You can almost see it from here.'

She was pleased that he didn't correct himself. 'My place is over in the other direction, just off Marylebone High Street. I'll get the Jubilee Line around to Bond Street.' Perdita said and wondered if he would immediately offer to drive her there, but the moment passed.

'I'm sorry, you don't know anything about me,' he said out of the blue. 'I'm an art dealer, I live above my gallery.'

'Successful, by all accounts', Perdita said, tapping the dashboard. The rich smell of leather from the large seat in which was sitting spoke of luxury and the car's engine was barely audible.

'In one way, very,' Toby responded cautiously. 'David Hockney bought me this. Not directly, of course, but I sold one of his pictures rather well. Not that it was difficult to do that. But this is one of the results.'

Perdita was on the point of asking in which way it wasn't successful, when she stopped herself. After all, he had been in therapy.

'I'm a composer.' She waited but the response she normally received never materialised. "How *wonderful*", people said. Or, "That's *marvellous*", as if talking to a four year old child who'd just drawn a picture of a smiling face. 'Well, that sounds a bit grand. A sometime composer would be more accurate. I am a musician as well. I play the piano and I get work when I can.'

Perhaps it was her imagination, but Perdita felt the atmosphere in the car change slightly. It could have been his lack of response, she wasn't sure. Normally people asked what sort of music she composed and rattled on about their favourite pieces but Toby Browning remained quiet and seemed to have retreated into himself.

He dropped her at London Bridge, as he said he would. As they got nearer, she took out what he had first thought was an iPod. She knew he would be looking at it and she explained about her personal navigation system. Putting it to her ear she mimicked the voice she could hear. 'You are now on Tooley Street south side heading west. It works to within two metres, although not beneath ground. Most of the Jubilee Line stations I know, but it can occasionally be a little difficult. Anyway, thank you for the lift.'

She was already out of the car by the time he came around to open the door. She stood for a moment to orientate herself and move surely towards the entrance to the Jubilee Line.

\*     \*     \*

Peter Harrington watched the Bentley nose its way down the narrow lane towards the cemetery exit before walking over to sit next to Marise on a bench surrounded by small headstones each displaying a picture of the person they commemorated.

'I don't blame you for not wanting to leave Marjorie's ashes here,' he said slowly. 'If I said it was a bit dead and alive, I hope you wouldn't think I was being flippant.'

'She wasn't that sort of women,' Marise said. 'She wouldn't have wanted a fuss, a fancy headstone and certainly not a picture of herself,' she said bitterly, gesturing towards the graves. 'It was never about her but always about others. That is why she was such a great doctor.' She spoke the words with a hint of anger which belied the weary look on her face.

'I don't suppose you know the couple who have just left, do you?'

She shook her head. 'I do, but Dr Nielson always respected her clients' right to confidentiality and I really shouldn't tell you anything more.'

'Well,' he said softly, 'you've let me know they were clients at least. That makes me feel better. I wouldn't have liked be the only one paying his respects.'

'Major Harrington, I cannot give you that information.' Suddenly she stood up. 'Particularly you.' And she turned and walked away from him, into the sea of graves and was soon lost amongst the stones.

Peter Harrington was puzzled at her outburst which was as sudden as it was unexpected and as he walked back across the corner of Wanstead Flats towards Manor Park station he could not make sense of what she had said. It had been an emotional day which now lay like a weight on his shoulders. He paused to watch a group of kids playing football on one of the many pitches which quartered the Flats, their varied and brightly coloured shirts reflecting their support for different clubs. The ball was kicked his way and he watched it dropping towards him. Adjusting his feet he met it on the half volley sending it back with some precision before continuing on his way to the station, a distraction he wished could have lasted for longer. The train rattled into the station, the metal wheels squealing protest against the metal rails. Although he knew it was only half a dozen stops to Liverpool Street, he fell asleep immediately his head lolling and occasionally knocking against the side of the carriage.

When he was jolted awake at Stratford he had no idea where he was and he had opened the carriage door before realising he had only completed half the journey. He had been dreaming of Marjorie Nielson and he had seen her clearly, leaning forward attentively. Even in his dream he knew there had been a point, a word, a look, a reference, that had changed everything, that had altered the balance between the two of them and he was searching for it now. His mind was working as Marjorie had said it would and he knew that he had unwittingly glimpsed a vital clue about her background. In the small garden of one of the terraced houses which backed on to the line, he watched a child fall off a bright yellow tricycle and saw his mouth open but he could not hear the cry of pain.

# Chapter 17

I have been thinking more about what you said and I realise that I never told you the end of the story about Taffy Jones coming to see me. I wonder if that is important?

He looks at me and I nod.

I imagine now that I stopped myself because I was entering a danger zone.

Again he looks at me.

Well, Taffy stayed for four days which I didn't find at all easy. I've looked back on it now and I cannot really say why, but it was clear he triggered something. I wanted him to go really. I have increasingly wanted to be by myself which is why my work in France suits me so well.

What do you think Taffy reminds you of?

Well, the army, I suppose.

But you didn't dislike your time in the army, did you?

Pause. No, I don't believe I did.

You're not certain, though?

Well, I feel that my time there has been coloured by, well, I'm not sure really.

I asked you if you had the black cloud when you were young and you thought not. Did you have it in the army?

Oh yes, he says without hesitation. I couldn't tell you when it began.

Isn't that the point of being here, though?

He considers me carefully wondering if my question is an admonishment. Pause.

I am here because I know I am unhappy and I know this sounds perverse but I don't consider myself a sad person. Sometimes I can't sleep or I suddenly wake in the middle of the night and I know I have been having a vivid dream, but the moment I'm awake is has gone and I am left, well, stranded.

What do you mean?

At a loss, trapped. Occasionally threatened.

So these dreams you can't remember distress you?

I suppose so.

And you didn't tell anyone of this insomnia in the army?

Good lord, no. I don't think that would have been a very good idea.

But it might be a good idea here, Peter. We're safe in here. He looks at me again, not sure whether I might be teasing him or goading him to speak. Well, the latter is true.

Seeking help is not an option you find easy, is it?

No, I have always prided myself in a degree of self-sufficiency.

So it must have been quite a step for you to come and see me? He nods.

Psychotherapy is an odd thing, Peter. In some ways it is simply the process of helping someone remember the forgotten material of their life, of tracking their unconscious. One of my colleagues believes in some instances psychoanalysis can be an encounter between two people as opposed to one person treating another.

Pause.

That we are in this together, you mean?

Pause. Or, you mean that you are not necessarily more important than me? Pause.

Is it that you can't remember or that you don't want to remember?

I'm not sure what you mean?

Let's imagine that an event, or series of events, has occurred at some stage in your army career and this has caused you distress but for some reason you cannot acknowledge this, so much so your body shuts down at the very thought of it. And you collude with your body by avoiding the issue yourself.

124

He gets up now and walks to the wall and back. He is breathing deeply.

Do you know, I can't bear any sort of violence any more? Don't you find that odd coming from someone who was in the army for twenty-five years? I can't watch films that contain violence. I can't even cope with seeing someone fall over. What's happening to me?

Pause.

What do you think?

Well, I don't think this is normal. It's as if I am frightened. Sometimes even noises can do it, can set off a sudden reaction in me.

In our first session you spoke of going to pick up Taffy from the airport. You were slowed by a road accident. Does this come under the category of violent?

He stands again and then sits.

I can't look, I don't want to look. I was trained to help and I can't. I won't.

Pause.

What did you do in the army, Peter?

Eventually I became the commander of a rapid response squad.

You were trained for a form of violence, then?

We never saw it like that. We felt we trained to make things better, not worse. To create order out of chaos. If there was violence – and we never used that word – it was to restore order.

You make it all sound so reasonable. But what happened to this ideal? What went wrong?

How do you know anything went wrong?

Pause. Did something go wrong?

Pause. He stands again and walks to the window. He is controlling his emotions.

Pause.

Peter, it will come to you. I have said many times before that remembering the past will stop you living in it.

But I am not living in the past. My army days are over and I have moved on.

Have you Peter? What did your mother say? Secrets are power, well they can also wear you down, become a burden.

What if this material, as you call it, isn't forgotten and that I do remember it but I don't know how important it is?

That's the point of talking about it. Talking is so different from thinking.

I have never had to explain myself like this at all. My mother didn't believe in it. She thought I ought to be able to cope by myself, stiff upper lip and all that. I thought it had worked.

But there is another side to you, Peter, as there is in us all. Perhaps you express yourself through your poetry. Pause.

More my painting, but I'm not sure it expresses what you're talking about. But that's another thing, I haven't been able to paint for some time now. It's like a tap was turned off inside me. I just don't want to any more.

Why?

Pause. Why?

Pause. He drops his head. I lost my touch. Pause.

I don't understand.

I found myself painting what I like to paint, the landscape but hating what I had done. The pictures didn't seem right and I know this will sound strange, it felt wrong painting them, as if they didn't reflect the way I was feeling.

How do you mean?

I remember going to the Thames near Marlowe to paint. It was a beautiful day with open skies and great white clouds. And I caught it pretty well, there in front of me. People stopped and admired it but I knew it was false, that it wasn't about me. I had chosen the wrong subject.

Pause.

What subject should you have chosen?

Something darker, much darker.

He drops his head again.

Can you remember when this was?

Pause. Yes, it was the summer after I came back from Germany.

And did something happen in Germany?

And he stands again but this time he does it like a soldier, with authority. He is signalling that the session is at an end.

What is it Peter?

His face is stretched, his eyes narrow, as if he is watching something. He looks at me and shakes his head and then leaves.

**End of session**

NB This has been an unusual session in terms of intervention. I cannot fully explain this yet to myself and nor do I know whether it will work. I am certainly very engaged with Peter, a complicated man. It is as if I am being pulled along with a narrative I both know and fear.

# Chapter 18

What had so recently been under her fingers had now deserted her, flown away to some distant and inaccessible corner. She was sitting at the keyboard wearing a short silk night shirt the same colour as her hair, ghostly in the pale light. She had been up since dawn hoping that the events of the day before would feed her imagination and enrich the composition which had begun so promisingly. But she had reached an impasse and all the certainty Perdita had just a few weeks ago was now drained from her. She wondered if it was guilt, her blatant use of the therapist's life and death for her own ends but, she told herself, the composition was just as much a celebration and tribute to her. From childhood, Perdita had been able to represent the way she was feeling in music and it was this gift that was causing the problem this morning for the music in her mind was not about Marjorie Nielson, but about herself, an amalgam of clashing, ill defined themes which she was unable to decipher and make sense of. In an attempt to break the stalemate she began to play one of Philip Glass's deceptively simple pieces, the relentless minimalist helping drive all other musical thoughts out of her mind. It was as if the new facts she had learned about Marjorie Nielson came without instruction on how to interpret them. What Perdita had written so far was based on an emotional response to the woman which had been inspired by the exchanges that had taken place in her consulting room, but now she had to absorb a lost childhood in another country and the reality of a war that had destroyed a family. She could only imagine what impact this would have had on a young girl, but she desperately wanted to hear Marjorie talk about it herself. She needed flesh to put on the cold facts, but it was too late. What would have been difficult to achieve even when Marjorie Nielson was alive, was impossible now, but it was more than simply her inability to absorb the new facts about the lost therapist. The picture was further occluded by Perdita's doubts about herself. And she laughed as she remembered telling Marjorie that she, Perdita, was a woman confident in herself well aware of her own abilities. Up to a point, perhaps and that point had now been reached. She lifted her hands from the keyboard and placed them over her breasts. She ran her palms down the smooth silk and from that to her thighs. Perdita Landberg. Could she really see herself? And if she couldn't, now that Marjorie was dead, would she ever be able to? It was doubly difficult for her to publicly acknowledge a sense of defeat for it was always interpreted as self pity for her blindness, but she did so privately now.

The phone rang and it took Perdita a second or two to find the receiver which she had failed to put back in its base the night before, an unusual omission for her.

'It's Toby. Toby Browning.'

Perdita felt for her watch. Although she had been up several hours, it was still only nine, so she was surprised to hear his voice so early.

'Listen,' he rushed on, 'just thinking about yesterday, we didn't really get anywhere and I wonder if I could see you again? You know, to talk about Marjorie.' He was nervous, she could hear, but the call was well timed for it was as if he had read her mind.

'I was just thinking about Marjorie, myself,' said Perdita.

'I wondered if you would like to come to the gallery?' he asked, hurrying on. She could detect no note of irony in his voice.

'Did you have a time in mind?'

'Would later this morning be any good?'

For a reason she could not immediately understand, she agreed. Later, when she replaced the receiver, she assumed it was nothing more or less than a way of keeping in touch with Marjorie Nielson but when she was showering she debated whether this was the whole truth. It was at this point that she turned off the water so that the silence would help her think better. She put her hands against the white tiled walls and felt the final drips of water splash onto her feet. When Toby Browning approached her in the church he had done so not realising she was blind. It was only now that she absorbed this fact because it so seldom happened and for the first time she saw Toby Browning as a person and not simply as an ex-client of Marjorie Nielson. The death of the therapist had distorted the way that she had perceived him. They were members of a private club having been approved by the committee and fully aware of the house rules. On this level, she had accepted him completely but after the phone call she was conscious that there might be other rules of engagement. She stepped out of the shower and rubbed dry her hair. St Bede had chuckled when he had first seen her bathroom because two walls were entirely covered in mirror. 'You look after your guests so well,' he had commented. 'It reflects well on you, ho ho.'

Naked, she went into the living room. She remembered St Bede's comments on these rules of engagement. 'Darling, it's often lust at first sight. Nice boy, no complications, a physical thing. I'm always frightfully cautious about the others, you know, the ones that might be serious. They sort of frighten me.' It was the other ones she was interested in and St Bede was wise enough to know why she was asking without being too obvious in his replies. 'It doesn't take me to tell you darling that looks aren't everything. Have you ever thought how odd it is that many couples – gay or not – who eventually get it together are quite different from one another. How can you tell that across a crowded room?'

She sat at the piano and played again the four big chords that began the second movement of her piece, hearing again the wonderful blend of notes and wondering where they came from. Then she shut the lid of the piano with a small bang which echoed through its frame and lingered after she had left the room. She dressed carefully.

'I wonder what advice St Bede would give me if he knew? she thought as she put on the grey linen suit which he had helped her buy. And why haven't I told him? Why haven't I told anyone?'

\*     \*     \*

It was only as he put down the phone that he realised the inappropriateness of inviting her to the gallery and he nearly called her back to suggest a more suitable rendezvous. He was, of course, now trapped for this would indicate that he was making an adjustment for her blindness which she in no uncertain terms had made it clear she would not tolerate. So he paced the floor and tried to anticipate how the meeting would go, wary of the speed and hostility of some of her responses. Apart from the Hodgkin which shouted its absence from one wall, most of the pictures in the exhibition had still to go to their new owners and this was the last week they would be together, a comfortable and eclectic mix which spoke well of his skills. Not that Perdita would be able to judge this, he thought regretfully. One part of him had anticipated that she wouldn't come, certainly not so quickly, so he was somewhat thrown by the fact she would be arriving in a couple of hours. He nipped out and bought some croissants and pains aux raisins and searched in his kitchen for some clean napkins but gave up in favour of kitchen roll. A large mirror hung on the back wall of the living room, tilted slightly forward, to reflect part of the Thames and the south bank of the river. He looked at himself and asked 'Isn't this meeting just a little artificial, Toby?' He raised his eyebrows and couldn't think of a reply other than 'yes' which he said out loud to himself at the same time deciding that they would take coffee and croissant downstairs in the gallery and not up here in the living room.

He returned to the gallery and moved the table away from the wall where the Hodgkin had hung to a position in front of a beautiful landscape from a much less well known artist for whom he had great hopes, so much so that he had bought this picture himself. It showed a series of fields flowing down to the sea, the lines in each field at a different angle, a patchwork of pale colours neither representative nor abstract, deceptively simple.

His mobile rang. 'I am outside,' she said and he looked to the glass doors to see her standing there and a taxi pulling away in the background. The twenty paces he took towards her gave him far too much time to condemn himself for the stupidity of inviting her to an arena where sight is compulsory.

'Welcome,' he said, offering his forearm to her outstretched hand.

'It's big,' was her reply, gesturing with her free arm.

'Yes,' he said. 'It used to be two warehouses which I knocked into one. It's about sixty feet by forty, if you'll allow me to use old money.' Occasionally, thought Toby, I can sound just like my father. He led her to the table but rather than sit down she surprised him by asking him if she could see the pictures.

'Of course,' he said and, beginning with the ploughed fields he led her from picture to picture and did what he had done many times before with prospective buyers, explained a picture and its provenance but this time he did it quite differently as if he was being asked, as indeed he was, to see these pictures even more carefully.

'This is a wonderful portrait by a young woman – unusual in itself – who narrowly failed to win the young portrait painter of the year award. In my opinion, she should have. The boy who won it did so with a terrible piece of photo realism, very clever and the rest of it but it didn't tell you more about the sitter at all. More, I should think, about the artist.'

'And what does this portrait tell you about the woman?' she asked, looking directly at the picture in a way that Toby found uncanny.

'This is a self portrait of a woman who has a lot of questions to ask herself. It's painted in harsh light which falls across her face but her black hair is almost lost against the dark shadows behind her. It says "Who are you?" and "What is behind this mask?" The painter is really excluding us. We are accidental bystanders who just happen to be passing by.'

'So we know no more about her than, say, Marjorie Nielson,' said Perdita making the transition to the subject much easier than Toby could have wished for.

'True enough. I didn't know how to take the extra information we learned yesterday. I will be quite honest and say that I wished she had told me some of those details herself. I wanted her to have confided in me.'

'Perhaps you would have preferred to be in a congregation of one,' said Perdita and at first Toby was prepared to take this remark the wrong way, but of course it was true.

'I suppose,' he said, 'that we are a congregation of one when we see a therapist and we find it hard, no impossible, to imagine that other people sit in the same room and receive the same careful attention.'

'Whatever, we are all seeking a sort of divine intervention in our lives, a wisdom beyond our own.'

Toby smiled at this and almost asked her what she was seeking divine intervention for, but wisely kept the question to himself. He poured her some more coffee and looked at her more closely. He was cautious in doing this since she appeared to know each time he did it for her stillness, which he knew he shouldn't take for calmness, was her way of picking up movement all around her.

'I found yesterday's information difficult to absorb as well.' Perdita said quietly. 'I, too, wished she could have told me the facts herself but not because I felt possessive of her.'

'Why, then?'

'I wanted to hear the emotion in her voice when she spoke of such things. I wanted to turn the tables, to be the listener if you like. Why do you think we want to know more about Marjorie?'

'I didn't at first,' he replied quickly. 'I was angry that she had left me in the lurch. Then I realised how unreasonable that was and now I wonder if the act of finding out more about her will somehow help me . . . ' He voiced tailed away. It was the admission he didn't really want to make to her, at least not so early.

She got up and walked to where the landscape hung. 'What you're saying is that you are really as blind as me. I think I am looking at your favourite picture, am I not? In one way I can't see it and in another way I can. You have explained it and given me a picture. Similarly, you can see it but you can't. You can only see it through the artist's eyes. He has interpreted the scene for you, given it meaning. Marjorie was on the way to doing that for us but . . .

She stood there looking at the picture, her drainpipe thin grey linen trousers with a light crease down the front and her high-waisted jacket emphasising her height and figure.

'He lives in the centre of London and, when he can afford it – usually when I give him some money – he rents a cottage in the west country and paints from morning till night, coming back to his studio here after a few weeks to finish them off. He won't leave London. He needs its energy, he says.'

'I am writing a composition inspired by Marjorie,' Perdita announced, cutting across him. 'At least I was. May I ask you a question?' She turned to face him. 'What was your first impression of me?'

Perdita Landberg, he realised by now, had a way of coming straight to the point.

'I was curious who you were, at least at the inquest. What had brought you there, were you a relative or a friend or, like me, a client.'

'And that's all?'

'It wasn't until I saw you on London Bridge making your way to the church that I saw you in a different light.' He paused, remembering the scene and the appropriateness of his description. He wondered if he should continue. 'That I saw you as a separate person. And then, afterwards at the church . . . '

'Usually it doesn't take that long,' she said. 'Most people realise that I am blind sooner.'

'My reaction to you didn't change because I found you were blind,' he said as he tried hard to remember his reaction in the church when she told him. 'It changed towards me because I felt a bit of a fool. And then I annoyed you and that was that.'

'It changes everything. It's a barrier.'

He assumed she was talking about her blindness. 'It didn't change what I thought about you. You were quite direct, almost brusque on the phone and you were the same when I met you. Those were the only judgements I'd had time to make.'

'And what do you think now?'

'After our extensive relationship, you mean, based on two cups of coffee and a tour around my gallery? Yes, you being blind does have a little impact on the owner of picture gallery. But it also helps because you can't see the two giant warts I have on my nose and you can't read the prices.'

She turned back to the picture. 'And how much did you pay for this landscape?'

'I paid ten thousand pounds in instalments based on the rent of a cottage near Fowey intermittently over two years.'

'Why were you seeing Marjorie?'

'For the same reason, I imagine, as you. Something was making us unhappy.'

'And it still is?'

'And it still is.'

It was later that he made the mistake. She had asked to see where he lived and he had taken her up to his large living room with its view over the Thames. She had gone over to the balcony and stood looking out over the river.

'If only you could see it,' he had said, innocently. She had her back to him and he could see her shake her head.

'I do not need life interpreting for me,' she said angrily. 'If only everyone would realise this.'

She had called a cab shortly afterwards and Toby was left, as he had been at the church, with the sense of having blundered but not being sure exactly how. The river was full now, which always lifted his spirits as did the thought of Perdita Landberg standing in front of his favourite picture, her hand on her hip, smiling back at him.

# Chapter 19

London can close in on you like a claw, Peter thought and of all the places to spend a night in the city, the chain hotel he was returning to after the funeral came pretty low down the list, close enough to Liverpool Street to not only hear the trains but to smell them as well. It had cost him more to travel from an outer suburb of London than it had to fly to the capital and there seemed no logic to this disparity. But these were minor thoughts as he came up the escalators at the station into the murky light of a London evening. Funerals should end with a wake but now he felt suspended between grief and celebration, a limbo which had begun when he saw the blind woman climb into the Bentley. They were leaving together, almost certainly former clients of Marjorie whilst he was left behind to be admonished by Marise for he knew not what. And then his thoughts in the train, that moment which Marjorie had anticipated would happen, a tantalising glimpse of a new way of looking at the furniture of his life and seeing for the first time why the arrangement didn't work, which of the pieces didn't fit. Your insights will give you the answer, she had counselled. These were competing emotions, jealousy caught up with frustration as incongruous as the soaring new skyscrapers were to the discreet terraces of Lombard Street. It was like the dissatisfaction he felt at the end of an unsuccessful mission and he was disinclined to go back to France feeling so disorientated. A practical man he knew there was only one route open to him and he called Marise's number from a bench in Finsbury Square. There was no response so he left a message and stood and turned back to the station. London is either the best city to be alone in or the worst and with nothing better to do he decided to take a risk. If it came to nothing it was better than sitting alone in a restaurant. He took the tube to Oxford Circus and walked up through Cavendish Square to its north-western corner where the pencil-straight Harley Street came to an end. Standing at its imaginary portal and looking up towards the Regent's Park at the end, the street had never looked less welcoming, the consulting rooms and private medical businesses closed, the windows dark. He walked up to Marjorie's door with little expectation that his ring on the bell would produce a response. In fact, he was just turning away from the door when it cracked open, the gap held in place by a chain. He could barely see Marise in the gloom until the light came on above the door.

Seeing who it was, she slipped the chain and opened the door. She had a glass of what looked like sherry in her right hand whilst the other hung on to the latch of the door. 'The wake was for friends, only,' she said with a frown.

It took a moment for him to assimilate what she had just told him, containing as it did two assumptions, one that he knew about the wake and the other that he was not a friend. Before he had time to explain himself she opened the door wider.

'Now that you are here, you may as well come in,' she said reluctantly, leading him through to a room he had never seen before, part living room, part conservatory which overlooked a small garden dominated by a mimosa. The room contained half a dozen people, old enough to be Marjorie's contemporaries, all in the process of leaving, finding and gathering bags and issuing goodbyes. He was not introduced and they slowly filed away as Marise showed them to the door. He wondered if this was a waiting room but it didn't have the feel of a public area. There were books and mementos and it had nothing of the neutral anonymity associated with doctors or dentists.

Marise returned and offered him a drink.

'She would have thought this entirely inappropriate,' she began, handing him a sherry and filling her own glass again. 'There was a fine line she did not like to cross,' Marise continued, taking small steps across to a chair in the window. Since Peter Harrington felt about as welcome as foot and mouth disease, he wondered why she had let him in. He still hadn't spoken and he knew he should wait because Marise was looking at him the way his headmaster used to when meting out punishment. There may have been pauses in his delivery but woe betides any one who interrupted.

'She rarely spoke of her clients. You were an exception, why I don't know.' Marise had put down her glass, her face grey and old and slack with drink. 'The occasional reference here and there but it was as if she contained it all in her mind.' Marise gestured with a finger to her head. 'She was brilliant, quite brilliant. She kept notes, of course, but she worked it all out in here.'

It was only the ambient light from the city coming in through the big windows that now defined her face. Peter Harrington decided that this was a waiting room after all and he sat and watched Marise decide what she was going to say next.

'At first you were just another client, but later she became more and more engaged in your story. It was as if she knew you. She had that ability, you know, to arrive at a destination before you because she knew where you were going.' She stopped here and played with her empty glass, perhaps deciding whether to fill it again. 'And where you had come from.'

In some ways Marise was confirming what Peter already knew, that Marjorie had guided Peter towards finding his own way forward like a parent placing a toy train back on the track after their child had knocked it over. But it was as if Marise was trying to tell him something else.

'I have asked myself why you, why you amongst the many.'

Peter absorbed this information, unsure of what she meant. He took a sip of his sherry and watched Marise fill her glass again, an old woman slowly letting go of the normal disciplines of her life after the death of her friend. Leaning forward, she turned on a small table light with a shade of faded pink silk and pushed it closer to him so that she could see him more clearly. She blinked slowly, her lids heavy and her focus unsure. He thought that she might fall asleep before long and decided that this was the time to speak.

'I wanted to ask you again if you could help put me in touch with the blind woman and her friend, the ones I assume were Marjorie's clients as well.' For a moment he thought he had been talking to himself as Marise appeared not to have heard him at all.

'They weren't friends. They aren't friends,' she said. 'And they shouldn't be friends.' Her shoulders slumped in weariness as though she was giving up some internal battle, as if suddenly she didn't care. 'I am too old and tired to care,' she said. 'Her name is Perdita Landberg. You can look her number up. There can only be one person in the book with a name like that.'

He waited for her to say more but it was as if she had given up the ghost. Shortly afterwards he watched her head loll forward, her mouth slacken and her breathing become deeper and slower. He let a few minutes pass before he got up and quietly left the room. As he shut the big black door to the street and heard its solid click behind him he considered whether he would ever enter it again. It was ten o'clock and he caught a tube back to the City, watching an empty bottle of alcopops roll around the carriage over the remains of a giveaway newspaper now scattered on the floor. He pushed away the bottle with his foot and a young man sitting opposite with shiny black hair held upright as if in permanent shock, smirked at him. He was wearing black mascara around his eyes which were looking at Peter Harrington's as if to say 'what are you going to do about it, mate?' He had seen this look often before, the insolent gaze of a young soldier deliberately pushed to extremes in a training exercise to see whether he could maintain his discipline. His spikey-haired friend opposite might have benefited from a similar experience.

Instead of returning to the hotel he turned in the opposite direction after leaving Liverpool Street and walked across Moorgate towards Spitalfields, where he had been told it was possible to eat until quite late. He found a restaurant, a glass cube with low bench seating laid out with geometric precision and ordered a carafe of red wine and a steak. Although it was just after eleven, the restaurant was half full of young people squeezing the last out of the day and Peter sat with their talk and laughter all around him. It was both a surprise and a consternation that Marjorie has spoken of him to Marise and he felt that some private part of him had escaped into the public domain. It made him consider the last session that they had together, the day before she died. Then, she was just a means to an end for him, yet to become a real person with a life of her own and a background. He hadn't fully understood Marjorie's statement that occasionally the therapeutic process was an encounter between two people and not simply one person treating another and he hadn't considered for a moment that their exchanges might have been two-way. At first he felt flattered that he had made an impact in this way and then a chilling thought came to him which caused him to stop eating and to push away his plate. What if she had been trying to tell him something which, in his obsession with himself, he had failed to detect? Perhaps she had crossed a boundary and stepped out of her role as a therapist, but he had been too preoccupied to see this? Was Marise hinting at this, blaming him for upsetting the protocols of Marjorie's work and maybe even accusing him of being partly to blame for her death?

It was only as he walked slowly back to his hotel that he remembered what Marise had said, that Marjorie had kept notes on her clients. It disturbed him to think that intimate details about him were out of her control, and as he walked through the deserted station he looked behind him but all he could see were the empty escalators on their endless loop.

# Chapter 20

It was almost eleven o'clock when Perdita phoned St Bede.

'I think I've done it again,' she said as soon as he picked up the receiver.

'Well, lucky old you, is all I can say.'

Henry never went to bed before midnight so she had no doubts about calling him this late. It was other doubts she wanted to discuss.

She launched straight in. 'I keep losing my temper.' She described what had happened at Toby's earlier that day, taking Henry through the stages of her meeting culminating with her abrupt departure.

'Well, I have several questions for you, my dear. What you call losing your temper seems a mild bout of irritability to me, something to which we are slightly prone.'

Perdita knew that he wasn't using the 'we' in the plural sense. 'You mean that you've noticed I can be bad tempered?'

'No, darling, irritable. There's a difference and, yes, I have noticed over the long span of our relationship that you don't tend to take prisoners and that your manner can be, shall we say, a little on the short side. But that's you darling. Oh, and by the way, since your therapist is no longer with us I shall be charging for taking her place.'

Perdita carried on regardless. 'The thing is, I'm not sure that my manner is not putting people off.'

'Darling, if people can't take the way you are then you shouldn't bother with them. It's part of the package, isn't it?'

'You don't think I can be a bit difficult?

'That's your charm, girl and don't let anyone tell you different. Listen, Perds, if you're free tomorrow we can talk about this. I was going to call you anyway. I've been asked to do a feature on

"The Symphonies", that new classical singing group of doll-like girls who make Barbie seem positively plain. They're recording a new album and I'm seeing them at the recording studio. It's not far from you, just the other side of the Euston Road, Blue Train Studios. I think you've used it yourself. Can you give up part of your precious Saturday? I wouldn't mind your musical ear on them. We can regard it as a quid pro quo for the ongoing therapy.'

It was at this moment an unexpected thought occurred to Perdita. It was now Friday night and she had hoped that this conversation with Henry would tell her if she should call Toby and apologise. She decided she couldn't wait for Saturday afternoon.

'Do you think I should phone Toby and talk to him about my sudden departure?'

'Ah, my gaydar is picking up something here. Are we just the teeniest bit interested in this man? Am I registering a bat squeak of *je ne sais quoi*? Now you *have* to see me on Saturday. Compulsory. Oh, and to answer your question, my guess is this. If he's got your interest then he already knows how to cope. That'll be twenty guineas please.'

And what St Bede predicted came to pass. The following morning, as she took her camomile tea in her familiar position at the keyboard, Toby called.

'Look,' he said, 'it's quite clear that I need a little more guidance on how to talk to you and I wonder if I might practise again soon?' He was quite serious and she listened hard to see if she could detect a smile in his voice. 'I wonder if we could have another rehearsal soon?'

'Well,' she said, 'it may not be entirely your fault.'

'Oh, I'm sure it is,' he said easily. 'But perhaps we can find out for certain. There is a curious exhibition of plant pictures on at Kew and, in case we don't get on inside, I considered the wide open spaces there perfect for another falling out. It's on Tuesday.'

The following day, she told St Bede how correct he had been

and he merely raised his eyebrows as if to say I told you so. The Symphonies were an entirely manufactured group both in composition and sound, put together for their looks rather than outstanding musical ability and then perfected in post-production. They were already very successful and hearing them put words to the slow movement of Bach's concerto for two violins was both disconcerting and impressive. Perdita watched Henry's masterly mix of praise and mockery, a performance in which the group, to their credit, played their part.

'It's all smoke and mirrors, darling,' he said afterwards, 'a case of spotting music amongst the marketing. Still, the Monkees became millionaires doing exactly the same thing and who's to knock it. Now, on to more important matters, the emotional life of one Perdita Landberg.' She took his arm and he led her through the back door of the Landmark Hotel and installed her in the ludicrously overblown sitting area. 'Darling, it's like a New Orlean's brothel on steroids, but it's comfortable and I'm all ears.'

'Well, it's nothing,' she began, despite having thought about what to say all morning.

'That won't do, darling and quite clearly it's not true.'

'It is, in a way. He was a client of Marjorie's as well and that's how we met. I really don't know much about him except he has a gallery in Wapping and is an art dealer.'

'Sounds intriguing, darling. You've been thrown together as birds wounded by life. How romantic.'

'I think your imagination is running away with you, St Bede. We barely know each other and – and, this is what I wanted to talk about, I sort of don't know how to deal with these situations and that's partly what I was seeing Marjorie about.'

'Darling, I've messed up so many myself I could keep a legion of therapists fully involved for years. But that's not the point, is it. We can't have you worried. You're simply too beautiful for that and the libretto won't allow for it.'

Although he tended to reduce everything to a joke, she knew

that Henry was listening and absorbing what she had to say and would, when he thought appropriate, intervene. She wasn't surprised, then, when he took her hand.

'You've never broached this before, Perds. You've always been forthright about the men in your life, few though there have been. Cavalier, if you can apply such a word to a woman, I would say.'

'Perhaps all that is just a smoke screen, Henry, a way of disguising what is really going on. Perhaps my bark is worse than my bite.'

'Well, of course it is, my dear. A lot of women – and men, let me tell you – have this as a quite natural stock in trade. It used to be called being hard to get in my day and this is my day, darling.' St Bede splashed fizzy water into her glass.

'I just worried that it might be more serious than that.'

'You're not ill, are you?' he asked, tightening his grip on her hand.

'No, well not physically, anyway. It's a mental block I have, not being able to see beyond a certain point in a relationship, a fear of what might happen next.'

'Now we are talking in riddles, young lady. I assume we are talking about that dirty yet glorious word sex.' She didn't say anything and he carried on anyway. 'Now we are entering a dark forest, if you'll excuse the obvious Freudian connotations. It is my considered view that there is no such thing as a normal sex life and people who insist that there is either don't have it, or have it in such a way that they don't know how to tell us. So, whatever sex life you have is fine, because it is normal to you.'

'I can't say there has been an abundance of sex in my life, St Bede. Normal, then, would be stretching it a bit far.'

He heard the tentativeness in her voice. 'Darling, I don't for one moment underestimate the added pressure your blindness brings on this situation – although I do remember being blind-folded once and it was, shall we say, most interesting, but that's another story – but, and I repeat myself – this is a two way street and this fellow that you've set your eyes on, as it were, will play his part in this. At least, he'd better.'

'Set my eyes on him. Do you think I have? And how did I do that? What has happened here? I used to ask Marjorie about this for it confuses me, trying to identify the process.'

'Maybe you try too hard, Perds. I feel like a parent sending a child off to take part in the school play. Just do your best, everything will be fine.'

'You do make me feel normal, St Bede. Thank you. He's asked me out to Kew next week and I suppose I am preparing my battle lines already.'

'Go to Kew with your man. If there's anything to this, then he'll be just as nervous. I'll be there in spirit, of course, lurking behind some giant tree, checking on progress. But you don't need instruction from me. I've never met a woman more sure of herself than you. And do you know something, I am quite prepared to share you with him. There. No greater magnanimity has man, even a gay one.'

And she giggled, joining in with St Bede as if they were teenagers in a coffee bar. It was only as they parted and she walked slowly down Marylebone High Street that she reminded herself that she really hadn't spoken to Henry about what troubled her most. If she had been seeing Marjorie today, what would she have told the therapist? 'I am seeing another one of your clients and I am scared rigid about what might happen.' And even as she had this thought she heard St Bede's voice in her head. 'Ask for reduced rates for seeing the pair of you together.' And, in front of Patisserie Valerie, she stopped and giggled again, causing an elderly woman waiting in the queue, to turn and smile as well.

When she got home she checked the phone for messages and was told that she had just one. She recognised the voice as Major Peter Harrington's even before he confirmed it himself. 'I saw you at the funeral yesterday. I was a patient of Dr Nielson and I have to return to France tomorrow. I would be very grateful if we could meet before then.' He left a mobile number, his northern accent repeating the numbers slowly and carefully. This was an afternoon of smiles for she had an image of a long line of men, all clients of the therapist, queuing up to meet her as though Marjorie had been running an escort service. As she had done with Toby, she called him back immediately.

'You must excuse me,' he said after their introductions, 'but my motives for wanting to see you are entirely selfish. I just wanted to talk about Marjorie with someone who knew her as I did.'

'I don't know that I can add to the sum of your knowledge,' Perdita told him 'but I am happy to meet.' And so it was that, two hours later in Patisserie Valerie she felt the warm handshake of Peter Harrington. The early part of their conversation mirrored that with Toby, the regret of not having known Marjorie and their disappointment of being stranded without her. She liked his easy manner, the unassuming way he explained himself but as they talked on he became less sure, his tone darker.

'Marise told me that Marjorie kept notes on her sessions and I had the impression that she may have seen them. I don't suppose it really matters in the scheme of things, but it did leave me feeling a little odd.'

Perdita felt that he was expecting a response to this news. 'I had never thought about this, whether she kept a record of what we said or not. I'm not sure I really care, to tell you the truth. But there's something more, isn't there?' Perdita had detected that Peter Harrington had more to say and there was more to "feeling a little odd" than he was saying.

'There is. Marise seemed to imply that Marjorie had been affected by me in some way, that I might have upset her.'

Perdita was aware of another layer of knowledge materialising about Marjorie which, paradoxically, only served to emphasise how little they actually knew about her. Peter had been afforded a glimpse of the real Marjorie, just as Perdita had caught the faintest hint of it during one of their last sessions.

'It is crass to say it, but I shall nevertheless,' said Perdita. 'It has come as a shock to realise that Marjorie Nielson had a life of her own. Why do you want to know more about it?' Perdita asked directly.

'I don't know, except to say at the moment I can't leave Marjorie. It is as if something happened which I only glimpsed through a crack in a door. I need to try and get a fuller picture.'

'I know exactly what you mean,' she said, for Peter's disquiet was her own. She, too, could not leave Marjorie Nielson alone and perhaps their reasons were similar. Perdita was trying to grasp the essential nature of a woman she hardly knew and Peter had perceived that there were events in his background that matched hers.

'I think I will have to return to the redoubtable Marise for further information,' Peter concluded, almost to himself.

Later, when Perdita sat at the piano, a Saturday night alone ahead of her, she was unable to move forward with the composition. The drifting air of uncertainty about Marjorie that Peter had introduced had not materialised into anything more solid and hovered, a distant sound, in the back of her mind.

# *Chapter 21*

**Notes on Peter Harrington. Age 48. Referred by Dr**
**William Jones at the Royal Scots Regiment. Problem**
**unspecified.**
**Session 12**

He arrives agitated, impatient, quite unlike himself and begins
speaking even as he sits down.

I bolted, didn't I?

That's an interesting choice of words, Peter.

Bolted, like a horse. I refused to take a fence and ran away. I know
the fence is there but I'm frightened to get over it.

Pause.

I don't know where to start.

You were talking about the army and you made reference to a
training exercise in Germany. Pause. His fists are now clenched, as if
steeling himself for what is ahead. Pause.

It was that winter in Germany. Pause.

What happened?

He stands. His hands are grasped together. He looks away into the
corner of the room and then abruptly sits.

It was a wretched affair. As a commanding officer it is not a good
idea to have friends in the ranks. There are soldiers you like more
than others, but distance is always advisable. You have to tell them
all what to do at some stage.

Pause.

I was against it from the start. There was no moon and the
weather forecast was foul, a force eight gale coming in from the
north. We would be protected to some extent by the trees, but the
paths would be treacherous.

Pause.

We were in a group of Warriors, support tanks, eight in all. We were split into four groups of two and I was in the second tank of the first group, with Freddie ahead of me. That's the chap I was talking about. Corporal Freddie Johnson. Came from nowhere, a dead loss background somewhere on the outskirts of Glasgow, but an absolute natural leader of men and destined for great things. It wasn't for him to express doubts about what we were going to do but I could see it in his face. Not fear, no. That would have transmitted itself to his group. There were four men in each of the Warriors. No, it was his concentration on what to do if things went wrong, the contingencies. He always wanted to be one step ahead. He did it naturally. We were in Germany, as I said and some of the terrain was good for the heavy tanks, but parts, where the trees began and we had to rise steeply, not good at all. A Warrior is not the biggest tank, but it still weighs around twenty-seven tons. As it is with the army, we were asked to go from A to B in the quickest time possible. No reason given, no questions asked. The rain was torrential and the amount of light we were allowed to use was minimal. Freddie was mounted in his turret ahead of me and I was in mine but it was almost impossible for us to see each other. Even if it had been a matter of life and death, we might not have set off. But this was only a training exercise, damn it.

Pause. He looks over to the corner again.

The first part, over the heath, was relatively straightforward and we made good speed but it became really treacherous when we turned up into the trees and the track, such as it was, became difficult to follow. Add to which, the Challengers – those are the really big, heavy tanks – had been up there the week before and churned the ground to pieces. We rose with difficulty, slipping a lot and the men behind me had the devil's own job keeping up. We pushed on for a couple of hours, climbing all the time, the weather in our faces now. We were in touch with each other and I could see Freddie slow to walking pace. I remember his words to this day. 'We have a steep camber to our right to I know not what'.

Pause.

To I know not what. And he didn't. The track was reasonably wide and he informed me that he would keep up to the left as much as he could, but that he was going to have to take it easy.

Pause.

A series of red blotches have now appeared on his neck, small islands on his brown skin.

I could hear the big engines rumble, inching the tank forward. I suppose in that moment I might have said something, ordered a halt, but I didn't. I'd like to think I couldn't, that there was no alternative but to move forward. But now I don't know and I never will. It will stay with me like a rock.

Pause.

Peter drops his head. He is frightened to continue, his face a series of grimaces.

I suppose Freddie weighed the options as I did. Creeping forward slowly, or moving forward quickly, either way trying to beat the camber. I had already decided on the faster option and I was about to tell him this when I heard him shout 'we're going' and then the roar as he opened the engines to try and counter the slide. I couldn't see it, but I heard the tank slipping rapidly sideways and I could hear his shouts in my headphones c'mon you bugger, c'mon get a grip, get a grip. And then nothing until we heard an awful crashing of trees even louder than our engines. I was appalled. It didn't seem possible but we're trained not to have emotions in these situations. I ordered a halt, dangerous on the slope but the best way of marking where the other tank had disappeared. As far as I could see, we were in a small clearing and the winds were whipping the rain into our faces. Looking down the slope there was nothing but black but we had to go down there. I asked the rest of the crew to secure the tank as best they could, driving wedges and pins against the downward side. It was easy to follow the slide of Freddie's tank. It had taken great slices out of the soft earth, but the further I got so the ground fell away more steeply until I could barely retrace my steps. When I got back to the tank I organised a rope feed and a harness and ordered an emergency call back to base.

He is back there now, completely and I feel his tension as palpably as he does.

It was a black void and I could see no shapes. Where the ground became steeper, not quite vertical, the skid marks stopped and I knew we had a major incident on our hands. It would have taken a miracle for the tank to have remained upright unless by the grace of god the trees, if there were any, had held it in place. Although I had asked for a light to be turned on the scene, it merely showed me the brow of the drop and made the blackness below even darker. I slithered over the edge and slid down. After about ten metres I came across the crushed undergrowth. There was no sound from below and I began to imagine what I was edging towards. With the torch I was carrying I could make out the jagged broken ends of larger conifers which had been snapped off by the falling tank. It was about twenty metres further on through the chaos of trees that I first saw it.

Pause.

He looks up at me, as if coming out of the memory.

You know that everything that I am telling you, I shouldn't? That I am breaking the Official Secrets Act? That I am doing something that I have been expressly told not to?

He was not expecting an answer. He had made a decision and it is clear that he has gone beyond the point where he could stop himself.

The underneath of the tank was facing me, like a great beetle tipped up and useless. Its fall had been slowed by the larger trees but it was the big outcrop of rock that had stopped it dead. It was terrible to be alone with it, terrible. The wind was screaming up the slope and the rain was relentless. For a second I felt useless, as if the logistics of the situation were beyond me and I looked back up the slope to where the light was vaguely outlining the shape of the cliff top. The top hatch of the tank was completely out of sight and all the time I was trying not to imagine the picture of Freddie mounted there. To access the hatch on the main body of the tank I had to get round and under it. Do you need me to tell you all of this? Do you? Is it necessary? Is it necessary to go through it all again?

*There is a break in his voice and he is willing himself forward*

I couldn't open the hatch. It was almost impossible to hold my position under the tank and get a firm enough grip on the lever. And I thought the tank might slip any minute, as if my pushing against the hatch would somehow dislodge all twenty odd tons. I could hear no sounds from the insides, just the roar of the trees and the water pouring down the slope and off the tank. I had to leave it and go back up and this was terrible for I knew I had to go back down and I dreaded what I would see. Do you understand? In this blackness in the middle of nowhere there would be men broken and mutilated. I took a corporal with me, using the same rope but carrying mallets and equipment. We sent further messages back to base saying this was a major incident and that medical back up was essential but it was going to be a long time before it arrived. Back under the tank we hammered open the hatch. I had hoped the noise would wake them, as if they'd been sleeping inside. One of the crew was directly on top of the opening, blocking it. It was a ghastly mess but by now I was beyond thinking, I was merely doing. We managed to manoeuvre him along so that his head was directly above us. He had a gash across the centre of his forehead and his nose was broken. We had to get him out in order to get in and it was awful to manhandle him upside with his body so broken. By now we had been joined by a third member of my crew with a stretcher but the slope was so steep that the only place we could put it was on the flat base of the underneath of the tank. He was dead. Quite dead. His neck broken and there was nothing we could do. By now the others had organised a rope line to allow us to haul up the stretcher. It was a sort of hell going in through the hatch. The floor, which was the ceiling, was covered in blood and the first of the men had broken his leg and his arm. But he had a pulse. We had a medic with us now from one of the other groups and he did the shots but all the time I knew what I had to face. And I can hardly tell you about it now.

Pause.

Freddie had been in the turret and he hadn't stood a chance. When I got round the other side of the tank, it was hanging over a vertical drop. At first, for just the tiniest moment, I wondered if he had been thrown free. But then my torch picked up the heavy drip of blood from the point where the upper hatch was wedged against the rock. His face was crushed and his upper body compressed. It was awful. And do you know what I thought? This is a violation. This should not have happened. This man's good life has been obliterated. For what? Tell me, for what?

An enormous revulsion is in me now, rising like a panic. I have to concentrate hard to keep it from Peter.

I wept, like I am now. I could do it there, in the rain and the noise. No one could hear, no one could see. But here, now, I feel such a fool. But there was worse, much worse. We had to leave poor Freddie there, crushed almost beyond recognition. Two dead and two seriously injured. It took us almost three hours to get the others up the slope and only towards the end did the weariness set in.

Pause.

But then they arrived. They found me in the rain and the dark. Even the way they spoke to me was ominous. We sat in the back of a truck, it was like a small metal office and the rain thundered like a warning on the roof. I wasn't to say anything about this. It never happened. They would create the official version and I was to tell my men not to say a word about it. I wanted to rise up and strike them, but I was a soldier. I had twenty years of taking orders. Freddie's parents still don't know the truth. Lost in a routine training accident, they were told. It was a lie and I did nothing. And now I feel Freddie's death like a cold wet towel around me, condemning me for what I failed to do. I'm sorry. I have spoken too long.

It is hard for me to speak, but he doesn't notice.

Pause.

And what do you feel now, Peter?

Empty. I feel almost as tired as I did on that hillside. And will this do any good? And was I right to tell you?

You were right, Peter.


**End of session**

As Peter was telling his story I had terrible flashbacks, images I have not relived for many years, some of which I cannot remember seeing before. It was as if his own tension, his description of the violation of young Freddie was a description of what happened to me. The army carelessly abusing someone innocently living their life. Afterwards I had to wash, like I did then all those years ago. I must write more about this, but I can't now. My hands are shaking. Did I think I had cured myself? Of course not, there is no real recovery from that. Freddie did not have a life to relive his trauma. That was taken from him. Would it have been better for me to perish in those ruins as he did on that bleak hillside? Was it Peter Harrington who carried the burden and the guilt just as I have all these years? Do I see in him a fellow traveller, someone who has unwittingly awakened the old wounds in me? I am an old woman now, not given to regret, but for a moment today I saw, too, that I have been carrying a black cloud, a legacy that has haunted me all my days, that has meant that I should be childless and sexless all my life. Is this something I should have put up with, like Peter did? Was I bound by the laws of secrecy? I have been clever enough to fool myself, to hide the truth and to pretend to others that somehow I am the sage one when all along I have been fooling myself. I did well to survive for so long, to keep it hidden. Peter will be free now, he will recover and the memory of Freddie will take its correct proportion in his life. But what about me? It is all too late now, too late to get back what I had, too far to go. In that terrible moment all those years ago I was given my life's work and my life's burden, the reason to live and the reason to die. I was crushed like Freddie but I had to carry on living.

# Chapter 22

He worked from what used to be a pram factory on the other side of the river from Toby's gallery, a first floor studio with bare concrete walls and floors and long metal windows which overlooked the rows of arches that carry the railway out of London Bridge station. The picture propped in the middle of the room recorded a very different view, a moorland top of purple heather and above it a rushing sky in greys and blues. Toby walked up to it and examined it closely and then walked back a few paces before turning again and looking at it anew. It always astounded Toby how the detail made up the whole, how tiny bundles of colour, like specimens under a microscope, made sense when viewed from a distance. It was like making sense of life, he thought. He had got stuck with a detail, whatever it was and it was preventing him seeing the whole picture and getting it in perspective.

The artist, Laurence Cooper, was sitting on a high wooden stool watching him.

'Thank you for buying in my picture at the gallery.'

'I didn't buy it in, as you put it,' Toby rejoined. 'I bought it for me, for my private collection. If I took pity on my artists, I would be broke. It may surprise you to learn that I like your work.' Laurence Cooper watched him quizzically, always in need of reassurance.

'You showed me some of your smaller work last time and there are one or two I would like to see again. I remember one in particular . . .'

' . . . beach and rock,' the artist picked up, 'at least that's what you called it.' He went over to a line of pictures stacked separately under the window with their backs to the studio. He held one up for Toby. 'This one, I think.'

Toby nodded. It was an abstract and the predominant colours, pink, white and mauve seemed in places to bleed into each other like the words running through the centre of a piece of rock, the sort he used to buy on holiday as a child. Again, a random series of lines, some running vertically, others horizontally defining he knew not what but entirely fascinating, drawing him into its interior. Perdita said that he was accepting the view of the artist, that Laurence Cooper had done the seeing for him, but this morning, viewing the picture again, Toby realised that he was bringing elements of his own to the picture and in some ways completing it.

At that moment Toby's mobile rang and he broke away to answer it having seen that the call was from his father.

'I'm in the middle of something now,' he said quickly, 'can I call you back.' He might just as well never have spoken.

'Listen, I need you here tomorrow. I want to run things through with my lawyer. He'll be arriving about eleven. Can I rely on you?'

'No, I'm afraid you can't. I am busy all day.'

'I thought you might like to be down here, tomorrow of all days.'

Toby paused for a moment and then realised the truth of what his father had said, playing the trump card, the passing shot as he so often did. Toby had forgotten that tomorrow was the anniversary of his mother's death, an occasion which Charles Browning always marked with faux solemnity and much red wine and whisky. Toby was surprised that his father was going through the dance this year with his second marriage looming, but then he wouldn't spare Penny Trottman's feelings any more than his son's.

'You had forgotten, hadn't you?'

Toby looked over to Laurence, who was watching him and who could see the discomfort on his face. And then he shifted his gaze to the picture and remembered the purpose of his visit.

'Are you there?' his father demanded, irritated.

'I am, but I won't be tomorrow, I'm afraid. I have a very important meeting which I can't, indeed don't want to, break.' His father had rung off even before he had finished.

The picture held him even as the phone buzzed in his ear. When he had first seen it, a few weeks ago, he had instinctively liked it, the accumulation of shapes and colours pleasing him in ways he chose not to identify. But now he thought he recognised why. He bought it and returned over Tower Bridge, the picture tucked it under his arm like a trophy.

When he arrived home he propped it on a shelf against a wall in the living room, the colours of the brick complementing the pinks and mauves of the picture so that it looked immediately as if it had always been there. Toby Browning felt unusually satisfied, a feeling rare enough for him to pause and register it with a broad smile which was noticed by the his two assistants carefully bubble wrapping pictures in the gallery below. The coincidence was merely accidental, thought Toby, but he always remembered Marjorie saying that accidents are reminders of unfinished business. The rational in Toby fought to down play the romantic, that it was just chance that he was going to Kew with Perdita on the same day that his mother died. Of course it signified nothing, but then again, wasn't it like looking at pictures? It was the way you looked at them. You could give them whatever significance you wanted.

*       *       *

For some reason, Perdita knew that he would be on time. She had tried to work without success and had been ready for ages before his call to tell her he was five minutes away. She stood in the middle of the room and checked herself, starting with her hair and then her clothes, feeling for creases, undone buttons, wisps of wayward hair. She could have done with St Bede now, but he had been too busy. 'You will have to go into battle without me, darling. Just think Henry V, or in your case, Joan of Arc.' She stood very still in the middle of the room so that when the door buzzer sounded she jumped, even though she had been expecting it.

'Good morning,' he said as he met her at the door. 'My car is about to be hijacked by a team of wardens so grab me and we'll make haste.' She walked quickly by his side, holding on to his arm.

'Oh bugger,' he said. And she heard him cut short the next sentence. 'But that's so unfair, I had to park here because I was picking up someone who . . . a friend of mine.'

'That's no excuse, sir.'

'Well that's a good way to start the day,' she said by way of commiseration as they drove away.

'Do you think that it is an omen for the rest of the day?' he replied.

'Oh, I'm sure it presages mayhem ahead,' she said, picking up his tone of voice. 'Perhaps we should turn back immediately.'

'Perhaps I should warn you about the pictures now, then,' Toby responded.

'I'm all ears.'

'Well, they're Dutch still lives. Lots and lots of pictures without people, great bunches of flowers by artists like Van Haysum, who might have invented the chocolate box cover. And masses of fruit, quinces and pomegranates, by Nellius. Beautifully done, of course.'

'You don't seem too keen,' she said, enjoying the way he spoke about the pictures. He was making no concessions to her at all. 'I wonder why you are going?'

'Ah,' he said, 'there is a little method in my madness. There are a couple of works I'm particularly keen to see that rarely get to be shown here.'

The car purred along as she listened to him. She knew that he was only slightly taller than her, with wide capable hands and from the hairs on those hands she imagined he had a head of coarse, dark, curly hair. And she was aware that he was looking at her now and she wondered again about the disparity of their points of view. He could absorb her appearance whilst she could only guess at his and it led her to ask again, since she couldn't see herself, what he was seeing when he looked at her? She didn't think it unfair that she couldn't see him, only that it made the process slower. Whether it was simpler or more complicated, she couldn't tell.

'Where are you now?' she heard him say.

'I was wondering what you saw when you looked at me?'

'Wouldn't the more interesting question be, what do you see when you look at me?'

'Well,' she said, 'it is the difference between the two perceptions that puzzles me.'

'Why? Aren't we both hindered in similar ways? You can't be led by my looks, such as they are, but I can be misled by yours.'

'So, let me ask my question again: what do you see when you look at me?'

The car thrummed along, a quiet cocoon sealed from the noise of a steady stream of traffic heading westwards. She waited for the answer.

'The first two times I met you, I really didn't see you. I looked, but didn't see. I was too wrapped up in myself. You asked me a similar question at the gallery and I didn't answer fully. Perhaps I didn't understand then, but I think your question is purely physical and the first time I saw you in that way was at the cemetery. I saw a woman of uncommon beauty.'

She sat and absorbed this statement.

'And the uncommon,' by the way, 'in no way relates to your blindness. I thought I would mention this quickly before you grabbed the hand brake and tried to get out.'

'Do you know, Mr Browning, that hadn't crossed my mind. But I need to answer your question now which, as it happens, I don't think is more interesting. Just different. When you phoned me I remembered instantly your voice from the pavement in Harley Street. I think, in the main, you are persuasive and kind. Attractive but, I think, guarded.'

'But you haven't answered the question,' he responded. 'Those are internal features, if you like. What about the outside?'

Exactly, she thought. 'I think you may have to do this for me, Mr Browning. To complete the picture for me.'

'Five feet ten, curly dark hair, rather swarthy in fact. If I was being kind, I would say stocky rather than fat. I have blue eyes and I tend to wear blue or grey clothes. That is a brief survey of the landscape of one Toby Browning.'

She again took his arm as they walked into the Gardens, a high wind catching the trees in a rush of sound. The air was warm and full of the smells of orange blossom and roses.

'What made you go into the art world?' she asked him, as she felt her hair blown this way and that, like corn in a field.

'It's a long story,' he said, 'but in short, the violin,' he answered.

She waited for him to continue but he remained quiet. 'That's a tiny bit of a non-sequitur.'

'I know it is, but nevertheless it is true. And, as I say, it is a long story.'

Perdita sensed his evasiveness come down like a fog, clouding his easy manner. She could even feel his body tense. They both seemed adept at getting under each other's skins.

'We are walking towards the Marianne North Gallery, named after one of those enduring Victoria women who managed to paint exotic plants in the middle of steaming jungles wearing a full crinoline.'

He was on safer ground now and she chose not to divert him. 'Quite a formidable woman, then'.

'Not in your class, though.'

They had walked into a large room with a musty smell which he escorted her around, briefly describing the pictures rather as he had in his own gallery, except this time he was much less complimentary. 'You cannot believe the amount of work that has gone into this painting. Flowers, fruit, insects and a spider's web in the shape of a skull. Some of the fruit is rotten and some of the flowers are half dead. This is the subtle symbolism of period. The transience of life summed up in oils.'

'And what of the paintings you do like?' she asked. 'Are they symbolic as well?'

'Well,' he said, and she could hear the smile in his voice, 'I should say so.'

They wandered on a little further and then she felt him stop. 'This picture is so modern,' he said, 'it could have been painted yesterday. It is wonderfully realistic, a bunch of white asparagus bound together with brown string on a thick wooden table. The asparagus seem to exude their own light. I would love this picture in my kitchen.'

She asked the question spontaneously, unthinkingly exposing herself. 'And the symbolism?' She could sense his glimpse towards her.

'Nothing subtle about that, you won't be surprised to hear. It's all sexual. The shape of the asparagus, of course, and the fact that asparagus was meant to have aphrodisiac qualities.'

'Of course,' she said.

'Not that I would want this picture for its connotations. It's just such a fabulous piece. Three hundred years ahead of its time. The artist, Adriaen Coorte, would have been very much at home in Hoxton.'

Perdita could not help but think of the white fleshy stalks and the spear shaped ends, the clumsy symbolism underlining her own vulnerability. In her mind she could see the graphic representation but not the real thing. Had it always worked this way round in painting? Was the symbolism a substitute for what you couldn't have or was it deliberately the other way round, a reminder of what you had experienced and knew?

'Your turn to be quiet,' Toby said to her, acknowledging at the same time his own quietness earlier. 'A little lunch, I think. And I believe the asparagus season is over.'

And so she took his arm again and walked back across the flat gardens towards Kew village, where he said there was a small café where they could eat outside. They sat under a cherry tree and she could feel the dappled light play on and off her face. He read her the short menu and she ordered an omelette and salad and Toby a plate of charcuterie. As an afterthought, he called for a half carafe of white wine.

'Are all your visits this quick?' she asked him.

'Looking at pictures is like wine tasting,' Toby replied. 'The more you taste at any one session, the more muddled you become. There is a great deal of art and not much of it is any good.'

'You sound very decisive,' she said, half mockingly.

He paused before answering. 'In this respect, I probably am, but in other ways I am hopeless. I often find myself in situations which I positively dislike which I just seem to blunder into.'

'Do you know, we have spent the whole morning together and neither of us has mentioned Marjorie Nielson?'

'Well, I was about to say, apropos my last remark, that I have only ever admitted that to Marjorie. So we've both brought her up, so to speak.'

Was Marjorie Nielson the reason why they were together today, or had their relationship moved on? Is there a point where this outing becomes a date, Perdita wondered and has that line been crossed already?

'So why do you think you told me?'

'I'm not sure I can answer that. It can't be your kind and sympathetic character, can it?' He laughed as he said this, putting his hand momentarily on the back of hers just long enough for her to feel its warmth.

'You may have been trying to tell me that this is another one of those situations you find yourself in but where you'd rather not be.' The wind rustled the leaves above her and carried with it a platform announcement from the nearby station

'No, you saved me from one of those,' Toby replied. 'And please don't misunderstand that. I can't think of anywhere I would rather be than here.'

She had instinctively been about to reply caustically that she was glad that she had been able to help him out but it was as if he had second guessed her reaction.

'It's odd,' he continued, 'but I would normally be down with my father celebrating, if that is the right word, the anniversary of the death of my mother. I'm puzzled that he does it. Perhaps it is to make me feel uncomfortable. That I am not going and that I am happy to be here instead is, well, I don't know . . . '

She waited for him to finish his sentence and she assumed he was looking away from her, trying to find what he wanted to say. It was as if a piece of important information was being offered over an invisible threshold, almost unnoticed.

'My mother was an attractive but somewhat indecisive woman who, I'm afraid, drew a rather short lot in life, namely my father. I'd like to think one of the reasons he wants me to mark the occasion of her death with him is guilt, but even that would be an emotion too far for him I think.'

'Do I gather that you don't get on with him?'

'I think what I was trying to do was give you an answer about why I was happy to be here today. You see, my father is a highly persuasive and manipulative man. It's often hard to say no to him.'

'But you did.'

'I think that's what I'm trying to tell you.'

She felt very comfortable with this man. 'You're giving me a sort of convoluted compliment, I think,' she said.

'And I am smiling in agreement,' he said.

As Perdita had admitted in a roundabout way to St Bede, her default setting was intolerance verging on indignation, at one and the same time both critical and defensive. It was made worse when people assumed that this was the result of her blindness: 'poor girl, no wonder she's like that.' Toby had dealt with this instinctive behaviour from her almost as if it didn't exist, that he hadn't heard. It allowed her to relax with him in a way she experienced only rarely. She could feel that her shoulders had dropped, as though her body had given up expecting to be on permanent alert.

'Is that why you were seeing Marjorie?' she asked. 'Your father.'

'I'm sure he's tangled up in it somewhere, he usually is. I think there were several issues I was seeing her about.'

He drove her back to Marylebone High Street. Although they barely spoke, she felt comfortable in the silence and it was only as they came to a stop that she fully realised that she wanted things to continue.

'Will you tell me about the violin, at some stage?' She didn't really know why she asked the question. It seemed at odds with the way she was thinking, but it just presented itself to her.

He took her hand and kissed it lightly. 'I'm not sure that it is not you who is going to tell me about the violin,' he said, before helping her out of the car and thanking her for the day. The line had been crossed.

## Chapter 23

Peter Harrington had cancelled his flight back to France, re-booking it for later in the week. He had tried calling Marise without success over the weekend and on Monday all he got was her recorded voice once again asking him to leave a message. Impatient, he went again to Harley Street in the vague hope that he would catch her there. Her remarks continued to roll around in his mind, incomplete and illogical and he knew he needed to talk to her before he returned to France. He was firmly in the grip of London now and on Monday night he ventured beyond Spitalfields, moving eastwards through the streets until he came to an old fashioned pub with fading gold letters on the windows announcing public bar and lounge bar. He chose the first and entered a world which appeared not to have changed for fifty years and raised his first pint to the memory of Marjorie Nielson. He hadn't known what to expect after he had told her about Freddie and the accident. Reliving the event and telling it to someone for the first time was a strange experience which seemed to involve two sides of him, one in control and the other being led by a compulsion he couldn't stop. Until he spoke to Marjorie, the conflict between the two sides had been taking place internally. He hadn't known what to expect afterwards and before he had time to be aware of any changes, she had died. It was like having climbed Everest with a colleague only for him to die on the descent, thereby taking away the joy of the achievement. Looking back on the time since that final session, there had been a change in him. From the smokey pub in Bethnal Green he could now see the garden at Natalie Dinan's, the thin cypresses and stubby palm trees. He had taken for granted his decision to go and paint there, to invite himself into her property. That in itself was out of character, but it was much more than that. Peter had never shared his paintings before and particularly not his sketchbooks. Above it all, though, he was painting again. The landscape of the Massif des Maures he had captured in water colour was a reflection of himself, he realised, calmer and simpler and more powerful. He had the confidence and desire to paint it, to express himself again and at that moment his art, until then a private passion, became a proper part of his life. He wondered if Marjorie had known this would happen, that the release of Freddie's story would free up his system and allow him to function again. But what had it done to her? He was still left with Marise's words, unresolved and threatening and he knew that he had to pursue this both for himself and for Marjorie.

Marise called him the following morning. Her voice was cold. It implied that she felt it was her duty to respond to his messages rather than her wish.

'I don't think I can help you any further,' she said, 'and nor do I think I should. It's not what Marjorie would have wanted.'

'Why not?' Peter could not keep the impatience out of his voice. 'How do you know what Marjorie would have wanted? You said that she spoke of me and you indicated that things I said may have had some impact on her. I don't like the feeling I may have been responsible for upsetting her.'

'Well, it's too late now Major Harrington. What is past is past.' She said this so bitterly that once again he was left feeling that it was he that was at fault for what happened to Marjorie.

'You surely can't be blaming me for her death?' Before he could finish speaking, she put down the receiver and he was left with the ring tone. He lay back on his bed in the hotel room. What is past is past, she had said. But Peter Harrington knew this wasn't true, that the past is often in the present, hidden in the system and stopping it working properly. He was not going to allow this piece of unfinished business to plague him and he began to think through the various stages he had been through since her death. He knew that Perdita wasn't able to clarify the situation any further but there were other people at the inquest and the funeral. Surely there was another way to move forward?

Half an hour later he called the Coroner's Office in St Pancras and was given a list of those witnesses who had spoken at the inquest. It was only then that a very simple fact occurred to him. Marjorie Nielson had died at home and not in Harley Street. It didn't take him long to find her address and since there are very few Vera Stanovics in the telephone book, the number of the cleaner who had found her body. He called it immediately and a voice-message told him to try a mobile number since she worked during the day.

'Yes, this is Vera. Who is this?'

He recalled now the thick accent and the face of the woman in the witness box. 'I'm Major Harrington, I was at the inquest into Marjorie Nielson's death and I wonder if you might help me answer a couple of questions?'

'I don't know how I could help, but if it means helping the doctor then of course I will try.'

'In one way it is all about helping Dr Nielson,' he said. He arranged to meet her when she finished her last job, at six o'clock, in a café in Hampstead. Since it was only midday, he took a sketchbook and some crayons and caught a tube up to the fashionable village to the north of the city. He walked to the Heath and made his way to the top of Parliament Hill, not far from where he knew Marjorie had lived. He looked down over London, impossibly large and unknowable.

There were a series of benches on the brow of the hill and from time to time different people would stop and look at the view and then move on. Seeing them in the foreground gave some scale to what was behind, so he began to make quick sketches of them: two young boys who had been playing with kites, an old woman and her equally elderly dog, a group of teenage girls with cigarettes and a radio. And all the time, at regular intervals, the planes roaring overhead, turning and beginning their descent into Heathrow. Marjorie must have sat here, he thought and he added a sketch of the therapist, trying to remember the contours of her face, the way she wore her small wire glasses on the end of her nose. In the end, he had drawn her on the right hand side of the sketchbook, overlooking the other figures opposite, as if she was regarding them with amused detachment. He then devoted the next two pages to the clouds which hung over the scene as if supported by invisible strings. He turned his sketchbook upright to give a sense of height, with just a hint of London at the bottom dominated by a massive sky. When he had finished he compared the two double pages, the first an observation of the particular and the second, the arena in which they lived. He hadn't planned either and yet they existed comfortably as a pair.

A wind was pushing up the hill as he made his way down off the Heath, between the ponds that were being shared by bathers and a pair of noisy coots. He arrived early at the café and he waited. He saw her before she saw him, a thin and determined looking woman in a coat that looked too warm for the day. It was an odd meeting, he thought, between the client of a therapist and her cleaner.

'It was good of you to meet me,' he said sincerely, seeing a degree of apprehension in her face. They ordered tea and he ventured a first question.

'I saw you speak so well at the inquest. You were quite clearly very close to Dr Nielson. How have you coped since?'

'It is difficult for me to forget finding her there, that morning. It is a memory I will not forget. Perhaps I don't want to forget it, I don't know. I have lots of other images of her, but this one always comes up first.'

'That's quite understandable. You had known her a long time.'

'I am Yugoslavian. I came here in the troubles, after I had lost my home and my husband. They were bad times. But she knew, Marjorie knew about me. I applied for a job as a cleaner and I met her and it was as if she knew my story before I told her.'

'How do you think she knew?'

'She had her family taken from her, too. She knew the pain of separation.'

'Did she tell you about this?'

'Not in detail, no. She just said that war does terrible things and that she had suffered like me'

'Do you think she ever got over this?' He was surprised that the conversation had moved so quickly to this point.

'That was her job, wasn't it? She had an ability to help others. She would have known pain herself to do this, but she knew how to do deal with it.'

Peter hesitated. 'Could you tell me again about that morning? When and where you found her.'

'Why do you want to know?'

'I will tell you the truth, Vera. Like you, I am puzzled why Marjorie died and Marise Dubarry hinted that there may have been something I said which had upset Dr Nielson.' He could see her regarding him, as if his doubts echoed her own.

'The Coroner said she had died of natural causes. I could not believe that. She was too strong, but then who knows what takes us away in the end . . . ' Her words trailed away and he waited for her to continue.

'She always worked early. She didn't sleep well, she told me. She always liked me to go up there when I arrived. She had a room with a beautiful view, right over all London. She used to sit in the window and that's where she was when I found her.'

'Could you tell what she had been doing?'

'When you are in shock, Mr Harrington, you don't see. You go blind.'

'But you said she was at her desk. Can you remember anything else?' Peter watched a faraway look come over her face as she attempted to recall that spring morning, to look again at the scene that had so shocked her.

'There was nothing unusual. She appeared to be working, as she usually did at that time of day. She told me she sometimes brought her work home with her because she saw things differently there.'

'How do you know she was working?'

'How do I know she was working?' She repeated the question to herself. 'I just did. She had papers on the desk and I assumed she was reading them. But she wasn't. She was dead. I can see it now.'

'What happened to the papers?'

She looked at him, as if trying to weight the importance of his question.

'I assume they are still there. I was told not to touch the room and I have not been back in there since. I don't want to.'

'But you still clean the house?'

'I do. I cannot stop myself. I suppose it is a way of staying connected. There appears to be no will and since there is no family . . . ' She shook her head. 'Except Marise, I suppose, but then she is not real family.'

Outside a bus pulled up with a hiss of breaks, the red bulk filling the window and Peter Harrington called for more tea. He wasn't sure how she would take his next question. 'Would it be possible for me to see the room? I would like to put this issue to rest.'

She once again looked at him, this time a penetrating stare into his eyes which he met without blinking. He wondered if she was searching for a reason to say no.

'In Croatia my mother used to say to me that when I was asked a difficult question that I should ask my heart and I should ask my head. My head says no, for reasons I am not sure, but my heart says yes, for Dr Nielson. And I suppose I trust you Major Harrington.'

They walked back towards the Heath, turning up the hill just beyond the station towards a development of large Victorian houses which had somehow been allowed to bite off a chunk of the precious green space. The house was at the top of the hill, a substantial villa in pale yellow brick. He felt slightly hesitant now, aware that he was about to invade someone's private space. He looked down at the York stone pathway that led to the front door and thought of Marjorie returning here after a day of hearing other people's problems. Was she able to leave them behind with professional detachment or did some stay with her demanding her attention, broken jigsaws insisting that she put the parts together?

Vera led the way as they climbed the four flights of stairs which narrowed the higher up the house they went.

'I don't think I can go in,' she informed him at the top. 'Already I am reminded of that day. I will be downstairs.'

Peter Harrington nodded at her and watched her thin frame disappear silently down the carpeted stairs. Breathing in, he pushed open the door and entered the world of Dr Marjorie Nielson. He stood still for a moment unable to take it all in, for around him now was the real evidence that Marjorie Nielson had another life, a world beyond her clients. He rested his hand against a tall wooden cabinet by the door as if needing to steady himself. He was beginning to focus now, to separate the detail, the pictures on the walls, the framed photograph on the table, the comfortable chair with the embroidered cushion and on the desk a doll with a polka dot dress. He surveyed the desk carefully from a distance as he might have done before approaching an object he believed might have been booby trapped. He could see the brown manila folder with the papers inside fanning outwards. Cautiously, he moved closer and then he froze in mid step, his knees slightly bent, one arm slightly forward, the other its mirror behind him. He could read his name: Major Peter Harrington and it shocked him so profoundly that for a moment he was unable to move. And then he turned and left the room, walking quickly down the stairs to where he found Vera Stanovic sitting at a table in the kitchen.

'Vera. There's a folder on her desk with my name on it.'

'I know,' she said, quietly. 'Take it.'

# Chapter 24

It was fine until the phone call.

Toby had spent the morning in the hands of his framer and he had experienced the double pleasure of watching an expert at work whilst carrying a feeling of bonhomie that had been with him since he left Perdita the day before. It was like, he thought, the excitement you had as a child on the morning of your birthday. The workshops were a jumble of run down buildings at the centre of an enormous north London roundabout, an oasis of craftsmanship infused with the smell of wood and varnish and decorated with a random geometry of frames and mounts. Even great art can be spoiled by poor framing and Toby enjoyed the process by which the framer arrived at the right shape and thickness of a frame and the colour and size of a mount. It was a delicate process of matching, a balance that, when right, is never noticed and taken entirely for granted.

The picture Toby had bought the day before now lay on the wide table in front of him surrounded by various samples of frame which were being shuffled to different corners of the work. Toby had no need to explain what he wanted, which he often did in the early days, because he was nearly always wrong. The framer explained how he was going to take an off-white streak, running vertically down part of the picture, as his guide and showed Toby a flat, unfinished, corner of wood over which he painted a thin wash of white paint. When it had dried, the grain of the wood had come through giving the frame a washed-out look. It was at one and the same time obvious and perfect. Toby was delighted and it was as he was waiting for the frame to dry that Perdita rang. He was smiling even before he heard her voice.

'I wanted to thank you for yesterday,' she said, 'and to wonder if I might return the favour by offering you a glimpse into my world?'

'I thought you had already.'

'The tiniest corner, Mr Browning, the tiniest corner. There is more, I assure you.'

'Of that I have no doubt,' he said, enjoying hearing the combative tone of her voice again. It was this very edginess that he found compelling. Perdita Landberg was the opposite of demure and did not rest on the wiles of her femininity. Perhaps because she couldn't see her beauty, she didn't believe it and therefore wasn't able to be seduced by it.

'I want to take you to a concert tomorrow. Well, concert is too grand a word. A recital. Some of my friends will be playing. There is one problem, though. It will be contemporary classical music. I don't know what you like.'

Toby hesitated just momentarily, as if his eye had been caught by an unusual and disconcerting movement in the distance which he could not identify, the merest shadow. As soon as it arrived, it was gone, pushed to one side as if it had never happened but Toby was aware that even in the short time that they had known each other, Perdita would detect this tiny pause.

'Is it me, the music or are you washing your hair tomorrow night? Or is there someone lurking in the background that I don't know about?'

'None of the above, Perdita. I was suddenly distracted. Of course I would love to come with you.'

'I can't say I am swept away by your enthusiasm. Anyway, you'll find me in the Barbican about seven tomorrow evening. In the foyer. Where the recital is taking place.'

And with a series of staccato sentences she was gone and he looked at his mobile as though he had been accidentally cut off. Above him the empty frames hung in their random disorder, moving slightly in the breeze of an open door, their blankness demanding his attention. For Toby, something had changed. Perdita Landberg had moved from being part of his peripheral vision to being the focus of his attention and in so doing Marjorie Nielson had taken the opposite route. Indeed, the therapist was not the only part of his life that had begun to take on a different proportion in his thoughts. It was as if the kaleidoscope had been shaken into a pattern that was altogether more comfortable, or a frame changed to better suit a picture. Nevertheless, somewhere in this realignment there was a flaw, leaving Toby with an uneasy feeling, as though he was being pulled somewhere he didn't want to be, towards a catastrophe he could not identify. It was a feeling he knew only too well, but he banished this uneasiness to the back of his mind. He could not deny, however, that a small cloud had passed between him and the sun.

*   *   *

Perdita was not sure that she had turned off the phone in anger or frustration, or both. She paused to examine what had happened in just the few seconds between calling Toby and ending their conversation. What trip wire had triggered a response that was almost beyond her control? She was aware that calling Toby had been an important step and she had approached thinking about it cautiously at first and then, in the end, almost compulsively. No matter how she and her parents had fought the traditional responses to blindness, at a certain point in Perdita's life it had caught up with her and she had been separated off from her contemporaries. It was only music that had stopped her disappearing into a ghetto of the blind but even so she was wounded by the knowledge that she could not do everything her sighted friends were able to do. The young are merciless about anything abnormal and Perdita's blindness was an easy target. It was during these days that she learned and perfected the instinctive defence mechanisms which she employed so freely now. But the fact remained that she was damaged in ways that she could only partly identify. Telephoning Toby was an important step, made even more so by her enjoyment of the trip to Kew. She was not experienced in reading the runes of a developing relationship so the call was, in more ways than one, an act of blind faith. She knew enough about voices to know that he had been pleased to hear from her but the spontaneous delight to her proposal was missing and she found this hard to bear. His hesitation was a vital clue to someone trained to interpret silence and to pick up the most subtle of changes in voice. Was this just part of the package that St Bede had said was integrally her, or did it speak of something else?

Her left hand sought the keys at the extreme end of the keyboard and she rolled five notes together whose deep tones told her as much as she needed to know about her mood. With her right hand, she now found a series of lighter notes which played against the reverberations of the bass which lingered under them. A mix of darkness and light made interesting only by their conjunction. She continued the experimentation, with the base clef sometimes dominating the treble and then the reverse. After an hour, she stopped and recorded the accumulation of ideas and then played it back, hearing unexpected patterns. She made further adjustments, leaning over the piano so that at times her ear was inches from the keys. Gradually she organised her emotions audibly so that when she played them back she could think what they might mean and where they fitted. Was this a continuation of what she had been writing about Marjorie? No, she felt it was a transition from what the therapist had inspired into a new dimension which, as yet, had an imperfect shape. She wanted to phone Toby again and tell him what had happened, but she didn't know how, so she turned again to the keyboard and tried to find a phrase or theme which would join the new work with what she had already written. She worked on but the conjunction was tantalisingly elusive and she went to bed with her head full of snatches of piano each suggesting a way forward but never quite coming together.

The following morning, she called St Bede for help.

'But, my dear, how exciting. A date. I shall be round *tout de suite* – well, at lunch time, at least. You can tell me all then.'

Later, she told him about the phone call.

'Well, darling, perhaps you were expecting quite a lot from him. Somersaults of delight and cartwheels of anticipation. Yes, I think your impatience can be a virtue, but in this case I think your fuse might have been a tad short. Tell me again what you said.'

And so Perdita took him through the brief conversation and St Bede pronounced himself none the wiser. 'I'm sure it will be alright on the night, Perds. And now, what would you like to wear?'

Henry Beadles never made this offer seem condescending and she was able to accept it from him in a way she couldn't from others. It was because she knew he enjoyed it and not because she needed it.

'Do we want to be more sexy tonight, my dear?'

'What do you mean by more sexy?' asked Perdita, slightly puzzled by his question.

'Well, you are quite sexy enough *au naturel*, but I wondered if you wanted to augment, er, the package?' And, before she could answer, he added, 'do you remember the black, slightly flared skirt we bought for that recital at the Wigmore a couple of years ago? Well, I did wonder whether it might go with that simply lovely short grey jacket you have. And then we can add the pinky scarf we picked up in Bond Street the other day.'

She changed and did a slow turn in front of St Bede but before he could speak she told him that she thought she would be more comfortable in her black trousers. Between them, they prepared her for the evening, St Bede helping with her make-up.

'Darling, you were born with eyes that simply don't need mascara, but just the tiniest hint.' About four o'clock they finished and he declared himself pleased.

'How you've survived until now without being snapped up, I can't believe,' he said. 'I don't know who's blind around here.'

'You're not just saying that, are you St Bede?'

Henry Beadles heard the faintest hint of anxiety in her voice, so unusual that he considered his response before answering, something of a first for him. 'I'm going to repeat myself,' he said. 'It is they who cannot see, not you. If your blindness puts them off, then more fool they.'

'But is it my blindness, St Bede. Or is it me?'

'Look at me, Perdita. Let's say it is both. The first you can't do anything about, the second you'll find out about, for anyone who is really interested in you will either confront it or love it. Now, I think my work is done and thank you for a most nourishing lunch.'

'But I haven't given you anything,' Perdita suddenly realised.

'Darling,' he said, as he let himself out, 'I have had a feast.' And he blew her a noisy kiss and tripped down the stairs.

\*     \*     \*

Toby stood on one of the upper walkways and wondered which way to go. Ahead of him, a skyscraper rose in uncompromising concrete, a series of balconies repeating themselves like teeth on a giant saw. To his left was a wide garden where hidden fountains sprayed water over bright and elaborate garden displays. Where the water leaked across the polished bricks which made up the pathways, the surface was slippery. He skirted the spill and followed the gardens in the direction of a conservatory which had been built on to the side of another concrete shoulder of the Barbican. There was a surprising absence of people which told him that he probably wasn't taking the most direct route to the actual Centre. He walked through a glass door to a corridor which began to carry him around in a very large circle rather as he imagined the great particle accelerator was like under a Swiss mountain. He had virtually completed three hundred and sixty degrees by the time he came to the larger door and the sign which indicated the Barbican foyer. He had now left the shiny bricks and moved on to a grey carpet lined with black which somehow clashed with the grey concrete walls. He was about to descend the stairs into the foyer when he saw her standing talking with a man and a woman, both clearly players for one wore black tie and tails and the other, who had her back to him, a long black dress. From the safety of the stairs he was able to watch her, as he had done in the cemetery, but what he had observed then simply as a beautiful woman he now saw as a woman towards whom he was drawn with a force he was only just beginning to comprehend. This time she didn't turn to face him, but carried on talking and listening and he absorbed again the line of her face, the shape of her body and the crop of silver hair which caused more than one person to turn and stare.

He was looking down into an arena of people, the sharp lines of the modern building dwarfing them, the rough concrete walls at odds with the softness of their shapes. Toby felt the first prickle of anxiety rise in him, an unease he recognised only too well and did not attempt to understand for it seemed beyond his control. He looked up and registered the green exit signs and then again at Perdita, his eyes moving between the two. This is ludicrous, he told himself and taking a deep breath he pushed himself away from the concrete balustrade and down into the foyer reassembling his thoughts as he walked down the stairs.

'Good evening, Perdita.' He gently put his hand on her sleeve as he announced himself. She turned towards him, her face lighting up with a huge smile. She found his hand, which had remained on her sleeve and took it in both of hers.

'Let me introduce my friends. This is James Clarke. He plays the violin and the saxophone and really is very good. And this is Samantha Hardy . . . '

' . . . who plays the cello. I've already had the pleasure of meeting her and hearing her play.'

'Toby Browning,' Perdita concluded. 'They're part of the Konstam Players who we're about to hear.'

'I hope you enjoy this more than you seem to enjoy my last performance,' Samantha said to Toby, before signalling to James Clarke that they should be getting on. 'We'd better go and get ready.'

'What did she mean by that?' Perdita asked, still holding his hands.

Once again, Toby Browning was at the confluence of two emotions, the unsettling memory of what had happened at the gallery and the huge impulse to lean forward and kiss Perdita Landberg. Ignoring the first, he chose the second and putting his free hand on the bundle containing his other one, he stooped and kissed her cheek, leaving his mouth there slightly longer than he would do if he had been merely greeting her.

'You look utterly wonderful,' he said and he felt the room go quiet as he said it, as if the only focus was them and the surroundings had receded.

'And so do you,' she said quietly. 'You'll have to take my word for that.'

'And as to your question, she played at my gallery for an opening recently. And I didn't feel very well.' He was about to add "and it was nothing to do with her music" but he stopped himself because he wasn't sure it would have been the truth. 'But I do now.'

There were about three hundred people in the foyer and they began to settle down as the members of the group took their positions on the makeshift stage. She took his arm and he guided her across the floor to the edge of low wall where there was space to sit. 'There are eight of them,' Perdita said. 'They're going to start by playing a piece by a Canadian composer, which is for the saxophone. Jim is also an accomplished sax player.' As she said this Toby watched as James Clarke slung a gold saxophone around his neck and played one or two notes from which the rest of the group tuned their instruments. 'It's normally for a bigger orchestra, but it still sounds fabulous.'

Like an animal picking up a scent, the discordant noises of the musicians tuning up focused Perdita for she was concentrating hard on the stage, caught in the thrall of what she knew. He watched her face and only then did he wonder what her eyes looked like and how he had kissed her earlier without realising that she was still wearing her glasses. He kissed her again now, on the corner of her mouth, whilst she still looked ahead and she responded by pushing her face slightly against his.

'Concentrate, please,' she ordered. 'This is a serious moment.'

'I think it is,' he said, but when she turned towards him he made sure he was looking at the group of players.

The foyer, a public area with bars and people coming and going, was not entirely quiet when they started but the force of the playing brought a silence to the arena. It was as Toby watched the intense concentration on the faces of the players, the interplay of the instruments and the light catching the gold of the saxophone, that the symptoms he had recognised earlier began to force their way back into his consciousness. At first he wasn't sure why but he now realised that, just behind the saxophonist, the girl with the cello was sitting. The music was an intricate interplay between the saxophone and the other instruments and it was as he watched Samantha Hardy's animated playing that the nausea began to rise in him. He shifted uncomfortably and looked away from the stage to distract himself but this only made it worse. His heart was beating faster now and he felt light headed. He knew he had only seconds and he abruptly got up and stumbled towards the exit sign. The perspiration was now rolling down his face and by the time he got to the door his vision was blurred. He pushed it open and fell forward onto the pavement, kneeling and retching with an ugly barking sound as visitors to the concert hall parted around him assuming he was drunk. The sweat had now soaked into his clothes and he with each bout of nausea he thought he would faint. On all fours, he crawled away from the door desperately holding on to consciousness. This is the worst, he thought as he tried to take deep breaths and force control over his body. He felt pathetic and hopeless but, most of all, as the nausea subsided and the sweat began to cool on his body, he felt embarrassed. How could he be like this, a grown man unable to control himself? He could now see that he was standing in the covered area where cars could drop their passengers before going on to park underground. He made his way slowly up the slope towards the open air, dishevelled and unsteady. A cool wind now chilled him and he thrust his hands into his pockets, seeking the protection of a doorway. A succession of taxis passed as London went about its business. He dropped his head, unable to think straight, furious that he should have been caught out again on this of all nights. He had left her down there and he knew he should return and explain, but he was frightened. He did not want to lose Perdita Landberg but what would she make of this pathetic man who could not control himself and was at the mercy of his own body. Would she not see him as a liability? How long he stood in the doorway, he wasn't sure but it was long enough for his sweat to dry. His senses had returned now but things weren't the same. His first instinct was to run, faster and faster, great strides taking him away into the night, into the darkness where he could curl up and escape. This is what he had done in the past, revising his own history and pretending it had never happened. Until it came around again, taking his legs from underneath him. He looked left along the darkened street and then right towards the entrance to the hall. Taking a deep breath, he headed back down the slope and returned to the foyer. He felt incapable of words, as if what had just occurred had no logic. He simply did not know how to explain it to Perdita.

When he pushed opened the glass door it was if he was entering a different world. The music had changed and the drive of the saxophone had been replaced by a subtle and quieter mix of piano and violin. The music, though, remained in the background as he looked for Perdita. She was standing close to where they had been sitting. She was looking directly at him, motionless, as if the music and the musicians didn't exist. He walked towards her and stopped.

'Toby?' she said.

He found it difficult to speak. He watched her take off her glasses. He noticed that her eyes were the palest of blues, like the water on a tropical beach. He held out his hand and touched her shoulder but it was she who embraced him, finding his shoulders, on tip toe so that her face was near his. They stood there not speaking, the music rising and falling around them.

'Please don't ask me about it,' he said quietly over her shoulder. 'Please don't say anything.'

# Chapter 25

It was as if he was about to violate his own privacy. Peter Harrington regarded himself as a private man and the idea that he could read intimate details of his life in the folder he was carrying both shocked and concerned him. Was it fear or propriety that stopped him opening it?

The Northern Line tube rattled towards the city, the folder lying on his knees held there by his large, capable hands. No one was ever meant to see what was in this folder except Marjorie Nielson, he thought, turning the buff file so that his name appeared in the top right hand corner. This had been on her desk when she died, a connection he found impossible to ignore. Was it coincidence or did the enclosed pages hold a clue as to why she died? At Camden Town he had to change and he was caught in a flow of people through the tiled corridors clutching the file, suddenly anxious that it should be amongst so many people for the idea of losing it appalled him. The tube to Moorgate was crowded and he stood pressed against anonymous passengers all carrying their own secrets and doubts, although not quite in the same way. It was dark by the time he got to the hotel and not wanting to return to his room he sat in the almost deserted lounge and ordered coffee. He looked around him at the dismal attempt to recreate one of the great Edwardian hotels, the dark mahogany veneer panels around the walls, the faux leather buttoned chairs and sofas, the tall palms hanging wearily in the corners.

As he opened the folder he felt his eyes stinging in apprehension and he looked up again to reassure himself that the lounge was empty. Curiously, at first, it was not like reading about himself, for he couldn't remember anything of the early sessions on which Marjorie Nielson had kept notes. The man he was reading about seemed simultaneously aggressive and defensive and, now that he could see the compressed narrative of an hour's session, very slow to appreciate what was happening. Reading on, he was a spectator observing someone who happened to be called Peter Harrington feeling his way through a process that was alien to him. From a distance he could see the other Peter Harrington's tentative steps towards the ultimate conclusion, a man almost wilfully avoiding what now seemed obvious. Marjorie must have sensed this, for as the sessions unfolded before him he saw her take more control and begin to steer him back towards himself so that he was forced to address the issue that he was most trying to avoid. It was like being able to watch his unconscious thoughts come to life, to be verbalised and to escape from the carefully patrolled place where he had been marshalling them. Blessed with hindsight, he could see the inevitability of Freddie's story emerging but what astonished him now was the dispassionate way he was able to read the account of the young soldier's death. He was not the anguished Peter Harrington unable to prevent himself talking about the ghastly events of that night, still trapped in the emotions of the moment, almost reliving the hours on the dark hillside. Although he wept quietly at the end of the account, it was not for Freddie but for the Peter Harrington who had kept all this to himself for so long. He sat on in the empty lounge as, somewhere in the bowels of the hotel, a distant vacuum cleaner went about its business.

It was inevitable that he had read the accounts of his sessions with Marjorie with the same selfishness as he had experienced them, focused entirely on himself. It was only as he began to re-read sections of the notes that Marjorie Nielson began to emerge and he became aware of the two-way process, often an elaborate dance where he was the unwitting partner. At the end of one of their meetings she had commented on the unusual level of intervention she had employed, something that had clearly surprised her. And what did she mean when she alluded to being pulled along by a narrative she appeared to know and fear?

Clearly, an element of his story, at that stage incomplete, had been glimpsed by Marjorie and like the sound of distant thunder, it had alarmed her. He turned to the final session and the unfolding of Freddie's death and at his ultimate querying challenge to the therapist: 'will this do any good and was I right to tell you?' And those very final words to him, assuring him he was right to have relived what he had kept at bay for years. How she had said those words he fought hard to remember and he looked again at the typed notes, trying to put a voice, a sound, to the black and white words. It was only then that he saw the numbered page had a forward slash followed by a (cont). He turned the page even though he knew this was the final sheet in the folder. Had there been more? Had Marjorie Nielson continued to make notes? Now the emphasis had shifted from Peter Harrington, the client, to Marjorie Nielson, the therapist and he tried to recall her face in those final minutes he had been with her. This was a woman with a life, a background, some of which he had heard in the church but it had somehow remained a distant history, disconnected from the present. He got up and paced up and down the lounge, hoping the movement would help dislodge a clue to Marjorie or a memory of a reaction that might be a tell-tale to why she had felt such a strong connection to him. Marjorie Nielson used to wear her hair tied up in a bun behind her head. She was graceful and attentive and her eyes, if they betrayed anything at all, revealed compassion and en-couragement. He struggled to see more in her face, but he knew that he, like so many others who sat opposite her, sought not to look at this face for clues of about her character and her history. No, they, like him, were concerned only for themselves. For them, Marjorie Nielson was only a means to an end.

He called Vera very early the following morning, before the noise of the city had reached its normal crescendo, knowing she would almost certainly be on her way to work. She appeared unsurprised to hear from him, almost as if she had expected the call. They arranged to meet in Cavendish Square at lunchtime and it was in the shadow of Lord George Bentinck that, a few hours later, he found her eating her sandwich lunch.

'My country is full of statues of people you wouldn't know,' she said to him, as he looked up at the imposing statue. 'Local heroes, forgotten politicians.'

'I've no idea who he is,' Peter added. 'But he certainly cuts quite a figure here, doesn't he?' He sat next to her on the bench and looked at the other Londoners enjoying their lunch break spread randomly over the garden square.

'You knew I would take the notes, didn't you?' he said, not looking at her.

'Of course,' she replied, still chewing on a sandwich. 'They should be yours, these notes. When you told me your name, I knew that they belonged to you.'

Peter thought about this for a moment, registering the straight-forward common sense of her response.

'And, no, I did not read them.'

'Did anyone else, do you know?' Peter asked, as a group of pigeons walked expectantly in front of them.

She didn't answer the question but answered another, as yet unasked question he was intending to bring up. 'I think they are all there, kept under lock and key. I have wondered about them since she has gone. But Marise will deal with all that, I expect.'

'Does Marise have keys to the house?'

She took a bite of her sandwich before replying. 'Of course. They were like this, those two.' And Vera held up her thumb and forefinger to emphasis her point. 'At least, that's what Marise told me.'

'When did she last come to the house, Vera?' He had now turned to face her, but she continued to look straight ahead over the lawns.

'I cannot be certain,' she said after a while. 'She could come and go whenever she liked. As far as I know, though, she has not been to the house since Dr Nielson died.'

'But she could have been without you knowing?'

'I suppose so,' replied Vera with a shrug.

'Do you think anyone might have touched the papers?'

Again, another shrug. 'What does it matter now? She's dead and you have your notes.'

What does it matter now, he thought, why should he care? The flag on top of a nearby store enjoyed the mild westerly wind which hurried the small white clouds across the blue sky. A woman with an elderly and very small dog under her arm paused to look up at a pigeon which had landed on Lord Bentinck's head and left a streak of white down his nose. Peter cared because the tables had been turned and instead of posing Marjorie Nielson with a problem, she now presented him with one. The unfinished business was hers, not his.

'I think there were some sheets missing from my file,' he said, again facing out over the square.

'I think you will have to speak to Marise, then.' She stood up, clipped the plastic lid onto her sandwich box and placed it into her large handbag. 'Now I have to work.'

Peter got up as she left and watched her disappear beyond the tall plane trees. He assumed that, as well as cleaning Marjorie's house in Hampstead, she also did some consulting rooms around there as well, perhaps even Marjorie's own. He ran after her and she was startled to see him, as if she had closed that chapter and did not want it reopened. She confirmed that she did in fact clean the Harley Street rooms.

'Why do you ask?' she said.

'I need to go there.'

'Marise is not there today.'

He waited, looking at her as she stared back at him. She shrugged again and turned from the direction she had been walking back towards Harley Street. He followed and when she reached the familiar black door and she took a large bunch of keys from her pocket and let him in.

'Major Harrington, in my country trust is a very important thing, as I have told you before. Close the door when you leave.'

He stood on the black and white tiles of the hallway and waited for his eyes to adjust to the gloom of the interior. It was both familiar and strange, the smell of the hall reminding him of previous visits. As before, there was an unnatural silence to the place, a solemn acknowledgement to what took place in its various rooms. He made his way towards her consulting room, remembering the times he had done it before wondering what he would end up saying. He paused at the door and then pushed it open, waiting again before he stepped inside. Only then did he realise the futility of what he was doing. Surely this was the room where he was destined to find absolutely nothing, its surroundings so deliberately neutral as to give no clues about the woman who used it. The two chairs were in the same position by the window, the small desk in the alcove where it had always been. He sat on the chair that Marjorie used and looked at the one where he had always sat, but decided that this was the wrong way round and so he switched. Now he imagined seeing Marjorie Nielson sitting opposite him, talking about her life as he listened. It was a difficult adjustment to make. How do you listen for the clues to someone else's life? How do you encourage them to talk, to get them to verbalise what they don't want to, or feel they can't or, most confusing of all, don't know they have inside them to say in the first place. He could hear nothing now for in the many hours that they had sat together in this very room, she had remained as anonymous as the room itself. It was only at the very end that she had lifted the veil enough to hint at her own life, the history that lay behind her impassive demeanour, the many years that had gone before she sat listening to his problems in a classic Georgian house in the centre of a capital city in a country a thousand miles from her own.

## Chapter 26

He had not offered to take her home and they had parted on the road outside the Barbican where he had put her in a taxi. She had done as he had asked and not questioned him about what had happened and he had remained silent. She could sense his disappointment and the wind, swirling down from around the tall Barbican towers pulled at her clothes as he helped into the cab.

'I'm sorry,' was all he said as he slammed the door.

As the cab rattled under the concrete tunnel she heard the whoosh of the cars passing the other way, their sounds intensified in the confined space. Although the evening had ended disastrously, she felt somehow relieved, as if a burden had been lifted from her shoulders. At first she couldn't define why, or perhaps wouldn't acknowledge the reason. So often in the past, Perdita's blindness had been the cause of difficulties, either logistical or, as had been happening more recently, the result of her fierce protection of her independence. Tonight had not been about Perdita but Toby and it was his problem, whatever it was, that had shifted the spotlight from her. Toby Browning had his own demons and these had put her own into perspective so that now, as she bounced along the Euston Road, she felt an equal partner. Here am I, thought Perdita, with a bundle of likes and dislikes, of experiences good and bad and there he is with his. And we are about to offer them to each other, to relinquish some and to change others hoping in the end to make them match, or at least not fight each other. She knew that an initial threshold had been crossed but that each of them carried the means to make the next stage work or to destroy it. Marjorie would ask her, after she had spoken of a dream or described something that had been on her mind, 'well, how do you feel?

What is the feeling you have in your body?' And, right now, Perdita felt good and not even the subdued voice of Toby Browning as he said good-night could override the memory of the two small kisses he had given her.

She phoned him as soon as she got home.

'I have decided to ignore you,' she said, before he had time to speak. 'And I'm going to ask you why. What happened?'

'I can't explain,' he said after a pause. 'It's why I am seeing – was seeing, Marjorie.'

'I know, you told me that. But tell me about tonight. Did I do anything wrong? Was I somehow responsible?'

'Oh, I don't know Perdita.' He sounded exasperated. 'Yes and no. Of course I wanted to see you, but something happened. And I hate it.'

'But what happened, Toby. What actually happens?'

'It's as if I lose my ability to reason, that the thinking part of me gives up and my body just takes over.' There was a resignation in his voice which made Perdita feel angry rather than sympathetic.

'But how long has this been going on? It must be intolerable? What did Marjorie say about it?' In the silence it was if she could hear him struggling to remember what he had said to the therapist.

'I don't think she actually said anything.'

'Toby,' she said abruptly. 'You have to talk about it. Especially now.' Whether she meant this because of the proximity of the last attack, or as a reference to their growing relationship, she wasn't sure. There was a further silence on the line but she pressed on. 'You said that when Samantha played for you before, you didn't feel well. What this the same thing?'

'Yes.'

'And is this all you have to say about it? Just tell me what happens.'

'I have,' he said, his voice smaller than ever.

'No, you haven't Toby. You have done your best not to.'

'She made me talk about when the attacks happened and when they started. As far as I'm concerned, they've been with me all my adult life, lying in wait to catch me out. And they do.'

'So you had no idea you might be likely to have one at the Barbican?' Perdita asked, more gently now, remembering, as if out of nowhere, his hesitation when she had telephoned him with the invitation. Maybe she had detected his early warning system.

'I don't think so,' Toby said vaguely.

'Think harder, Toby. Were you completely happy to come to the Barbican and meet me? What was your first reaction when I called you?'

'I had two feelings, as I recall,' Toby replied. 'Real happiness at the thought of seeing you and then, I don't know, a faint whiff of apprehension.'

'Why, Toby?'

'I don't know why, do I?' Toby's reply was almost petulant. Perdita's reply was calmer.

'Marjorie would say that you do, but you don't know how to put it into words.'

'I began to talk about my father with her,' he said, 'but that's all too simple, that it might be something to do with my parents.'

'It's nearly always something to do with parents, though, isn't it?'

'My father is a bully and my mother suffered. Is that what it is about?' She hadn't heard this resigned bitterness in his voice before.

'It certainly seems to matter to you,' she said.

'It's all the past,' he said tiredly. 'What's the point? I can't do anything about it, can I?'

Her reply was instant and direct. 'You're wrong. It's all in the present and you're letting it be. You must do something about it. Let's start here. You came to the Barbican, you said you wanted to but with a reservation somewhere. When did it get bad?'

'About half way through the first piece. I began to feel it rise in me and knew I had to get away.'

'Get away from what, Toby?'

'I wanted to get away from people, from the crowd. I didn't want them to see me.'

'See you do what?' Perdita could hear his anxiety, but pushed him nevertheless. 'What were you doing the exact moment it got bad?'

'I was just looking at the players, at the saxophone player and behind him the girl. And then it was on me and I have to flee.'

'From me? From the music? From the concert? From your father? C'mon, Toby, ask yourself. Don't just accept it.'

'From all those things,' he said and she felt her heart jolt a little. 'You made it worse because you were there and somehow I thought you might have made me invulnerable. But I was wrong and my shame was all the worse.'

'Shame for what, Toby?'

'For having broken down and left.'

'But you didn't break down, Toby. You had a panic attack, or claustrophobia, or something similar. But you didn't break down. Why do you choose those words?'

'I don't know. Perhaps that's what it feels like to me.'

Perdita suddenly understood what it was like to be Marjorie Nielson, sniffing the air and listening for clues in what was both spoken and unspoken. This was the first time she had put herself in the shoes of the therapist and it seemed like an important moment, one where she stepped out of her shadow to see her as a real person with a job, like everyone.

'If there is a common denominator at the moment, it is music and crowds.' The memory of Marjorie Nielson pushed her on. 'Can you think of any attacks you've had and you might have told Marjorie?'

'I told her that I had one on the top of a bus and the other going to a funeral.' Did Perdita detect a new interest in Toby's response, as if he was beginning to engage properly in this exchange?

'So that's two crowds, two public arenas. Is that right, Toby?'

'Well, I suppose so. The bus was quite full and I was in a car loaded with people going to the funeral.'

'Can you tell me anything more?' It was as if Toby was releasing information under torture, holding on to as many facts as he could. Only, thought Perdita, he doesn't know he is doing it.

'Whose funeral was it?'

'A musician friend of mine.'

'Well, there's another connection with music. Tell me more about him.' Once again she could hear Toby organise his thoughts and she imagined a series of connections being made, some consciously and others in the darker recesses of his mind without him realising it.

'We played in the same orchestra together.'

The news, given in such an offhand way, took Perdita aback. 'You never told me you were a musician,' she said, unsure if her tone reflected her hurt or indignation, or both. Certainly she felt let down that he hadn't spoken of this before.

'Why didn't you tell me?' she continued.

'Because we talked about other things: Marjorie and my work at the gallery and your composition. There is nothing sinister there, surely?'

Perdita thought about this and realised that it was perfectly true and yet some vestige of dissatisfaction continued to bother her, particularly as he did not offer to tell her more. He knew that she was a musician and that she composed, but he had kept his own involvement from her.

'What did you play?'

'I played the violin.' He said this almost reluctantly and Perdita picked up his discomfort immediately.

'But you don't want to talk about it?'

'What is there to talk about?'

All the easiness which Toby had exuded on their visit to Kew had now evaporated and his answers were short and defensive.

'I can think of about twenty questions, Toby, all of interest to us both. Do you still play?'

'No.'

She let his answer pass. 'Who did you play for?'

'In the end, the National Youth Orchestra.'

'So you were good.'

'My father didn't think so.'

'What's that got to do with it? Your father didn't play your violin for you and you got to the NYO which meant beating at least twenty thousand other violinists. I don't understand.'

'He didn't want me to play the violin for a living, or do what I am doing now, in fact. He's hard to please.'

Perdita weighed these words and wondered why Toby could say them in such a matter of fact way. Or perhaps he wasn't totally aware of how odd they seemed to her.

'So did he stop you playing the violin?'

'No. I gave it up. It was too much, reading art and practising for the orchestra. It was one or the other.'

She didn't believe him. 'So you just gave it up? Stopped practising one day and laid down the violin and decided to do art instead?'

'Yes.'

'That must have pleased your father?'

'Not so as you would notice,' Toby said, his voice now more distant again.

'What's the matter Toby?'

'Nothing,' he said. 'Nothing. I'm just tired.'

'Think about it, Toby. Don't just push it out of the way.'

'I won't. Thank you for phoning and listening to me.'

And he was gone, leaving her. It was as if the expansive man she had seen just days earlier had been a figment of her imagination. The Toby she had just spoken to was flat and evasive, a man who had closed in on himself and shut down and was apparently unwilling to let her help him.

*     *     *

It was dark in the living room and so he could see across to Shad Thames and the apartments on the opposite bank lit up, different rectangles of white and yellow reflected in the slow flowing Thames. There was no river traffic and for these few hours now, the gulls would be quiet. He walked out onto the decking and felt the fresh wind in his face. All the fight had gone out of him and he abhorred his own abdication, aware that he had not engaged with Perdita in a way that might have been more helpful to him and, he supposed, to them. There is no real darkness in London but the river below him, where it disappeared under the old moorings, faded into blackness and only water sucking at the edges of the slippery wooden legs revealed its presence. There was a darkness in him and somewhere there were hidden movements, currents of doubt, battles of attrition which remained beneath the surface of his consciousness but which caused him to act like he did tonight. He knew this, of course he did, but wasn't it like having asthma or suffering from migraines, burdens that you have to learn to live with? Marjorie didn't think so, for she had challenged him, once he had described his attacks, to ask himself whether he wanted to live with this condition. The fact is, he thought, he had learned to live with it, to take it as part of his lot in life. Now, though, it was Perdita challenging him and he felt both defensive and vulnerable. To the east, high on top of Canary Wharf, a triangular wedge of mist had formed where the cold air from the night mixed with the warm air from the building's extractors. In the middle a single red light flashed its warning, diffused and weak in the grey cloud. Some days it disappeared completely, the enormous building absorbed into the sky, shrouded and lost as if it had never existed. It was there, though, just as the bulk of Toby's problem lay somewhere beyond his vision, lost in the shadows but waiting to emerge. And just as he knew that Canary Wharf existed in and beyond the clouds, he realised that his problem lay within him, always there however dormant and out of sight.

He got on his bicycle and rode between the cast iron supports spread through the living room, the tyres making the lightest protests as he glided across the wooden floor. The act of maintaining the balance and flow between the objects concentrated him, as it always did, emptying his mind for the moment, allowing him, as it were, to start a new paragraph or a new chapter. He was describing two figures of eight, one on top of the other and he attempted to keep his movements smooth and exact, as a circus performer might. As suddenly as he started, he stopped and dismounted, resting the bike against the wall. He picked up the phone and called Perdita.

'It's me. I want you to keep talking to me even if I don't like it.'

'You think you can stop me.'

He could hear the relief in Perdita's voice which in turn encouraged him.

'No, I don't suppose I could if I tried. You see, I know that I run away from this thing like I do from lots of situations and I don't want to.' It was like a statement of intent but one he hadn't known he was going to make.

'Well, that is half the battle,' Perdita said.

'How strange this is,' he told her, 'you taking over Marjorie's role. She did the same thing, pushing me to think more about what was happening.'

'But there is a big difference, Toby. I am prepared to trade myself in the bargain. This is not a one-way process. I will have to do it with you in a way that Marjorie didn't.'

Toby thought about this, not sure exactly what she meant and, as always with Perdita, she seemed to understand his silences.

'Marjorie was not going to be changed by seeing you. But I think I will be if we go further. I have to give up something if we are to move forward and so do you.'

And for the first time since he returned home, Toby smiled. 'I think you will have to take me through that one more time, Perdita.'

'I'm serious, Toby.'

'And so am I, Perdita. I have to go to see my father this weekend and I wonder if you will come with me?'

Now it was his turn to hear her pause so he added: 'This is what is called taking the bull by the horns.'

It was only after she had agreed and rung off that Toby wondered why he had decided to go to Norton Hall. He had not discussed it with his father and they had no prearrangement for this weekend and, in so many ways, risking his fledgling relationship in the cauldron of his father's home was foolhardy and thoughtless. Yes, he decided, thoughtless. He had done it instinctively and as he rode the bike once again between pillars he did not know whether to be pleased or worried. He was certain, though, that he wanted to see Perdita Landberg again.

## Chapter 27

Peter had fallen asleep on the couch in Marjorie's consulting room, the quietness of the house and the calm, almost church-like atmosphere, combining with his emotional fatigue to embrace and somehow to reassure him. When he awoke, the skylight, which he had been staring at earlier, was darker. He had been dreaming and at first he didn't know where he was and he sat up disorientated, looking around the gloomy room for clues. Just as it had felt strange to read the notes about himself, it now seem odd to be sitting in this room, an intruder not only into his own life but also the territory of Marjorie Nielson. He needed to legitimise this pursuit and there was only one person who could help him do this.

'Marise, it's Peter Harrington. Could we meet again please?'

'Why?'

Marise Dubarry's question to Peter Harrington was sharp and aggressive and was aimed to discourage him.

'I would like to find out more about Marjorie Nielson's life,' he said, truthfully.

'For what reason?' she replied coldly. 'She is dead and no good can come of talking about her now. I've told you this before.'

'What do you mean, Marise? I'm not looking to harm her but just to find out more about her. She was, after all, reading about my case when she died.'

When Marise spoke, her tone was different. 'You know about those notes, do you?'

'You told me she kept notes, Marise, but I wasn't aware until recently that it was my notes she had been reading on the morning she died.'

'So you have been to the house, then?' Marise asked cautiously, as if still piecing together the chronology of what she was hearing.

He chose not to reply to her question, but to continue with his theme. 'You can understand, then, why I feel a certain connection with what happened and would like to talk further about it.'

'I doubt it will help,' Marise said, but without her earlier conviction. Peter waited.

'OK. I will see you again,' she said reluctantly. 'But I don't want to meet at the house or in Harley Street. I will see you in Regent's Park, at the café on the Broad Walk. One o'clock tomorrow.'

Peter Harrington was beginning to realise that his involvement in the life of Marjorie Nielson was a reflection of how he was beginning to change. The temporary abandonment of his life in France had been done almost without thinking, except for a call to Natalie to extend the time she was looking after his dog. This desire to so readily engage with other people in the pursuit of something so personal was unusual and clearly stemmed from the sessions with Marjorie. He didn't know quite what he was looking for now, but it dawned on him that he was enjoying this interlude in London and he was starting to feel at home in the city.

As he entered Regent's Park the following day he recalled having had a dream in which Freddie had spoken to him, his handsome face as clear as the trees around him now. It must have been when he fell asleep in the consulting room and the conjunction made him shake his head at its obviousness. At the very place he had finally given up the secret of his death and the terrible images of his broken body, so Freddie returned in the form he wanted to remember the young soldier. The simple logic was there, but how it happened, how his mind had switched its priorities, was beyond comprehension.

An avenue of lime trees escorted him along the dead straight path first through the ornamental garden and then between the open playing fields beyond. Families were making their way in disorganised groups towards the Zoo, which was signposted ahead. The leaves on the trees were beginning to reflect the changing season and as the wind worked its way through the overarching branches, a dry rustle accompanied his progress.

He saw the café over to his left and beyond it the wide undulating green swathe with the golden dome of the mosque on the far horizon. She was already sitting at a table, neat in a blue overcoat.

'I took the liberty of starting without you,' she told him and he nodded a welcome at her before entering the café to return with a coffee and sandwiches to match what she had already bought.

'I used to come here with Marjorie, even in winter when the wind would whistle from the west over the football pitches. But she used to love it, as if she didn't feel the cold.'

'She came from a much colder country, of course.' Peter said, his voice encouraging her to continue

'She spoke little of Russia to me, sadly. I knew the stories that I told the vicar; a little of her father, some more of her mother, but not much. She just never referred to those times.'

'Did this surprise you?'

'Given what I know about the war, probably not. So many of my contemporaries were unable to talk about it at all, it was so terrible. No, it doesn't surprise me.'

She looked at him, almost daring him to continue and it occurred to Peter that she had been preparing herself for this meeting, deliberately controlling her emotions.

'I meant,' Peter ventured, 'in order to have become a therapist, part of her training would have been talking about her past.'

'Some things are buried very deeply, Mr Harrington. Too deep to dig them up. And too dangerous.'

'Was this your experience as well?'

'Very few people from Europe came through the war unscathed. It is hard to imagine those times now, but it wasn't a question of living from day to day, but minute to minute. But you don't want to hear my stories.'

'Did you talk about them to Marjorie?'

Marise looked down at the half finished sandwiches on the small round table and then switched her gaze across the fields to the west where the clouds billowed above the stuccoed terraces of the Outer Circle. He waited, his sandwich uneaten.

'I did, I did,' she said cautiously, as if the very act of confirming the fact might release the past. 'We were fellow travellers, in more ways than one. We had both escaped. Do you understand, Major Harrington?' She was not expecting an answer.

'She was younger than me and yet it was as if she knew. She wasn't even a doctor, she had not trained yet but she had the instinct of understanding. Yes, I told her my story and she knew what it meant to lose everything. You can see why she was so important to me. We had a special bond.'

A heron flapped lazily towards the lake and somewhere behind him Peter could hear the whooping of monkeys.

'But she didn't talk to you about herself?'

'She didn't have to. I understood her. We shared a bond.'

'I'm sure you did. Her death must have been an awful blow for you.'

She looked at him now, a cold wintry look, her old face pale and lined even more so than he remembered at the inquest. 'More than you can know, Major Harrington, which is why I find your persistence so difficult. Can we not let her lie in peace? Must you continue to persecute her? She was helping you, now you can help her. Can't you let her be?' Her eyes looked directly into his, not imploring but threatening, without emotion. He had seen eyes like this before, eyes that dared a response and were full of hate, warning him not to exceed his boundaries. Marise Dubarry, surely in her late seventies, but far from frail and determined to protect the memory of her friend.

'Marise,' he said, meeting her stare, 'I believe some papers might have been removed from my folder, the one on Marjorie's desk. I cannot be certain and I thought you might be able to help. This is a personal matter, as I'm sure you understand and it was your assistance that I wanted. I do not intend any harm.'

'Huh,' she exclaimed. 'Harm. What do you know of harm? You've done your damage, Major Harrington.' She spat these words at him as she got up to leave. He put his hand on her forearm.

'You cannot leave without explaining what you mean,' he said. 'I am aware that something may have affected Marjorie and that's why I wanted to talk to you. It appears that you are confirming what I thought. Can't you tell me more?'

She was standing now, not looking at him but facing the open playing fields. 'Some of the happiest days of my life were spent just here. We would walk up from the noise of Harley Street into this,' she said, gesturing with her hand. 'It was peace, real peace, the sort I never knew. And now it's gone.' She turned, angry still and looked down at him, her contempt for him clear.

'But how could I have harmed her, Marise? What could I have done?'

'I don't know, Major Harrington. But you did and she changed. Even here, sitting here,' she said pointing at the table, 'she was different. She wasn't happy. She had gone into herself. She disappeared, from me, her friend.'

Peter stood up. 'But how do you know I was responsible for that?' He spoke quietly, not wanting her to go. 'Why would I want to hurt Marjorie Nielson?' But, of course, this is not really about the therapist, he realised, but about her first client, Marise Dubarry. Somehow he had come between the two of them and broken their bond and Marise could not forgive him. And now he asked himself the question that he had put to Marise: what had he done?

She went without a word, her steps small but firm, walking across the grass to the neat row of limes and he watched her until she disappeared. He tried to put himself in her shoes and see her dispassionately. For half a century Marjorie had been more than her companion, she had been her family and her support. And now she was gone and Marise was a child again, an orphan, blaming him for Marjorie's death. If the broad logic was there, the details were missing. He looked at the two chairs on which they had been sitting and imagined the two women there, talking and sharing their lives. Did their relationship ever change? Was Marise always the patient to the therapist? Did she ever discover about the past of Marjorie Nielson, or was she like all her other clients, kept deliberately in the dark?

Several sparrows were now pecking at the remains of the sandwiches on the table and they remained impervious to his presence as he sat down. She is blaming me for the death, he told himself and for this to be the case it was clear that she knew something that he didn't. It was remarkable to be involved so intimately with someone's life, he thought, and yet to understand so little about them. Marjorie Nielson was no more or less than the image he recalled in his mind, without substance or background, a virtual figure that it was impossible to touch. But he had touched her, unknowingly, and Marise knew how and she blamed him for the loss of her friend.

He stood and the birds scattered.

# Chapter 28

Something had shifted in Perdita, a landslip which had changed the contours of her thinking. She had been given another reference point against which to gauge her position, but it wasn't until she played back her continued work on Marjorie's composition that she was aware that it had taken place. It had crept up on her and it emerged through her fingertips. She had slept only intermittently after Toby had called her back and when she got up she knew that it was still dark and only the occasional car broke the relative quietness of the High Street. She was tired and for some minutes she sat on the piano stool with her back to the keyboard, as the chill of the room slowly embraced her. She returned to her bedroom and slipped on a dressing gown and still only half awake, sat at the keyboard. In her mind she could hear the rattle of the taxi that had taken her home the night before, an irritating jumble of noises accompanying the steady drone of the diesel engine. It was the sound that contained and held in place her thoughts about the evening which had begun so well and then collapsed around her. She began to play a series of repetitive notes with her left hand and after a while she found a shape for them which she then looped into the computer. She listened to this driving, somewhat uneasy background and as she did she closed her eyes and with her right hand improvised a series of single high notes, melodic and wistful, high in the treble clef. She found a pattern to these which she also looped before playing the two tracks simultaneously. At first they didn't match and she slowed even further the harmonious right hand, adding a series of flowing scales. Time disappeared and the dawn came up around her, the sun eventually reflecting itself through her windows to warm her face and remind her that an outside world existed.

Fours hours had evaporated and her body felt stiff and cold. She moved over to the window and allowed the sun to warm her, standing still in the bay window, the light shining in her dishevelled hair. It was here that she realised that the reference points for her thinking had been changed. Earlier that morning she had assumed that she was continuing her composition for Marjorie but the piece that she had just created was prompted by Toby Browning and her reaction to what had happened the night before. She went over to the computer, feeling herself step out of the shaft of sunlight into the shadow of the room. Returning to the sunlight, she heard the music again and listened to the way the sounds reflected her thinking, the angry monotonous drone of the taxi and, sometimes fighting it, occasionally complementing it, the lighter, distinct melodies coming from high up the piano. But as she listened now she could hear different conjunctions in the music, several points where the base that she had laid down combined with the treble to produce a harmony that she had not planned. She shook her head a smiled, for she knew she did not, could not, have planned these moments of unexpected beauty. They had emerged accidentally without any apparent guidance. It was the musical equivalent of saying the first thing that came into her head, something that Marjorie had encouraged her to do. The therapist would have been delighted and Perdita acknowledged that Marjorie was the catalyst for what she had just written and that it was a natural progression from the earlier movements dedicated and inspired by her.

She stood and listened to the music again but now she heard something beyond the unplanned harmonies which had initially pleased her, the darker, colder left hand which increasingly seemed to dominate the piece and give it a certain menace. Within the lurking, rolling sounds she detected her own confusions and doubts.

And now she was awake and the world beyond her music rushed in, thoughts and sounds that took her out of the capsule she had been in for the past five hours. She saw how Toby's problem had allowed her to push her own fears to one side and these now began to assail her as she recalled their telephone conversation. How could she possibly go with him to his father's when he knew so little of her? Surely this was a step too far, or at least too soon, and she put her hand to her stomach as she felt the unease in her body. It was this involuntary gesture which brought her face to face with herself. She had encouraged Toby to talk about himself, to confront his problem and yet she wondered if she could do the same herself, to talk to him about the root of her anxiety. Her rational side could see that they had both arrived at the same point, where to go further would involve an act of faith on both their parts, a trust that any revelation would allow them to grow rather than be cause for distrust and separation. They would have to meet in no-man's land and leave their weapons of self-defence behind. With these thoughts came the awareness of just how much her thinking had changed. Suddenly, it seemed like hours rather than days, she was with a man who interested her like no other and who had become the focus of her thoughts. She picked up the phone.

'Did I agree to go to your father's with you last night?' she asked without preamble.

'I can't imagine you having cold feet, Perdita?'

'Will you meet me for coffee? Now?' It was a statement masquerading as a question.

It was Toby's turn to be unsure. 'I'm a little uncertain of my ground, following yesterday.'

'I can't imagine you being uncertain, Toby,' she replied, mimicking his tone to her. Even in this moment, she realised how little he knew about her. Toby had never heard her music, had never seen where she lived, had little or no knowledge of her background. What was the substance of his interest in her? He cut across her thoughts.

'Do you trust yourself to be with me today?' he asked lightly, although she could hear concern lurking there as well.

'That is a remark that could be taken two ways, Mr Browning. The answer is the same either way. I shall take my chances.'

'Then, shall we have lunch?'

'I thought I was inviting you.'

'Fine. You choose.'

And all of a sudden she was at a loss, as if her impulse had caught up with her and called her bluff. Could she step into the no-man's land unarmed or was she too vulnerable?

'Let me help,' continued Toby, 'if you'll let me. I could pick you up at midday and I'll take you somewhere I like. Again, you'll have to trust me.'

Afterwards, it all seemed so perfectly normal. As she waited for him it was as if their lunch had been planned for a long time and was part of the fabric of the day.

*     *     *

Can I really fool my body, thought Toby, or will it rebel when asked to perform an unnatural act for one time too many? As he became more aware of his patterns of behaviour, Toby was beginning to recognise that, over the years, the act of suppressing his emotions had resulted in him sometimes not being aware of what his true feelings were. As he put down the phone to Perdita, knowing that later he would have to talk about his attack the night before, he saw that this was a way his body was asserting itself because he wouldn't. It wasn't a surprise then that as he drove towards Marylebone High Street he experienced the same apprehension as he had in the early days with Marjorie, when he worried about what he was going to say. He could not imagine how he would begin to account for what happened, or explain it and yet to ignore it would be like denying the existence of a major landmark.

If departure is all we need to know of heaven and all we need to know of hell, then the arrival of Perdita at her front door had a similar affect on Toby. It was as if he was seeing her for the first time as a woman and he was gripped by the way she looked, her pale face and white blond hair, her body behind the pale blue shirt and her smile. Then, hard on its heels, came the thought that his inability to come to terms with whatever caused his attacks, might be a barrier between them. He had to make it work.

'Toby?'

He realised he had been staring at her and so he stepped forward and kissed her cheek, as he might have greeted his goddaughter. She took his arm and he said the first thing that came into his mind.

'You look beautiful.'

'So do you,' she replied, smiling.

They drove westwards out of London and he told her that he was taking her to a small pub in the Chilterns. When she asked if it was one of his favourite haunts, he failed to see that she was teasing him and he replied seriously that a client of his lived nearby and had taken him there for lunch. Less than an hour later they pulled into small village tucked in between the swell of two hills topped by beech trees and speckled with sheep. As she got out of the car, Perdita stopped and looked around.

'This is so different from London,' she said, 'and yet we've hardly come any distance.'

He wanted to say something clever about their relationship being similar, that although they had only just started things seemed to be very different for him. The pub was almost empty and they sat in a snug at the back with a view to the distant chalky hills.

Perdita opened negotiations. 'It is curious,' she said, taking his hand and echoing his earlier thoughts, 'that although we've hardly started this relationship . . . ' She paused and looked at him and he responded by squeezing her hand. ' . . . we have an advantage that many couples don't have.' She paused again. 'We both know that we have had to confront certain problems in our lives by going to see a therapist. That, in a way, we are both damaged.'

Until that moment, Toby had not thought about why Perdita had been seeing Marjorie and today he had expected to continue their telephone conversation of the night before. At first he didn't know what to say.

'I don't see you as damaged,' he volunteered. 'At least, not as much as me,' he added spontaneously, probably the first time he had acknowledged this out loud.

'I just wondered,' she said, nodding to show that she had taken in his last remark, 'if you ought to know a bit more about me before we go to your father's.'

'Ah, yes, my father. Here beginneth another story. I'm sorry. Perhaps I was getting ahead of myself in asking you to meet him, particularly after the build up I have given him.'

'No, it's not him,' she said. 'It's you. Or, should I say, it's me. I just feel that I have been unfair, making you talk about what happened last night. It was easy in a way, because it meant I didn't have to tell you about me.'

Toby was not practised at exchanging personal information and for a moment he looked at Perdita as if searching for a clue to her predicament, whatever it was.

'It doesn't matter to me,' he said. 'You don't flee public gatherings to the embarrassment of all, at least.'

'It might be worse.'

Toby did not know how to go further, so he took a deep breath and decided to try to talk about himself. He didn't quite know what he was going to say and it felt as though he was standing on the top board at the swimming pool about to jump off.

'I don't know why I have my attacks,' he said quickly before hurrying on. 'I hate them and I want to be rid of them. I thought about what you asked me last night and it seems to me that one way or the other, music is a link between them all. But I'm not sure where that gets me.'

'And how do you feel about music?'

It wasn't a question he was expecting. 'How do I feel about it? Funny.'

She waited and he watched her looking at him, expectantly. 'Difficult. It makes my chest uneasy.' He wondered if she knew he was shaking his head and screwing up his face.

'I know this is painful for you, Toby.'

Again, it was as if she could see him and knew instinctively how he was reacting. The face that looked at him now was calm and encouraging.

'Tell me about it, Toby. Tell me where it went wrong.'

It was the idea that it went wrong which made Toby drop his head in an attempt to stop the tears which were forming just behind his eyes.

'It's OK Toby.' But it wasn't, and he cried, quietly, his warm tears falling on their hands. He waited until he was sure he could talk.

'I played the violin. You know that. At the beginning it was all about pleasing my father, if such a thing is possible. I associate it with being alone and, for some reason, cold. Maybe it was the practice I used to have to do when I was away at school. Maybe the association is the misery of those early days. Anyway, things changed when I found I was quite good. I was encouraged by a very nice master and in the end he persuaded me to audition for the National Youth Orchestra.'

He paused and looked out of the window where a pair of red kites wheeled above the hills, their forked tails ominous against the milky blue sky.

'So what went wrong?' It was Toby who asked the question of himself. 'What did go wrong? Maybe it's something else and music is just a decoy? I don't know.'

'You said you gave up the violin because you didn't have the time to practise. Is that right?'

Toby waited, because no answer immediately came to him. He searched his mind for a response but like an empty radar screen, he could identify nothing.

'You've stopped Toby. Why?'

'I don't know. I remember once playing the slow movement of

Bach's A minor violin concerto and thinking how absolutely wonderful to have this under my fingers. What a gift. What power, in a way. I've never said that before. I'm not sure I've ever thought it before.'

'Why do you think you said it now?'

'Perhaps because I am trying to tell you that it wasn't all bad.'

He paused and she waited and the birds continued to wheel in the summer sky. Around them the pub was quiet, as quiet as any consulting room in Harley Street.

'It's too obvious to say that my father hated that piece of music. Too melancholy, he would say. Give me something with a bit more backbone. And do you know, I always think of that when I hear it, as if the association is indelible, that I can't get back to the way I originally thought about the music.'

'You said he wasn't proud of your success.'

'He took it for granted, I think. He kept on moving the bar higher so he was never satisfied. The competitive instinct in my father is ingrained. Life is a matter of the survival of the fittest and the tougher you are the better it is.'

'So you never had any satisfaction for doing well?'

Toby gave a dismissive snort. 'No, that's not a currency my father knows, praise. The only time he ever came to one of my important concerts, he did so because he knew that he would be sitting next to one of the patrons of the orchestra, a well known politician.'

Toby thought back to the night at the Albert Hall and suddenly several memories came rushing back to him, as if they had been let out after long hibernation.

'What's wrong, Toby?'

'Do you know, I had an attack that night? I didn't mention it to Marjorie. I have only remembered it now.' He stopped and although he was looking out of the window, he saw nothing of the view for he was searching for the details of a night over a quarter of a century away in another world which he thought he had left behind.

'Tell me about it,' she said again.

'He never once spoke about it afterwards and he never knew the truth. He only told me he was coming a few days before the concert. He was so off hand about it. I'll be able to catch up with Tubby, was how he put it. Tubby Moyes was Minister for the Arts and he wangled a seat next to him. I doubt if he ever told him I was playing.'

'I'm sure he did, Toby.'

'To impress him, you mean?'

'Yes.'

'But in the wrong way.'

'Yes.'

Toby waited as he took in what she had just said. 'I saw them arrive from the back of the stage. I had been warming up and I wandered to the wings and looked up to where I knew they would be. It was a black tie night and my father was standing with his back half turned to the stage talking to the Minister.'

Toby stopped. He could see the scene exactly as it was and as he did he felt his pulse increase and his breathing quicken.

'Talk to me Toby. Now. Tell me what is happening.'

'I was scared. I was more scared than I have ever been. The idea of failing appalled me so completely that I shrank back into the bowels of the Hall. Perhaps it was seeing his back. The total indifference of the man.'

He was beginning to sweat now but she held his hand more tightly and encouraged him to speak. 'C'mon Toby, you can tell me.'

'I didn't know what was happening to me. I could hardly breath and I was sweating everywhere. My dinner jacket was soaked and I could not see properly. I managed to get to the loo and I began to retch. It was ghastly. It was the worst feeling I have ever had. I sat against the wall outside the loo with my head between my knees and I think I would have stayed there all night but for John Lockyer. He played the trumpet and we were friends. He sat down with me and said he knew what I was going through. Stage fright, he said, was terrible and it was really getting him down. He told me he was leaving the orchestra and packing it all in. I could barely take in what he was saying, I was feeling so tired. But I do know this. I realised his diagnosis was wrong but that his solution was right.'

'But you played that night, didn't you?'

'I did and I don't know how I did it. I certainly didn't want to go through it again. And what did my father know of it? Nothing. There were four other soloists that night and my father mentioned them all. Some fine players there, he told me. Not much room at the top of classical music. Are you sure you've got it in you? You look pretty washed out to me.'

'What was the correct diagnosis, Toby? What did you know back then?'

'That I couldn't please my father no matter how much I sacrificed myself.'

He watched her pause and check herself, opening her mouth and then turning away as if having second thoughts.

'What were you going to say? I want you to be direct with me.'

She turned back to him. 'I was going to say that perhaps you are still trying to please your father, but then I wondered whether this was fair. There is part of us that always wants to please our parents.'

'I'm sure you're right, but what makes me react so violently?'

Again she paused. 'Perhaps it is because you never reacted before, you kept all your frustrations tightly contained and they had nowhere to go.'

'I once described it to Marjorie as like having bombs strapped to me that were likely to go off at any moment, that I carried with me the permanent threat of self-destruction. It's pathetic really, isn't it? A man in his forties still bleating on about his father.'

'I can hear you saying that to Marjorie as well and if she didn't tell you it's rubbish, then I certainly will.'

'When I first went to her I wanted to pretend that the attacks didn't exist, that they were some sort of blip that came and went and didn't really matter. It's only now that I can see that they are merely symptoms of a larger malaise. You know,' he said, changing his tone of voice, 'that I have never really talked like this, except of course with Marjorie. But that was different.'

'Well, Mr Browning, it's about time you did because I wouldn't mind going to one or two concerts with you.'

'And what about going to Norton Hall to see my father?'

She smiled. 'I would consider it a pleasure. And a challenge.'

On the way back in the car he told her about the house and its history and, grateful that he was driving, added, in a matter of fact way, that his father wanted to give it to him. She remained silent for a moment as the car hummed towards London.

'That must be difficult for you,' she said quietly. And then, looking across to Toby with a smile on her face, she added. 'I wonder what he's up to?' And they both laughed and for the first time in as long as he could remember, Toby felt that he had an ally. It was only as he dropped her in Marylebone High Street that he remembered what she had said to him earlier.

'I still don't know much about you, do I? I have spent the day talking about myself. I'm sorry.'

'Yes,' she said, getting out of the car, 'you have hogged the conversation. But we have a long ride to Norfolk to put that right.' And she slammed the door. He watched her put on what he still thought of as an iPod, before turning and feeling for the passenger door. She kissed the palm of her hand and placed it flat against the glass. He stretched across and placed his hand against hers. He was sure she knew that this is what he would do.

# Chapter 29

The windows in the cream stuccoed houses by the exit to the Park reflected the western sky, pink with streaks of grey neatly framed like printed blinds, for a moment an optical illusion. It caused Peter Harrington to stop and look up the cobbled street to the fine double fronted house topped by a wide, low pediment. The windows might just as well have been mirrors so finely was the sky they faced defined in them. Just as this was a *trompe l'oeil* so he considered that all was not what it seemed to be with Marise. He now recalled what she had said at the inquest, that she could see no reason why Marjorie Nielson should have taken her own life. For the first time he wondered had she been lying? He had been too soft on Marise. If she had lied before, she could lie again.

Peter Harrington was an orderly man, both by nature and by training and as he walked back to the City he felt like a soldier before an inspection knowing that his kit would not pass muster. There were too many loose ends and it irked him. Marise had refused to answer his questions, particularly the one about the missing pages. Was it simply jealousy that made her so resistant to him, or was she frightened of something? He turned down into Cavendish Square heading towards Bloomsbury, his regular pace encouraging his thoughts. He knew enough about the therapeutic process to understand that there is an important line between therapist and client, although occasionally this can be crossed. Is that what had happened between them? Had she stepped over the line that separated them? He walked eastwards towards the night, past the bars on the Clerkenwell Road already spilling customers onto the pavement, on to Shoreditch and then down to his hotel. And as the darkness settled on the City a thought came to him which made him slow his pace and resulted in him sitting on a marble bench, part of the small amphitheatre in Broadgate used for ice skating in winter. The coroner might have got it wrong. If Marise had lied when she said that she had no reason to think that the therapist might have taken her own life, perhaps she had been there at Marjorie's home on the morning of her death. She could have seen what Marjorie had written about his case and removed it. It would account for the fact that she blamed him for her death. As he let this thought sink in, he imagined the skaters gliding and tumbling in front of him, the good skaters drifting easily around the small arena, neatly weaving between the more clumsy novices, their bodies leaning and swaying in perfect balance. He was caught in a loop but he was stumbling not gliding.

His first thought had been to call Vera but then he remembered that tomorrow was Thursday, the day she regularly cleaned at Marjorie's house. Although it was still dark when he woke, the dawn chorus was already in full flood by the time he reached Hampstead and a still, pale light defined the big yellow brick house. A silver tabby cat licked its paws on one of the gateposts and a milk float whirred its way up the hill behind him. Peter assumed she would not start work before six and he waited patiently, with the cat, for signs of her arrival. Not long after, he saw her approach and as she walked past him she nodded but did not stop. She climbed the stairs to the front door and let herself in. She left the door open and Peter followed. She had her back to him removing her coat as he entered the wide hallway.

'You want something more,' she said, placing her scarf on one of the line of pegs along the wall.

'I do, Vera. Something was missing from my folder and I want to find it.'

She shrugged. 'You know the way,' she said. 'And you remember what I told you.' She turned to face him now. 'I believe you are doing this for Marjorie.'

He nodded at her as he went up the staircase towards the study at the top of the house. He felt quite different this time, his focus not blurred by apprehension. Nevertheless, he hesitated at the entrance to her room and, as before, pushed the door open before stepping in. The painting of the therapist looked down from the wall in contemplation of his arrival. He quickly went over to the desk in the window and checked that he hadn't missed anything on the old wooden surface. Without pause, he opened the drawers and looked carefully though their contents. This time he didn't feel that he was trespassing and under her watchful gaze he moved across to the filing cabinets the other side of the door. He pulled at the brass handle, like a hollow upturned segment of orange, of the top drawer but it was locked. Standing in the same position, he looked left and then right. He put his hand on a small lustre jug just to his right and gently shook it before turning it over. Nothing. He felt along the tops of two prints of Leningrad which hung just above the cabinet and moved them slightly away from the wall. But no key fell to the ground. His gaze moved slightly wider and on a small wooden table he looked behind the elaborate frame holding a black and white photograph of a woman wearing a long black coat and a tall black hat. It was only when he drew a blank here did he turn around and face the fireplace and the mantelshelf. He took two steps forward and looked along its surface, under the candlestick and the narrow lamp with its parchment shade painted in zigzags of mauve. And then his eye came to the portrait and somehow he knew it would be there. Sliding his hand up the right hand side of the painting, to the point where it began to slope away from the wall, he felt the key hanging from the tiny hidden hook. He took it off and pausing in front of the portrait as he might have done an altar, he said quietly 'don't worry' before stepping back to the cabinets.

She was an organised woman and the eight drawers were filed alphabetically. So many lives, so many secrets separated by so much more than brown manila. He went to where his own file should have been without much hope of finding the missing pages. There was nothing there. He didn't exist and in a sense he took comfort at this, as though his removal was a sign of recovery and release. He was about to shut the drawer when he noticed, further along from where his dossier once lay, the name Perdita Landberg. He stared at it before slowly sliding it out of its position and laying it on top of the wooden cabinet. He then took out his phone and without thinking called her number. He waited, forgetting at first that she was blind and that it was only seven thirty in the morning. Eventually she answered.

'I'm sorry to phone so early,' he said. 'This is Peter Harrington and I have something for you and a question I would like to ask you.' He waited but she didn't say anything. 'I have some papers which belong to you and your colleague, the one at the funeral. I can't remember his name.' Again he waited.

'His name is Toby Browning.'

Whether she had guessed what he had for her, for them, he couldn't tell. 'Will you be at free later, say eleven? Could we meet in the same place?'

'OK,' she said, with no query in her tone as if this was all matter of fact.

He put the mobile back in his pocket and pulled open the first drawer and found Toby Browning's file. He slid the drawer shut and turned to replace the key, carefully slotting it onto the hook. As he left the room he looked back at Marjorie and said, with a slight bow, 'thank you'.

Downstairs he heard the sound of a vacuum cleaner and he opened the door to a large living room to find Vera at work. He called to her and she switched off the machine.

'Vera. I cannot find the missing pages, but I have taken the dossiers of two other of her clients, who I know. You must trust me when I say that I will not read them. They will go to their owners.'

'You will tell me what happens, won't you?' she said, looking at him.

'I promise Vera. But you will have to help me one more time. I need to have the address of Marise.'

Vera went to her handbag and pulled out an address book. 'Trust is a strange thing, Mr Harrington. It is instinctive.' She wrote the address on a card and gave it to him. 'I don't think she will give you the key to her home,' she said again fixing him with her eyes.

'No, Vera, I don't suppose she will. Thank you.'

It was only nine-thirty so Peter Harrington walked down Haverstock Hill, from the village of Hampstead into Camden Town. He cut through another village, Primrose Hill before entering Regent's Park by the east side of the Zoo. He watched the wolves lope along the boundaries of their enclosure and he was aware of the big owls marking his own progress from their perches below him. He passed the café where he had sat with Marise and looked over half expecting to see her huddled up in her coat. After the relative quietness of the Park came the roar of the Euston Road and he waited for the pedestrian lights to stop and part the roaring traffic before he crossed and entered the top of Marylebone High Street. He was early arriving at the café and he ordered a coffee and waited for Perdita to arrive.

So assuredly did she appear at the entrance to the patisserie that he was certain she would see him and come over and join him. Instead she was shown to a table in the corner, the same one they had sat at before. He got up, leaving his coffee and announced himself to her before sitting down. She had a calmness about her and he realised that she was expecting him to explain why they were here. He came straight to the point.

'On the morning of Marjorie's death she had been reading my dossier, notes on my case. Marise led me to think that I had somehow been responsible for her death. When I went to retrieve the notes I found some pages missing.'

Perdita had turned her head slightly as if to hear more clearly what he was saying.

'Anyway, I went back to try and find them but with no luck.

What I did come across, though, were these two folders which belong to you and Mr Browning.' He pushed them forwards until they touched her fingers. 'They have not been opened.'

She looked at him before she spoke. 'Thank you Mr Harrington. I can understand your curiosity about what happened. I have thought about it since, but of course all we can do now is speculate. Who do you think has your missing papers?'

'Marise. I think she might have been at the house the morning that Marjorie died.'

Perdita frowned. 'You don't think she had anything to do with her death, do you? Didn't the coroner say she died of natural causes?'

Peter chose his words carefully. 'I think Marise is very involved in the death of Dr Nielson, but I am not quite sure how. And I think I have something to do with it. I will find out. I have to find out.'

Perdita shuffled the two folders in front of her, putting one on top of the other and then the other way around, as though she was about to do a card trick. 'Our anxieties reduced to a few pages,' she said quietly before smiling. 'I don't suppose I shall ever read mine.'

At first he didn't know what to say. 'Whatever, it should be yours and you can give the other one to Mr Browning.'

She chuckled. 'He'll be thrilled about that.' And then she laughed, a rich and quiet sound and he watched as her shoulders shook. 'I'm sorry,' she continued, 'I'm grateful and I hope that when you get to the bottom of what did happen you will let me, us, know.'

'And I trust that if you, or Toby, remembers anything that might help me, you'll get in touch.'

When he got up to leave, she was still smiling.

# Chapter 30

Somewhere their thoughts must have coincided, she decided afterwards, for the worries that began to nag at her after their trip to the Chilterns seemed to find an echo in the phone call she received from Toby late on Thursday evening. She could tell immediately he was uncertain and at first she wondered if he was calling to cancel their trip to Norton Hall on Saturday. He approached what he was going to say like an inexperienced pilot about to make a landing in a light aircraft, skimming uncertainly just above the runway afraid to actually touch down.

'Firstly, can I say that I found it a great help to talk to you the other day.'

'I found it a help as well,' she said and he continued his erratic descent.

'I've been thinking about Saturday,' he went on, with no great confidence, 'and I just wonder, well, I just wonder if you are free to go down a day early, tomorrow and perhaps stay over somewhere before we get to my father's?'

'Have you told your father that I'm coming?' Perdita guessed where the conversation was going and two senses were alerted in her at one and the same time. Excitement and fear.

'Well, yes,' she heard him say uncertainly. 'And he sort of thinks we are a couple already. And,' he hurried on, 'I think we are in one way but not in another.'

Perdita unpicked his clumsy approach. 'You mean we haven't slept together?'

'No. Well, yes, I suppose.'

'So you want to sleep with me before we get to your father's, is that your plan?'

'No,' he said quickly. 'Well, yes and no. I just think it might be a good idea to know just a bit more about each other before we are thrown into the lion's den, as it were.' Toby's wheels had touched down briefly but had bounced back into the air.

It was now that Perdita realised that Toby's fears were a different version of her own. If Toby could not imagine them sleeping in the same bed at Norton Hall then Perdita had a real fear of it happening anywhere. They had achieved one sort of intimacy, which she had found easy, but thinking of the other sort caused her a swirl of uncertainty.

'I didn't mean we should sleep together tomorrow night. No, I didn't,' he emphasised, 'but I would appreciate being alone with you before we get to Norton Hall. I wouldn't presume the other, you know that.'

She thought she did. And she wondered again about the mystery of attraction. What was Toby 'seeing' when he looked at her? What shapes, what proportions, what conjunctions made her attractive? She could not see herself any more than she could see him but it wasn't just this that was making her pause before answering him.

'What did you have in mind?'

He still had not quite made the landing although he had better control now. 'I thought I would pick up you up around eleven tomorrow and we'd stay somewhere on the coast not far from Norton Hall. There's a hotel I know.'

'You're quite good at knowing these little places to go,' she said in a tone that belied the way she was feeling.

'It's a place I sometimes go to get away from my father,' he said, not really picking up on her tentative teasing. 'I walk along there to have a solitary pint after a particularly gruelling Sunday lunch. And there have been a few of those over the years.'

It surprised Perdita that Toby allowed himself to be so bullied by his father, but she kept this thought to herself.

'I'll book two rooms,' he said finally, as he taxied to a halt. And again she felt contrary emotions, relief and uncertainty. He had taken the honourable course of action, which, given that they had barely kissed, was perhaps inevitable but a lingering anxiety, like the draught from an open window, played around her.

'Fine,' she said. 'I'll be ready.' But whether she would be, she couldn't be sure. Later she told St Bede the story, under playing her doubts and seeking to draw on his abundant enthusiasm.

'My dear, you're going away for a dirty weekend. I'm so jealous. And to meet his father. My, we do move at a rate of knots. It'll be marriage the next week and babies the week after. Now, I take it that madam has given full consideration to the packing?'

'Well,' said Perdita, 'it might *not* be a dirty weekend, as you so delicately put it. He's even booked two rooms.'

'My, how gallant. But, darling, we have to plan just in case it is. So we have a father and a son to please. I think we can meet that challenge.'

'Strangely,' said Perdita, 'his father doesn't bother me at all. Toby paints a pretty foul picture of him and evidently he has always flirted with Toby's girlfriends. He certainly gives his son a hard time, but I'm sort of prepared for that.'

'And, by default, there is something that you aren't prepared for?'

Perdita knew he sensed her unease and she blessed him for not pursuing it.

'Darling, we're all racked by doubts all the time. What we need to be into is damage limitation. So I suggest being prepared for all eventualities. The sexiest of clothes, just in case and some jolly sensible stuff for those bracing walks which I gather are compulsory in that part of the world. So part Barbour girl and part, well, your lovely sexy self.'

And so it was that when she finally came to zip up her case she did so having not really expressed herself to St Bede. In the case she placed the two dossiers that she had been given by Peter. It was as if she was trapping her doubts in the bag and trusting to fortune that whenever and wherever she unzipped them she would be able to cope. She had no desire to read Toby's notes, out of a sense of propriety and because she wanted to form her own opinions, untainted by an intermediary. As to her own dossier, she acknowledged a sense of fear, an apprehension of what might be revealed.

Twelve hours later she thought of this as she orientated herself to the bedroom which Toby had just finished describing to her. Although they had left London in pouring rain, by the time they had arrived at the coast it had stopped and the mild air was tinged with the smell of salt and seaweed. He would knock on her door again in fifteen minutes, he said and then he would take her for a short walk. He had been quiet and non-committal in the car, speaking of the journey which he had made many times and not alluding to the difficulties they had discussed in the Chilterns. He was keeping himself in check as well.

She felt for the zips and slowly undid her case and smiled at the idea of her demons rushing to get out and flying around her like zephyrs. She left the case open and continued to familiarise herself with the room so that by the time he knocked on the door she could move around it with comfort. If only she could do this with her thoughts.

She took his arm as they left the hotel which he told her was built of flint and brink and fitted neatly into a meander of a river which was slowly being cut off from the sea by a mile or more of salt marshes. She could hear the sounds of many different birds, some, like the plaintive cry of the curlew or the piping of the oystercatchers, she knew but it seemed to her that the air was alive with new and strange sounds. He took her out along the sea dyke and unusually for the flat landscape, it was windless and warm. He talked of the churches they could see and of the village they were walking towards and how the low, cultivated fields to their left came down almost to their path which formed a division between them and the wild marshes beyond.

'So you like it down here?'

'Oh, I love it here,' Toby replied immediately.

'Despite the little local difficulties?' Perdita asked.

'Ah, well, yes. Pleasure does come with an element of pain.'

'Does it?'

'Seems to do in my case,' Toby said and she knew that he had said this facing away from her towards the sea.

'That's a bit pessimistic,' she challenged. 'Isn't it possible to have pleasure without the other?'

'There is a group of rabbits scattering in the fields, heading for the hedges,' Toby said. 'And a couple of hares, if I'm not mistaken.'

'And what do they think of the pleasure pain equation?' Perdita persisted.

'We're doing it again,' Toby countered. 'We're talking about me and not about you. I'm sorry.'

Whether this was another evasion, Perdita couldn't be sure, but she did recognise that he might just as well ask her the same question. And in a round about way, he did.

'Don't you think that there is no such thing as unalloyed pleasure, that somehow the consequences always linger close by?'

Her instinct had been to deny this, but she hesitated, realising that this was exactly the predicament in which she found herself. If sex with Toby was an exciting prospect it came wrapped with anxiety which might easily, she feared, turn into pain.

'Well, perhaps I have my answer,' Toby said, putting his arm around her.

'Don't be so sure, Mr Browning,' she countered, not wishing to concede to the assumption of his practised scepticism. But she didn't know how to continue, to tell him that in one respect he might be right. She had yet to unzip this case and show its contents.

They walked on in silence until Toby told her about the path that led up from the marshes which had been used to take salt inland. It was clear to Perdita that Toby did not know how to make her challenge her thinking and for the moment she was grateful for this and she deferred to a different sort of conversation. He was an easy and fascinating companion and she marvelled at how quickly she had adapted to his company.

'You can feel the debris under your feet now,' he told her,

'which shows just how high the tide can come here. Last time I came here it had just lapped against the boundary wall of Norton Hall. It's hard to imagine it today, but the wind is normally so strong that all the trees here are bent away from the sea, deformed by the ferocious storms coming in off the North Sea.'

As Toby talked on, so Perdita began to relax into his illustrated guide to the landscape and as she did she imagined the wind and the trees and endeavoured to translate this to music, the idea that a repetitive series of events could warp someone into an unnatural shape. In some ways it had happened to both Toby and her and their ease with one another, the fact that they were walking along this path together, was recognition that they had been slightly misshapen by life.

Musically, this was the conjunction she liked, distortion with melody but it was only on this path with Toby that she realised, somewhat obviously, that it was a reflection of the dissonance in her own life.

Later, over dinner, she mentioned this to Toby and she heard him pause before he replied.

'Of course,' he said. 'It is your gift and your misfortune to be able to express yourself in a tangible way. Like my artists. However obscure, their pictures are all reflections of themselves. What dissonance, as you call it, does your music represent?' He asked the question slowly and very gently and as he did so, she felt his hand on hers.

Perhaps this is what Toby felt in the Barbican, she thought. A rising fear, an unstoppable tide, that was engulfing her. She, so sure in so many ways, so ready with a quick fire response and solutions to other people's problems, unable to answer this question about herself. She dropped her head in silence.

'You know,' she heard him say. 'That I don't care. That, whatever it is, will not deflect the way I think about you.'

'But what do you know of me, Toby?' Could he see more in her, because he was able to see her as a physical entity? Did this distort his perception or help it? She looked up at him.

'And what do you see in me, Perdita? Perhaps I should be frightened that you can see straight through me? Or is that the very thing which attracts me? That you can.' He leant over the table and kissed her, but not as he had done before, but with a fierceness which was quite different.

They left the table, Perdita holding his hand and slightly behind him as they climbed the stairs. Instead of turning towards her room, he took her in a different direction along the corridor. He stopped and kissed her again before opening a door and guiding her inside.

'I have something for you,' he said, taking her by the hand to an armchair in the corner of the room. She felt a mix of excitement and confusion. A moment later she was handed a rectangular package which she knew could only be a picture. It was wrapped in paper and she felt the string or ribbon which encircled it. She looked up at Toby.

'Open it.'

As she peeled back the paper he knelt down in front of her. 'I saw this before I met you and once I had, it seemed to sum up many of things I felt and worried that I might not be able to say.'

She had the picture on her lap and ran her fingers lightly over it, feeling the roughness of the paint, the different textures of its surface, the smell of the oils.

'It is an abstract,' Toby continued, 'but the colours and the shapes seemed to represent the way you made me feel. There are bright pinks and whites and lines and dots which, I don't know, spoke of what I couldn't put into words. I thought you would love it.'

'It's beautiful,' she said and leaned forward so that he could kiss her again.

'It reminded me of the seaside, gaiety and freedom, clear blue skies and bright colours. In a sense, there is no doubt in this picture.'

It was his way of talking to her, she thought, through an

intermediary, someone, something that could translate for him. Did she need the same with him? Was she able to talk directly to Toby Browning, or did she need a go-between?

'Now,' he said, 'I shall accompany you back to your room.'

She stood, holding the picture by the edge of its frame in her right hand, a symbol in so many ways of the point they had reached. It touched her in more ways than she could say that he had given her a picture and that he had done so unselfconsciously as if he took for granted that she could see it and appreciate it.

'Do you know?' she said, looking up at him.

'I know that there is something that is making you uncomfortable, and I don't want to make it worse.'

She leaned forward against him. 'Thank you. I want to talk to you but I don't know how.'

'It appears to be a familiar story between us,' he said into her hair.

She followed him back to her room, knowing exactly where she was and when she would arrive at her door. About this she was sure, but beyond the door lay a territory that was unexplored and menacing, but she sensed that he knew this and that she could cross the threshold with some tiny shred of confidence. He let her into the room first and he turned to go.

'No, don't,' she said, not looking at him. 'Wait a moment.' She felt his stillness and for a second neither of them moved. And then she moved towards him and he took her in his arms. This was not passion, but a state beyond it, almost post-coital, suspended between emotion and rationality. They stood there a long time and she felt the heat from his body and the steadiness of his breathing.

'It was this that I went to see Marjorie about,' she said quietly. 'My inability to get beyond this point. To know why anyone would want to go further with me and my uncertainty about what to do next.'

'I know,' he said, in a near whisper. 'I can feel it in you. For a woman of such wonderful confidence, it must be very important.

I have never really wanted to know what is happening in the lives of those around me. Until now.'

She heard him and she knew it was true and for that instant she felt safe as if his arm around her embraced so much more than merely her body. There were no darting hands feeling her, groping her breasts, eagerly tugging at her clothing. She was being allowed to pause, to take stock and draw breath and make her own decision. He kissed her and wished her good-night. She heard the door click quietly shut and she sat on the bed and lay back against the pillows. The bag was still to be unzipped but perhaps Toby Browning knew what was in it anyway and was prepared to deal with. She fell asleep fully clothed, her feet crossed, her arms resting over her heart and her white hair on the pillow making her look like a marble carving of an earl's wife in one of the local churches Toby had described to her on their walk. Only she was warm and alive and was dreaming of being carried on a high wind, weightless and free over a landscape of patterned fields in a sky full of thousands of different birds each singing a different tune, a great cacophony of sound. It was only when she woke three hours later, chilled and uncomfortable, that she realised Marjorie's notes lay undisturbed in her suitcase by the window.

# Chapter 31

Marise lived between Regent's Park and Paddington station, in a tall non-descript block with an old fashioned lift which rattled as it slowly took him upwards to the eighth floor. He felt no impatience at its ponderous ascent for he was sure that this was the last act in the drama that had led him over the past weeks to drop his normal life and pursue the truth about a woman he was only just getting to know but who still remained a mysterious shadow somewhere just ahead of him, elusive and compulsive. To know the truth about what happened to her was more necessary than ever, a piece of unfinished business which refused to let him go. Earlier he had spoken in these terms on the phone to Natalie, putting together for her an assembly of the story of the dead therapist and asking her to understand his absence. It was only now, in this shaking lift with its concertina gate, that he fully understood how out of character his call had been, for during it he had explained about his need for therapy and the story of Freddie and what had followed. It was as if what had secretly haunted him had become matter of fact, a part of life and not removed and separate from it, like an unacknowledged bastard child. She had listened with sympathy, gently nudging him this way and that for further clarification and it was only at the end that he had realised what a comfort it had been to talk to her, to express himself in such a way. It felt like the end of a journey, with this the final climb.

Peter Harrington shut the lift gate and looked along the narrow, ill lit corridor, the air still and stale. He walked slowly, looking for the number of her apartment until he stood facing a pale green door with an old Bakerlite bell under which was a small metal frame which contained the name 'Dubarry'. He was startled by the noise the bell made. He waited. Could he hear movement behind the door, or was this his imagination? He resisted the temptation to say her name for fear that if she was there she might never open the door to him. He waited again and eventually the door split open and he could see her eye looking at him, holding his stare, not blinking. He remained still.

'I knew you would come,' she said and she stood aside from the door so he could push it open. He walked into a small flat which should have been in the centre of Paris, the living room dominated by a dark wood dresser and several plates in metal holders hung on the wall ahead of him. A round table by the window was covered in a white lace top with patterned edges. Through the door to the right he could see an old enamel stove and on it a metal cafetière bubbled, filling the small rooms with the aroma of coffee.

'What happened, Marise?' He heard the door shut and the security chain slid into place. Marise ignored him and walked into the kitchen and poured two cups of coffee which she put onto a small lacquered tray with a small china cup of milk and a silver bowl of sugar cubes. She returned and placed the tray carefully on the round table. With a gesture of her hand she offered a cup to him and he took a sip of the bitter, black coffee. Marise left hers untouched.

'You want to know about Marjorie Nielson.' She wasn't looking at him, but over to the dresser where there were two photographs in silver frames, a black and white picture of the therapist as a young woman and the other a faded colour photograph of her with Marise sitting in what Peter presumed was Regent's Park. She went over and pulled open a drawer and removed three sheets of paper which she handed to him without meeting his eyes.

'Read,' she said. 'Read and understand.'

He looked at the typed papers and confirmed that they were the sheets that continued on from his dossier. He glanced up at Marise, as if seeking permission to read. She was still staring at the dresser.

'Go on. Read,' she ordered.

Notes on Marjorie Nielson. Aged 78. Referred by
Marjorie Nielson. Problems various but specific.

I am speaking this aloud on the evening of April 1. The date is more
than appropriate. Today I have heard the story of Peter Harrington, of
how he finally tracked down the cause of his own depression, the
event which was spoiling his life. To hear his anguish and to witness
his release has had a profound effect on me and I feel I have to give
this account of my own experience which I have so expertly denied all
these years. Fool me, perhaps, but would it have made any difference?
Would it?
Pause.
Would talking about what happened have changed my life? Of
course, of course, but what was taken from me can never be given
back. Perhaps hearing the misery of others was in a perverse way a
comfort for I could see that there were others as badly off as me. I
could hide behind them.
But why did Peter Harrington's story have such an impact?
Ah, here is the rub and for me to fully understand it I have to go
back to my childhood, where we all have to go at some stage. I was
eight. Do we see ourselves at that age? Looking back now I am
watching a beautiful young girl with blond hair carrying a doll,
Mischa, with her blue polka dot dress and her plaited blond hair.
What happened to that girl? Where did she go? That terrible day
you could say that she grew up immediately, or you might say that,
as a woman, she never grew beyond that point at all. Intellectually I
know all this, but what good is that?
So can you be that little girl again?
Pause.
The siege has been going on for months. The city is falling around
us and we are fighting not just the enemy, whoever they are, but for
our lives. We are eating cats and dogs and the cold is almost too
much to bear. But I have Mischa and somehow we have to get

through. Our beautiful house with my father's violins is windowless and the ceilings have fallen in two of the rooms. We all have to hunt for food. We are desperate and each day it becomes harder and more dangerous. There are bodies everywhere, broken and mutilated, foul smelling corpses, even in the freezing winter. Is this an upbringing for a child? But this is nothing. This, after a while, we took for granted. That is the special skill of children, to adapt and adjust, to bend with what is happening. It soon became normal.

Pause.

But at a cost.

When it is happening to you, you do not think of cost or damage. But somewhere you store it, deep down. I was an expert scavenger and I was good at exploring the rubble and squeezing through gaps in the broken houses to the smashed kitchens and cellars. Through that first terrible winter we stayed alive until finally we pushed them back, the Germans. And that is the sadness. It wasn't the Germans who did it, but Russians. Pause. But does it really matter? They were men. I can see it now as if it was yesterday, playing out to me like a newsreel in black and white. There was no colour in the city then. It was all grey and black and white. And there is no colour when I remember. It was harder and harder to find food and I went further afield, scrabbling over rubble and through broken doorways. I had found a store of tinned food in a cellar lit from above by tall windows. I can see the shape of those metal windows now. It was all I had to look at, all I had to cling to. I returned to the cellar for more tins, but they had discovered the store too and were waiting when I arrived. There were six of them, dirty, swarthy, uncouth Russian soldiers who had been fighting nonstop for over a hundred days. But why should I begin to excuse them. They may have seen terrible things, had to do terrible things, but it did not mean they should do what they did to me.

Pause.

So what did they do to you?

I was raped, although then I did not know what rape was. They played with me, chasing me and touching me and I was frightened.

There was a fierce and unusual look in their dirty faces, an awful obsession in their eyes. There is not a nice way of telling this story, but it is what happened and it has to be told. One of the men took out his penis and asked me to touch it. I had never seen such a thing and I shook my head and he pushed me to the ground and he tore at my clothes. And then there was a pain such as I had never experienced before as he forced himself into me. Holding me down, pushing into me. I could not scream. My voice had gone and all I could see were the windows moving backwards and forwards as he did on top of me. And then, afterwards, the others, each in turn, silent and furtive. I looked beyond their faces. I had to. And so it went on and on. And then perhaps I fainted and I think now that this might have saved my life, if my life was worth saving after that, for when I regained consciousness they were gone and I was left alone with the pain. Left alone with the pain forever. I was bleeding and torn, my legs awash with my own blood and their sperm, although I didn't know what it was then. I was ashamed. It was my fault that I had been caught down there in the cellar and this was my punishment for stealing their food. It was agony to walk and I dragged myself into the snow so I could wash the evidence away, to pretend it had never been there. When I eventually got back to the apartment, I told my parents that I had fallen and I refused to let them touch me. I screamed. I screamed the screams that I should have in that cellar. But if I had, I might have died. And I didn't, my screams went inside. In the morning I could not move and there was blood on the bedding. And then my parents saw what had happened and the image of my father recoiling is vivid in front of me now, his hand going to his mouth, his eyes turning away. I think it was to kill him, for he never seemed the same again. Or was it me? When he died a year later I knew it was because of me. I lost my father. And I lost sex. And the children I should have had.

Pause.

But I have told this story to myself before. Why am I putting this down now?

Perhaps it is age. Perhaps you cannot carry your scream forever. It

235

is strange to have one client to disturb your carefully laid defences, but two . . . I could see in Perdita the struggle to tell me about her sexuality. I suspected she was a virgin, well a virgin of sorts and I wanted to be her, to claim back what had been wrenched from me and to anticipate what she was now anticipating. I never had that, never would have that. And then there was Peter Harrington, handsome and sure, a man prepared to examine the other side of himself even though he found it profoundly difficult. And I knew that I could never have had him, or anyone like him. But it was when he told the story of the boy, the natural leader, the youth whose life was so carelessly ended that I felt the waste of my own life rise in my chest like never before, for I felt the pain that Peter Harrington felt, the shock of destruction. And I wanted to share it with him, my own shattered life. For the first time I wanted to say, as I understand you so will you understand me? Peter had to conceal his emotions, to deny the smashed and broken body of his friend, to pretend that it had never happened. That was his secret, like mine. But it stayed within us, working through our systems, never letting us rest. We organised our defences well, but the events of the past lay like dead weights on us, condemning us always.

Pause.

I was so damaged that I could never have children, never enjoy sex. At eight years old I became a spinster lady, a dry old stick whose only use was to give advice to others. When I did my training I was as clever as that little girl in the rubble of Stalingrad. I told stories, true stories, of the horrors. But not that horror, not the horror of the men in that cellar on that cold floor under those blank windows. No one knew this, not even Marise who has been my closest friend for these many years. But I felt I could have told Peter Harrington and that he could have absorbed my story and somehow helped me through these final years of my life.

And why can't you?

He stopped reading and he could feel his heart beating, the thunder in his chest both a reflection of the anger he felt on behalf of Marjorie Nielson and at the reminder of what had happened to him on the hillside in Germany all those years ago. In this dim room, the twin traumas, hers and his, had finally met. He experienced an overwhelming remorse for the woman he had barely known but who had now connected with him so personally and profoundly. He felt touched by her, not as a client, but as a friend, an ally and it pained him to think of her isolation and the loneliness of living with her burden. He hadn't been wise enough to help her, to recognise the signs that she might have been giving him, just as he had revealed himself, knowingly or not, to her during their sessions.

Marise remained motionless by the dresser.

'Do you think she committed suicide?' he asked her and she remained facing away from him when she replied.

'Wouldn't you? Could you have lived with that?' Marise spat out the words, her words strangely harsh in the neat little room. 'It was disgusting what they did to her and she had the memory of it all her life. She carried it with her, that terrible . . . ' Marise searched for the word ' . . . that terrible intrusion. I hate them.'

Peter watched her say this, and heard the coldness of her words and the venom of her delivery. There was no compassion in her voice, no sadness in her loss or emotional recognition of what her companion had been through. Her anger, like her gaze, was directed elsewhere.

'You were there that morning.'

'You will not let it be, will you? Does it matter now?' Marise continued to look towards the kitchen, her hands, white and veined, gripping the back of the wooden chair in front of her.

'It matters, Marise, it matters even more now that I have read this.' He held the papers towards her and she turned to look at them and then, at last, towards him.

'She was dead when I arrived. She called me late, very late the night before and said that she wanted to see me. She sounded tired and perhaps a little drunk. We both get up early, so I arranged to come over the following morning and that's when I found her.'

'She was already dead?'

'Yes. I think she had injected herself twice.'

'How did you know?'

'At first I wasn't sure, and then I read the notes in front of her and I made the assumption that this is what she had done.'

'But why didn't you call an ambulance, or the police?'

'Because, Mr Harrington, I knew she was dead and I hoped that by taking the papers away people would assume that she had died naturally, from a stroke. I did not want people to think that she had committed suicide. And I certainly didn't want anyone finding what she had written about herself.'

'So you left before Vera arrived.'

Marise nodded and Peter got up from the table and walked over to the grey haired woman.

'I don't think you are telling me the truth, Marise. It wasn't the horror of what Marjorie went through that appalled you, it was the fact that she hadn't told you about it, hadn't confided in you. But it was even worse than that, wasn't it? She wanted to tell me, to confide in me because she thought I would understand. You were jealous and you felt betrayed. How could she do this to you, you thought, after all our time together?'

She steadfastly refused to look at him, her bleak face set in denial.

'I think you were with Marjorie the night before. She had been drinking and she told you something of her thoughts about me, about the peculiar impact I had made in her life. Perhaps she even told you that she had been writing about it. Maybe she went to the lavatory, maybe she dropped off to sleep, but you saw what she had written and you were angry, at me and at her.'

Marise's face betrayed nothing and he continued.

'I imagine that sometimes, especially after she had been drinking, you administered Marjorie's insulin. Am I right? And that night you injected a double dose, either in one go or in the same puncture mark again. Is that right, Marise?'

There was a long silence and the old woman was still looking into the distance as if transfixed by an object far away.

'You will never know, Mr Harrington. She was my closest friend, my only friend, and you took her from me. She could not cope with what you told her about yourself, with what you stirred up in her. You killed her as much as anyone.'

'No, Marise, it was you who could not cope with what happened. I merely reminded Marjorie of what she knew all too clearly about, the misery of trauma. In the end it was you who stopped her talking to me, of helping herself by talking to me. You could not have borne that, could you Marise? That I might become more important than you. So you made sure it could never happen.'

She made no response and he turned to the seat at the round table. He suddenly felt exhausted as if the pursuit of this moment had taken all his resources, physical and emotional. He wanted to be alone to mourn the death of Marjorie Nielson, not as a therapist but as a friend, albeit it one he never knew until after she died. He had a choice now and he thought quickly and clearly, as he had been taught to do. No purpose would be served by revealing the truth about Marjorie's death. He looked over at Marise, a diminished and bitter woman and he thought of Marjorie and the pain of her memories. He wished he could have helped, to give back some of what she had given him. It was too late for them both, the therapist and her first patient. He let himself out of the door and rattled slowly back down to the ground. He crashed the lift shut and pushed through the doors into the bustle of London and breathed in the air. He felt he had stepped from the past to the present.

# Chapter 32

He watched her from the bottom of the stairs sitting in the bay window of the restaurant, the table in front of her spread for breakfast. She was looking out of the window at the view over the tiny harbour and she gave the impression that she could see the jumble of boats on the bend in the river and the children playing on the sandy banks. In one way he believed that she could see what he saw, just as he was convinced she would turn in his direction now, even though he had not announced himself. Sure enough, she looked towards him and he walked across the carpet towards and sat opposite her.

'Good morning, Ms Landberg.'

'Good morning, Mr Browning.'

It was as he sat down that Toby noticed the two folders on the table in front of Perdita. He put his hands on hers.

'What have we here?'

'Secrets,' she said. 'These are Marjorie's notes on us, on our sessions with her.'

Toby glanced down at the folders and looked at Perdita, waiting for her to continue.

'Peter Harrington gave them to me and yesterday I forgot all about them. He thought we should have them. Are you interested in seeing yours? Or mine, perhaps?'

Outside, Toby watched as an elderly woman walked past with several large dogs on leads. 'To tell you the truth, no. A month ago I might have said differently, but now,' he emphasised the word by patting the back of her hands, 'this seems a little like history.'

'For Peter, they were part of a jigsaw puzzle. Marise has made him believe that he was somehow responsible for Marjorie's death for apparently she was reading his notes the morning that she died. He wanted to, needed to, find out more. In that way, his notes were more important to him than perhaps ours are to us. Perhaps that's why I forgot about them yesterday,' she added.

He looked down at the manila folders and knew that his lack of curiosity was to do with the woman sitting opposite who continued to regard him evenly. 'They seem as incidental as the woman who has just walked by with her dogs.'

'And you don't want to find out more about me?' Perdita said, with a tilt of her head.

'Do you think I would?' he said. 'If there are things I should know, I'm sure you would tell me.' It rather surprised him that he had made this assumption but he felt that it was true. She regarded him, as if weighing up what he had just said.

'I never did tell Marjorie, but I think she knew. It was getting me to say it, that was the problem. The gap between what we think and what we say can be enormous and seem unbridgeable. And unbearable.'

He took her hand. 'I would hate to see your notes,' he said. 'It wouldn't seem right. Just tell me when you feel like bridging that gap.'

'This has a neat symmetry, don't you think? The arrival of the folders on the same day that we are going to see your father. It's like an ending and a beginning.'

'Ah, my father,' Toby exclaimed. 'It could be the beginning of the end, more like it.'

They drove along the coast to Norton Hall, the road taking them through a series of small flint and brick villages and Toby continued his potted history of north Norfolk, perhaps in an attempt to mask his apprehension about the encounter ahead of them.

'The old railway line used to chug along the coast here. Our village is about a mile or so ahead of us, the church on the hill looking down on the house,' Toby said.

'Can we go up to the church first?' she asked and Toby turned up the narrow lane in the direction of the round flint tower and its majestic views of the flat lands all around. He stopped the car and before he could get out she put a hand on his arm.

'I just wanted to say that no matter how your father is today, he won't be able to mess up what we've already got.' She moved her hand to his face and leaned across and kissed him. In the shadow of the thousand year old tower, he felt the passion in her kiss, the sexuality beneath the body that was now arched towards him. As much as he wanted to touch every part of her, he also experienced a huge sense of release, as if a tether had been hacked away and allowed him to drift free. He helped her out of the car and they kissed again. 'I don't know what Saint Margaret would have made of this,' he said.

'She would have been jealous, Toby.'

He took her through the graveyard outlining the view spread in front of them, the village just below with Norton Hall at its edge, butting into the marshes.

'You love it,' she said.

'I do, but it comes at a price.'

Charles Browning met them at the door and ignored Toby in favour of an excessively effusive greeting for Perdita.

'My dear, how simply wonderful to meet you. Welcome, welcome to Norton Hall. Come in. Now let me introduce you to my fiancée, Penny.'

Although Toby had not been expecting this, he had predicted that his father would contrive some situation which would make their stay in the house more awkward.

'I believe you've met Penny already, Toby,' Charles Browning said with his back to Toby as he helped Perdita take off her coat.

'Hello, Penny. Nice to see you and congratulations. I don't think you know Perdita.' The two women shook hands. There cannot be more than three or four years between them, thought Toby and yet one is my stepmother to be and the other is about to become my lover.

Toby watched as his father led Perdita in the direction of the living room, his arm firmly around her waist, something he knew Perdita hated. 'It's marvellous that you don't let your handicap stop you getting about,' he heard his father say and he winced. Toby expected a withering response from Perdita, but instead she turned to her host and said. 'Ah, that's the trick, Mr Browning, I don't regard it as a handicap.'

Charles Browning dispensed drinks with his usual gusto, keeping up a running commentary about the house and its predecessors. It was several minutes before he asked Perdita a question about herself.

'And what did you say you do?' he said, whilst raking ice out of a bucket to drop into his whisky.

'I didn't,' Perdita replied calmly. 'I'm a composer.'

'A composer. How do you manage that?'

'Oh, I manage fine, thank you. I will send you some of my work on CD.'

'It's not that modern rubbish is it? Squeaking violins and strange instruments all out of tune.'

'Probably,' she said and Toby couldn't help smiling. He hoped that Perdita would register it, as she usually did.

'Isn't it marvellous about your son selling the Hodgkin,' she said, switching subjects. 'I believe the show was a huge success.'

'Can't bear that artist, myself. What do you think? Oh, but you wouldn't know, would you.' Charles Browning didn't say this with any sense of embarrassment, Toby observed. He was merely stating a fact and bowling along regardless.

'What I know of his work, I like very much,' Perdita said calmly. 'Your son has just given me a beautiful picture as a present. Don't you think that is wonderful? Although it is abstract, he says it should be called Beach and Rock because its chief colour is the pink of the rock he used to eat as a child. He has happy memories of his days at the seaside. I will show it to you.'

Toby watched Perdita circle his father with deliberate yet gentle attempts to get him to address or acknowledge Toby in one way or the other and he marvelled at her guile.

Over lunch, Toby made polite conversation with Penny about

Clayburn House and the forthcoming marriage but continued to be aware of Perdita's extended encounter with his father.

'Won't make decisions, that boy,' he heard his father say in his stage whisper. 'Offered him this place, but he can't seem to make up his mind. Beggars belief.'

'He loves this area and this house,' Perdita countered. 'Perhaps he considers this place too big a responsibility. We've not really talked about it.'

'Exactly,' Charles Browning jumped in, 'he needs to take responsibility.'

'You don't think buying and selling pictures for millions of pounds is taking responsibility? Anyway, what makes you want to give your home to your son at this stage?'

'Let me open another bottle.' Charles Browning stood and went over to the sideboard where he made a great show of uncorking a bottle of white Burgundy whose virtues and provenance he made sure everyone understood. 'Some of the vines that helped make this bottle are as old as this house, or at least the house that used to originally stand on this site.'

Toby listened to the familiar showmanship, doubting as he often did the truth of what his father was saying. Charles returned to the table and splashed wine into everyone's glasses.

'So how did you meet this son of mine?' he asked whilst still standing.

'We met at the funeral of our therapist,' Perdita said after the merest of pauses and he watched his father hesitate in mid-action, missing just a beat in his virtuoso performance.

'Well, there's a turn up for the books,' he said.

'Do you disapprove?' Perdita asked.

'About time he sorted himself out, if you asked me.'

'Anyway,' Perdita pressed on, 'I've been writing a composition about this therapist. Her name was Marjorie Nielson. Your son has helped me enormously. Only yesterday, for example we were walking along to Wells and Toby was describing how the prevailing winds have shaped the trees along the coastline, twisting them out of shape. And suddenly I could hear the last part of my composition, a reference to how a force of nature can make us grow unnaturally and how sometimes we need help to straighten ourselves out.'

She said this looking directly at Charles Browning, but her comments sailed past him unclaimed. 'This can be a difficult coast,' he said, raising his glass to her. 'It's not always as gentle as it is today. The last high tide lapped against our boundary wall.'

Perdita glanced over to Toby and smiled. If he hadn't known before, Toby now knew that he loved Perdita and he came around behind her and put his hands on her shoulders. 'Brilliant,' he said. 'I would love to hear it when you have finished.'

'Oh, you will, I assure you.'

As far as Charles Browning was concerned, they might have been speaking a foreign language. 'Can you make any money out of your compositions?' he asked in a way that presumed the answer.

'Indeed, Charles. I have made money from my writing. Nothing like your son earns, but enough. There's not a huge demand for contemporary classical music, I'm afraid.'

'I'm not surprised, from the sound of some of the stuff I have heard.'

'Some of that might have been mine,' Perdita said in mock indignation, but once again Charles Browning hadn't heard, or pretended not to.

After lunch, Toby took Perdita along the sea embankment towards the fields where the geese came to roost, so that she could hear the beat of a thousand wings in flight and the chatter of the birds as the night fell.

'Do you know,' she said as soon as they had left the house as she slipped her arm through his, 'I am not at all surprised you were in therapy.' And they both laughed. 'What's more,' she continued, 'he's a wily old bugger and I wonder why he's giving the house to you. He's probably frightened of global warming and rising sea levels, if you ask me. He tends to stick to his own agenda, doesn't he?'

'Could you imagine living here?'

She stopped and turned to him. 'I could imagine living anywhere you were.'

'That is a very big statement,' he said.

'It is,' she said.

Later, the geese gathered in the sky in front of them, wheeling and diving in a great swarm, darkening the blue grey sky before dropping as one to the ground to fill the dusk with their strange and engaging clamour. They kissed again then, intimately and separately as if no one else existed.

'You will have to help me tonight,' she said, close to his face.

'As you have helped me,' he said. As they walked back in the diminishing light, no one else did exist for Toby and this refocusing of his life had crept up on him as imperceptibly as the tides rose and filled the surrounding marshes.

'When can I hear your music, your new composition?' he asked her.

'When I have finished it, of course. I don't think it could have been written without you. As I told your father, not that he listened, the last part will be inspired by this weekend. I now see that it is about a journey, a journey from Marjorie to you, as if her dying was not in vain. I think she would have liked that.'

'You know my father has put us in the same room. I'll get him to make up the other spare room for me when we get back.'

'No, don't Toby. But remember what I said.'

Back in the house lay the two files containing their notes and Toby wondered what Perdita would make of his collection of fears and ramblings. In turn, could he unscramble what she had spoken about with Marjorie, the concerns which were still troubling her now? Never having been good at second guessing other people's emotions, he was forced to think about the woman on his arm who had marched so forcefully into his life to pitch camp at the forefront of his thinking. She seemed so unafraid of life, so able to spot its frauds and deceptions that it was hard for him to imagine her being brought low by anything.

Toby's father made a great fuss about dressing for dinner and he insisted that everyone follow his example. He had hired a chef and an assistant for lunch and dinner and when they returned, Toby described to Perdita the dining table that had already been laid for dinner: crystal glasses, heavy silver cutlery, a tall candelabra with six crimson candles along an old elm table with dark green napkins on beautiful blue patterned side plates.

'My father sees himself as an Edwardian patriarch whose every instruction has to be obeyed. But I think you've guessed that already.' They walked up to their room where their luggage had already been taken and immediately Toby felt self-conscious for them both.

'Would you like me to leave you while you change?'

'No,' she said uncertainly, 'I would like you to help me prepare. I have a friend who often does this,' she continued, 'Henry Beadles, or St Bede as I call him. He's really the only person, other than you, who doesn't really see that I am blind or if he does chooses to ignore it. I would like to have a bath. My things are in my case.'

Toby showed her the geography of the bedroom and bathroom before running her bath. Just before she shut the door she felt for him and kissed his hand and then his lips. He kicked off his shoes and lay on the bed and moments later she called from the bathroom.

'What are you thinking?'

'I'm thinking about you and what a slightly strange situation this is.'

'I've never done this before,' she called from behind the door.

'Well, nor have I.'

'No, I have never done it before.'

It took him a second to realise what she had said and then he suddenly sat up. From behind a closed door she was admitting to Toby a fact every bit as important as Toby's own story to her about his panic attacks. At that moment, so much of what she had said and alluded to in their time together made sense. How do people see me, she had asked, what do they see in me? What are the rules of attraction? And, since I can't see, how do I gauge these things, what criteria shall I use? But what was important to Toby was that she had said it at all, that she had trusted him. He looked at the closed door and he imagined her clenching her fists as she spoke.

'Toby, can you hear me?'

This was a Perdita he had not encountered before, tentative and wary, speaking from behind a barrier in a small voice.

'I can,' he answered.

'How did it get like this?'

'You only have to look at me to know the answer to that,' he said.

'How did it become such a problem for me? Why does it loom so large?'

'I think you told me that I felt the way I did because I kept all my frustrations inside me and that they had nowhere to go.'

'It's as if I begin to move forward but then I recognise the signs and I begin to close down. I defeat myself from the very start.'

'What signs?'

'Oh Toby, it's so difficult to talk about.'

Toby, unaccustomed to playing this role, was feeling his way carefully. 'What do you want to tell me Perdita? Whatever it is will be OK.' He waited and he could hear the tap dripping into the water behind the closed door.

'I have only had two reasonably serious relationships before this but you must know, Toby, that what I feel for you is quite different.'

Toby thought about this for a moment before replying. 'But I take it that the problem is the same and the signs, as you call them, have happened again?'

'Yes and no,' she said and he could almost hear her taking a deep breath before continuing. 'I have found sex a problem,' she said in a rush, 'and it is all to do with being blind.'

Toby knew what a concession this was for Perdita to make, an acknowledgment that her blindness might in the end have hampered her.

'I didn't know why the boys wanted me,' she hurried on. 'And, more to the point, I didn't know why I wanted them. Why should I let them touch me, I used to think and then it just got more and more difficult. It was as if I never had the chance to be certain of anyone before the sex thing came into play. I lost all my sense of judgement and I found it best to avoid any situation where it might happen. Or I became abrupt and dismissive.'

Toby walked over and stood by the door. 'Listen, Perdita, I can answer the first part of this. They wanted you because you are good looking and I know that this isn't a term you can use to describe, well, us, men.'

'But I've been lucky with you Toby. I feel that I have got to know you before now, before we . . . '

'I want to come in now but I won't if you say so.' He waited and then he pushed opened the bathroom door and walked in and knelt down and embraced her. They remained like that, the water seeping into his shirt and then he kissed her.

'I feel such a fool in saying it,' she said. 'Although I am not sure I have actually said it. It has become like a millstone and each year it seems to get heavier. You know, don't you?'

'I know,' he said. 'I know so well. I think you are going to have to shut your eyes and trust me.'

She stood up and he saw her naked for the first time. He took a towel and wrapped her in it and walked her through to the bedroom where he slowly dried her, taking great care not to touch her intimately. He led her to the bed and pulled back the covers and she got in. He took off his clothes and followed and for the first time he felt the strength and size of her body, her large breasts and wide shoulders. Her skin was pale and smooth and as he kissed her dark nipples he could feel her tense.

'Don't worry', he said, 'we can stop.'

She shook her head. 'Can I feel you?' she asked, as she ran her hand over his chest and down to his penis where, with great care, she defined its shape with her fingers. And then very quietly she said 'OK'. When he entered he did not know if the grunt she gave was of pain or an exclamation of triumph. He kissed her pale eyes and he felt the strange conjunction of desire and tearfulness, of abandonment at the instant of clarity. He wanted to hold on to this moment as long as he could, to remain suspended in the comfort he now experienced. They remained locked together, hardly moving.

'I should stop,' he whispered. 'I am not wearing a condom.'

She gripped him and he remained inside her and then he felt her fingers slowly release him and as he left her she exclaimed and again he wasn't sure why and he turned her face towards him.

'Now let me look at you,' he said as his eyes took in her wonderful white body and his finger defined a line from her lips, over her breasts down lower until it stopped in tangle of dark hairs between her legs, made even more startling in contrast with the paleness of the rest of her body.

'What shall we do?' he asked.

'What do you think?' she replied and when he re-entered her she smiled. He felt he was floating in a space he'd never been to before, in complete safety. It was a sensation he could never remember having before. He leant forward so their lips were almost touching. 'I would like to come with you,' he said, 'but we will have to wait. I think you know why.'

'Did you assume we'd make love?' she asked.

'No, I wanted to make love, but I assumed nothing,' he replied.

She continued to touch his body, to move her hands over his chest and legs, defining his contours and her hand came to rest between his legs. 'Thank you for your care,' she said. She turned her head away from him and he could feel that she was crying and he put his arms around her. When she turned to face him her lips were wet and she was shaking her head.

'Sometimes, how flimsy our fears are,' she said, her words not flowing, but disjointed. 'But they don't conform to reason, do they?' And then, in amongst the tears she laughed, expressing out loud the absurdity of her doubts and the joy at the beginning of their departure.

'So where on earth have you been?' Charles Browning demanded as they arrived in the dining room. 'I was about to send a search party.'

'No need, Charles, we're found,' Perdita said and she squeezed Toby's hand as they sat at the table.

Perdita was winning the verbal ping-pong with Charles Browning and Toby realised what a comfort it was to have her drawing fire from his father and relieving him of the relentless assault he normally experienced.

'I suppose it takes you longer to do everything,' he said to Perdita as he waved in the first course with a napkin in his hand.

'In this case Charles, you're right. Absolutely right. It has taken me a long time to get where I am tonight.' Charles frowned and turned his attention to his son.

'Well, Tobias, you've not had a lot to say for yourself this weekend. Have you thought about the proposal? Are you happy to take on the house?'

'Do you know, father, I love this house and all that it stood for over the years.' As he spoke he rested his fingers on top of Perdita's. 'And it would be churlish for me to turn your generous offer down.' He pushed Perdita's fingers slightly apart. 'And I'm not going to. I accept Norton Hall. Thank you.'

'At last,' exclaimed Charles Browning. 'Not one for making quick decisions, I must say,' he chided. 'What changed your mind, let me ask?'

'The woman on my right,' he said. 'Simple as that.'

'Couldn't make up your own mind, that it,' his father persisted.

'Ah, my own mind. There's an interesting topic. But, yes, I think you're right. She helped me make up my own mind. It's an on-going project.'

Later, as they were laying in bed together Perdita propped herself on her arm and faced him. 'We've sort of approached this the hard way, haven't we? So often it seems to me that sex comes first these days and only afterwards do you find out more about the person you have been so intimate with.'

'Maybe sex is not always intimacy,' Toby replied. 'Intimacy was when I touched your hand at the dinner table. Intimacy was when you spoke to me from the bath. I'm glad we did it this way round.'

'Sex is intimacy with you,' she said. 'And I'm glad you have decided about the house. I could never give up the place where I first made love to you.'

'Perdita Landberg, how you have changed my life.'

'Work in progress, I think you called it.'

'Work in progress, indeed.'

# Chapter 33

'Are you ready?'

He sat in Perdita's sparse living room and recognised the arrival of another milestone in their relationship.

'Yes,' he said.

'I want the truth,' she said.

'You will have the truth,' he replied.

Sitting at the piano, she was about to play the music she had composed for Marjorie. Behind her was the picture he had given her, lit by the only light in the otherwise dark room. He watched her take a deep breath as she started the CD and immediately the rolling, repetitive theme from deep down in the piano seemed to spiral its way towards him and wrap itself around his senses. Was it easier for him to receive this music because he knew what it was about, because he had met the woman who had inspired it and because he had fallen in love with the woman who created it? Yes, but the music had a power of its own and it was driven from somewhere deep inside Perdita, expressing both her vulnerability and her power. He was drawn further into the overlapping themes and the density of the piece and the events of the previous year came to him as he listened. He saw the face of Marjorie Nielson, leaning forward in her chair as she so often did, concerned and involved. He realised how the discordant notes represented not only the mystery of her life, but the problems that beset him, that had disrupted his life and Perdita's. And he saw Perdita herself, reflected in the sunlight of London Bridge, the first time he had really recognised her beauty and her existence. The huge chords that pulled him into the second movement, massive, ominous statements indicated not only doubt, but the awareness that somewhere deep down in the unconscious there was activity, felt but not seen or understood. Playing against the great chords were the lighter themes and melodies coming from high up the treble clef so that they appeared to be escaping, to represent the promise of a different path at one and the same time connected but separate. Toby was entirely trapped within the music which filled the room with a rich and magnificent noise. It spoke of hope and confusion in equal parts. The next movement began with the evocation of wind sweeping unfettered over the flat land, remorseless and unforgiving, pushing aside everything in its path and with it the ugly, twisted noise of saxophones bent against the wind, struggling to fight their way into the music, hard and uncomfortable. Here were the difficult truths about life laid bare with their consequences. When this section ended Toby felt as if he, too, had been fighting the gale force winds, head down, pushed here and there by their violence. In contrast the last movement was a delicate interplay between piano and violin, supported by a small string orchestra, which hovered between great sadness and complete joy. The solo instruments complemented each other, swapping with great politeness so that neither one dominated the other, the falling cadences of the piano picked up and augmented by the violin. Gradually the themes from the earlier movements were represented as reminders of the journey that had been taken. Toby raised his hands to his face and cupped his nose and mouth in a prayer like gesture, feeling the tears form in his eyes. The orchestra swept in now, emphasising all the melodies in a great welling of sound and at once he could see the image of Perdita at Norton Hall, her face full of tears and laughter. Then the orchestra stopped and the piano and the violin were left alone to gently escort each other to the end of the composition, the echo of their final notes slowly drifting away into the darkened room.

Toby got up and walked over to Perdita who was motionless by the piano. He knelt down and raised one of her hands to his face so that she could feel his tears. There was no need to say anything else.

\*　　\*　　\*

Toby adjusted his bow tie and stepped back from the mirror. He could hear the audience upstairs and he went through to the green room where Perdita was sitting with other members of the orchestra. He kissed her on the forehead and touched her lightly on the shoulder and left the room to climb to the auditorium. He took his place amongst the crowd in the Barbican main hall, not quite full but respectable for the premiere of a new work. He watched the players come out followed by the conductor with, on his arm, Perdita in a long dress of black silk. He felt no nerves for her but instead a complete comfort in what she was about to do and he settled back and waited for the music to embrace him once again. And it did, taking him back over the journey they had made together, but this time his picture of Marjorie and Perdita was even more vivid and he heard elements in the music that he had missed the first time. He regretted again not knowing Marjorie and silently acknowledged his, their, debt to her. He thought how the music that Perdita had created caught the power of the landscapes which had shaped the therapist. He recognised that there was a melancholy that ran throughout the composition, the presence of unmistakable sadness which even in the triumphant ending was not entirely dissipated. He looked down on Perdita, completely absorbed in her music and marvelled at how she had captured the mood of the piece absolutely correctly, hovering as it did between joy and sadness. When the music ended the audience rose to its feet and the applause was long with whoops of delight. One by one, the other players went over to shake Perdita's hand and the clapping became even louder as the conductor hoisted Perdita's arm before stepping back so she could take her bow. Their journey had become public. In the rise and fall of the music, the eddies of sound and the play of melody and dissonance, lay the story of their time together. Some would take from it the messages of despair and redemption, others would find echoes that touched their own lives and for some the music would pass them by wasted and unwanted.

Afterwards, in the green room, he watched as she received the praise of her peers and friends, a woman whose pale beauty shone from her black dress. As before, she seemed to sense him through the crowd and he moved forward to greet her.

'Were you OK?' Perdita asked and it wasn't until that moment that he realised he had sat through the concert without experiencing even a hint of a panic attack.

'Oh, Perdita,' he said, taking her in his arms. 'How lucky I am that in this moment of success you should think of me.' They clung to each other and he felt the firmness of her grip. 'The piece has never been better,' he whispered in her ear. 'You have captured something for everyone, but most of all for me, for us.'

Afterwards they ate in a restaurant overlooking the Thames close to Toby's gallery. It was late and many of the tables were empty but Perdita was alive and the success of the music pulsed through her.

'When did it start to go right?' he asked her.

'Now you ask,' she said, taking his hand, 'I think it was in the church, but I didn't recognise it at first. You never noticed my blindness and you never commented on my looks. I wasn't defined by either. And after that, for some strange reason, I always knew you were there. It was as if you gave off a signal which I could detect. Later, you showed me your pictures and that meant so much to me, that you knew in some ways I could see. And there was one other important point.'

Toby looked at her.

'You're the only person who has never asked me how I got my name.'

Toby smiled. 'Perdita. I've always liked it. It seemed to fit you. Where does it come from?'

'It means "lost" in Greek.'

'Ah, then it suits you only up to a point.'

'And, for you, when did it begin?'

'It was me who couldn't see, Perdita. I was the one who was lost, if you like. It frightens me now that it took so long for me to see what was in front me, that I was content to exist in parallel with you, never touching in any way. Then, slowly at first, I began to recognise you and suddenly, in a rush, the rest of the world shrank back and there was only you. Perhaps it began when I saw you on London Bridge when the sun seemed to pick you out as you crossed. Yes, it was then.'

'In the beginning, when I first began to write about Marjorie, she loomed so large in my life. I think her loss troubled me more that I liked to admit for I had still so much to tell her, or for her to discover.'

'And then,' Toby picked up, 'as I came into your life she seemed less and less important.'

Perdita nodded.

'The same thing happened to me,' Toby continued. 'But you have written your thanks to her. And I have been thinking.' He stretched forward to put his hands on her forearms. 'I have been thinking that I would like to play Marjorie's piece with you. Would you allow that?'

'I would love that Toby.'

# Chapter 34

Toby watched Perdita's hands float over the keyboard and not for the first time marvelled at her skills on the piano and at the origins of the music she had created and which they now called Marjorie's Piece. He was waiting for his cue to pick up the theme and carry it through to the end, rising and falling with the piano. It was a glorious summer's day and the big French windows were open and the tide was high so that it was possible to hear the Thames lapping against the piers. Since Perdita had moved into Wapping they had been practising and today, for the first time, he felt that he had the composition under his fingers. The last notes slowly dissolved and the sounds of the river took over.

'Yes,' Perdita said, 'that was really very good.'

It had been Perdita's idea to offer to play the piece as a duet at his father's wedding, as a present from them both. Toby could only smile. It was typical of Perdita to come up with such a brilliant idea, he thought, since it contained both her mischievousness and her good sense. At one and the same time, it would allow her to reveal to Charles Browning both her style of music and his son's prowess on the violin, wrapped as a present. The fact that Toby could entertain the idea was proof of the distance he had travelled with Perdita towards what she called his 'recovery', his recognition that his father had taken a different proportion in his life. As she had told him, he had put down the violin for his father and picked it up for her.

'Amongst your many skills, Perdita, you are a very good teacher. And I don't just mean of music.'

'And you play a mean fiddle, Mr Browning, although I don't suppose we'll convince the elder Mr Browning of that.'

Toby heard the front door buzzer and he went down to the

glass front doors in the gallery to sign for the delivery of a registered letter. It was addressed to them both and he began opening it as he climbed the stairs. He was walking back into the living space when he called out Perdita's name and as she turned towards him he knew that she could detect the concern in his voice.

'What is it?' she said. 'Something's happened.'

'It's a letter from Peter Harrington. It was addressed to both of us. I didn't know he had my address.'

'It was on Marjorie's file about you,' she added and it was at that moment they both sensed that this was no ordinary letter. Toby sat down next to Perdita and as he did so he could feel the apprehension rise in him and the summer day outside recede. He began to read out loud.

'Although we only met twice, Perdita – and Toby I have seen you but never talked – nevertheless I feel I have to convey to you the contents of this letter for I believe that Marjorie Nielson played as important a role in your life as she did in mine. However, as you will see, in one sense my time with Marjorie produced consequences which went beyond that of most therapist/client relationships. I want you to read this letter before looking at the attached notes, which were written by Marjorie shortly before her death and are powerful and shocking.

As you know, the coroner's verdict was that Marjorie died of natural causes. It is more likely, in fact, that she was killed by Marise but before you rush to judgement I think I should give you a little background. It is my conjecture that Marise was Marjorie's first patient. They met in London in the early fifties when they began a lifelong friendship. Marise was devoted to her, almost obsessively so and I believe that she became acutely jealous of the impact I was having on her friend. I told you, Perdita, that during one of my sessions – I enclose copies of that session so that you can fully understand the true repercussions of what happened – I was aware that my description of the death of my friend Freddy was affecting her also. Anyway, Marise found my notes, which Marjorie had been working on the night of her death. She left them on the desk but removed some important sheets, which you now have. Marjorie had been drinking and I contend that when Marise administered her insulin injections, as she sometimes did, she gave her a double dose which induced the coma and death.

One of the truths I have learned over the last year is how little we know about each other and how cleverly we hide what we are and what may be troubling us and, what is more to the point, how few people really care. Marjorie was trained to care, to detect what was really going on inside us, a forensic expert in emotions, if you like. It came as a shock to all of us, I know, how little we knew of her after we heard of her death. Just how little, you will sadly be able to read. Marjorie carried the truth of her dreadful childhood to her death and it is our fortune and her misfortune that those events made her so aware and so able to detect the disabling factors in others. My story is a simple one and I send it to you in good faith, but Marjorie's is the tragedy of a life that was lost in childhood but which had to be endured for the next sixty years. I cannot tell you what it was like for me to discover the truth for at that moment when I was beginning to emerge from my own tunnel I discovered the real story about Marjorie. I have kept it with me now for many months, but remembering the advice that she used to give, I want to share it with you now and I believe that in her story and our part in it, however small, there is a message for everyone.

Personally, I think there is no point in confronting Marise about this. Nothing can give Marjorie the life she deserved and Marise will be living with her own punishment forever.

Yours,

PETER HARRINGTON

Toby put down the letter and stretched out to touch Perdita's hand in the way that a parent does to a child before an injection. Whether he was looking for support for himself or offering it to her, he wasn't sure. He felt, though, that there was worse to come. He picked up the copy of Peter Harrington's notes, a verbatim account of their session and read them, as best he could, for Perdita. The story of Freddie's death was compulsive and deeply upsetting, but it did not prepare them for what was to follow. He found Marjorie's notes even more difficult to read and had to stop several times as the account of her rape unfolded. In the end it reduced them both to silence and tears. They had both wanted to know more about Marjorie Nielson and now they did and the image of the little girl abused had shocked them to silence.

The past, trapped in the present, can be a terrible thing, hobbling us through life, thought Toby. Marjorie, trained as she was, was never released from those awful events in the cellar and endured a life in which so many pleasures were denied.

'How appalling and tragic,' said Perdita, holding her head in her hands, 'that Marjorie should have helped me understand my sexuality when her own was so appallingly ripped from her.' The conjunction was hard to accept and Toby put his arms around Perdita.

Toby himself felt humbled by the story and ashamed, not just of his ignorance of what occurred in Marjorie's life but at the memory of his own lack of interest in the lives around him. Without Marjorie he would not have been aware, even in the limited way he was, of the importance of Perdita. In a sense, Marjorie had saved his life and he realised this was her role, to give back to others what had been denied herself. He shook his head, as much for himself as for the dead therapist.

The events that had begun that fateful day in April over a year ago had begun when he wasn't looking, when he was preoccupied with his own life to the point of exclusion. What was to overtake him, to change him irrevocably, had stolen up on him unnoticed.

It is difficult to be precise about the start of any story, to say exactly when it began, to imagine the routes that led him to where he was today, but as he sat there holding Perdita's hand he tried to do just that, to make sense of what had happened, for it frightened him how closely it all might have passed him by. Life is what happens when you're not looking, but now, as he sat in the sunlight, he was haunted by the fact that, even when the truth was staring him quite literally in the face, he almost let it pass, failed to read the signs properly. He could now see that he almost missed that chance to save his own life.

'Is a life interrupted by events or are the interruptions the life itself?' Toby said quietly to Perdita. 'It's something that Marjorie once said and I didn't really understand at the time. I can now. We can't pretend that bad events don't happen, we can't just sail on regardless. Not without dire consequences, at least. She helped me see that.'

'Poor Marjorie,' said Perdita. 'I wonder if she could hear the music? All the time I was composing it, I felt I was pulled along by something much larger than I understood. Of course, I didn't know Marjorie personally but perhaps unknowingly she did convey elements of those dreadful events in her childhood and now in some mysterious way they have emerged in the music.'

Toby listened and he knew that it was true. If Marjorie's tragic life was to have any sense at all it was in making him understand that behind each and everyone of us there is another story waiting to be discovered and that we would do well to listen and to watch and to discover what it is.

Perdita began playing again and Toby picked up the violin and joined in. They played the piece as they had never before and the mingled sounds of the piano and violin floated out of the open windows as the sun slipped from the spire of Rotherhithe church and the river dropped in the departing tide.

# *Thanks*

With special thanks to psychiatrists Dr Greg Stewart and Dr Gerald Woolfson and Doctors Carolyn and Bob Wilkins, for their technical guidance and support and to Jean Harrison, without whom it would have been impossible to create Perdita. I am also indebted to John Fairclough for his insights into army life. Further thanks to Richard Barber, Chiara and Gary Brown and Rachel Pollard whose support and criticisms are immensely helpful. And, of course, to my wife Sally, who has had to cope with my behaviour, unwitting or otherwise, for a good few years.